passageways
SHORT SPECULATIVE FICTION
Lisa Fox

Crystal Skipper Press

CONTENTS

To Mom and Dad, Godma and Uncle Jim

Heaven is an endless library;

I know you're reading, and I know you're smiling.

INTRODUCTION

A "passageway" is defined as a means of getting into, through, or out of something—usually depicted as a long hallway or corridor connecting two distinct settings. Simple, right? But in literature, and in life, the passageways that connect past, present, and future are far more complicated.

Rarely is the corridor between Point A and Point B smooth. Sometimes a passageway is so cavernous that we can hear our own hearts beating in the empty echo of its walls; other times it's so tight and constricting we need to wriggle our way through, praying the claustrophobia leaves us just enough breath to make it. We know where we've started, we know what we *think* is on the other side, but what bridges the two together—the journey there and the joy/sadness/shock/fear/jubilation that awaits in the ultimate outcome—it's what builds us or destroys us as human beings.

The characters brought to life in this collection of speculative short stories all venture through their own unique passageways. Some stories are short, quick-hit microfiction pieces that carry a theme, an emotion, a moment as if on a curt autumn breeze. Others enable the reader to linger with the characters and their dilemmas, walking the path from one point to the next with trepidation, with empathy, or perhaps even joy through tears (one of my favorite emotions).

I hope you enjoy the journey presented in this collection of short fiction—that it, in itself, represents a passageway for thought and self-reflection; and when you turn the last page of this book, you are left with an experience that stays with you.

Is Getting Out like going Someplace Else?

-Lisa Fox, Summer 2024

Her Memory Uncloaked

CLASSIFIED AND CONFIDENTIAL

**MindMap® Whole Brain Emulation (WBE) Therapy
Subject: Cassie Syland, 27-year-old female, Caste-Alpha
Investigative Cohort: Malcolm Syland, 30-year-old male,
Caste-Alpha**

*MindMap Anomaly #1 of 3
Her Moment of Catatonic Entrapment
23 September 2189*

My consciousness embeds within Cassie's lucid mindscape, and her inner world blossoms around me like a plume of eternal spring. The breeze dances in a perfumed mist and lingers, sweet as the scent of her, my beloved wife. I breathe in her essence—swathed in the smooth coolness of her favorite silk dress, tickled by the supple blond curls cascading down her back. Our minds conjoined—concurrently hers, concurrently mine—I struggle to separate she from me, wife from husband, soulmate from soulmate.

I never would have revisited this day had there been a choice.

On this day—the day my Cassie had fallen—we'd been shopping at an open-air market on the outskirts of Caste-Alpha proper. Complex tapestries hang from racks tall as treetops, their intricate stories woven and unfurled in the vibrant fabric. Firm in Cassie's memory, I can taste the sweet nectar of a ripe pear she'd sampled from a vendor's stall, hear the crunch of her teeth biting through the crisp skin of an apple that shined as if lacquered in sunlight.

Cassie's tinkling laughter fills the lull of a wind chime that dangles from a merchant's kiosk. He's selling lilies. My Cassie loves the way their petals open, unencumbered, unabashed; preferring more 'interesting' flowers over the ornate arrangements of red roses my caste has conditioned me to associate with love.

On this last day—this horrible day—I'd been haggling with a shifty Caste-Theta vendor over the price of a bouquet when I saw Cassie standing rigid, empty-eyed and slack-jawed, in the bustling square.

Then the screaming began.

All the young women patronizing the bazaar—all Caste-Theta, aside from Cassie—had frozen, catatonic, dropping parcels and small children with a thud to the marshy ground.

They named this affliction Blight. Scientists identified it as a parasite that feasted on the brain synapses of its victims. Conspiracy theorists labeled it a bioweapon—governmental population control targeting the lowest classes, given its laser-precise mark on Caste-Thetas. Though its origin was an enigma, some speculated that a caste-targeted, bio-engineered organism had been released into the water; others spoke of a mysterious substance sprayed over the alleyway gardens that bore the fruits and vegetables that sustained the populace of Theta Proper.

Regardless, Cassie was the only Caste-Alpha afflicted with Blight—a statistical oddity that shattered our lives.

I'd transferred millions of terranotes into the accounts of top Caste-Alpha clinicians to extract the parasite before it reached Cassie's brain stem. Currently, an advanced vitalBot algorithm is mapping her mind's data stores, repairing her corrupted memories through the hippocampus so my Cassie can be—Cassie—again.

Yet, incongruities persist across three key memory points in her MindMap. Without their accurate restoration, Cassie's essence will remain shuttered; to the outer world, she'll be nothing more than a silent conch shell lacking the resonance of the sea.

I am the only one who can save her from the after-effects of Blight.

Malcom, you are under a contractual arrangement as an Observer. The tinny vitalBot voice reverberates through my brain. *Any direct engagement with the subject violates MindMap's terms and conditions and is subject to prosecution under the fullest extent of the law.*

"Understood," I think. Or whisper. Perhaps both.

You have sixty seconds to identify each Anomaly in Cassie's memory.

Sixty seconds to find a single misfired detail inside Cassie's mind. One minute for each of three anomalies before her broken subconscious initiates a permanent interlinking sequence with my own. The Map's developers speculate that after too much time elapses, the mind of the subject, *Cassie*, could swallow that of the investigative cohort, *Me*, or that our two consciousnesses would crash into each other, Big Bang-like, ceasing to exist, or perhaps creating something entirely unique, like a new universe born. Yet the bodies of both subject and cohort would live on, subsisting on oxygen and intravenous fluids until the government terminated them.

Of course, they have not studied the effects of such an interlink in the MindMap, all being theoretical—the disclaimers state as much—but for Cassie, the risk is worth it.

She is worth everything.

Please verify your bond to her psyche is secure.

"It's secure."

Mother had admonished against this procedure. Let her go, she'd told me. But I cannot. I'll risk anything to save Cassie, even if it means reaching into the depths of her soul to bring her back.

Commencing.

My mind sighs at the familiar visual, that moment before I'd lost her. Dirty, ragged Caste-Theta miscreants glaring at me. Cassie, in the distance, crouched down, running a jeweled hand over the back of a mangy dog as she feeds it a crust of bread. Cassie standing, brushing away crumbs. The dog wandering off.

I've never understood her affinity for this specific market on the border of the Theta Slums or her fondness for strays; it is a quiet quirk that makes Cassie so uniquely her. So different from other Caste-Alpha women.

Find the Anomaly.

The market lights with color, royal hues painted in brisk brush-strokes over the dismal sepia landscape I recall.

But this is Cassie's construct, not mine.

Then I see it, an imperfection in Cassie's attire. Tattered, muck-filled canvas sneakers replace her fine leather designer shoes. Bloodied and filthy, her perfect toes peek through holes worn by rot and despair.

"There," I say.

Anomaly confirmed.

Cassie's light dims. Again, I watch her body stiffen, frozen in this random, implausible moment that never should have been. I reach out, yearning to touch her as my consciousness tears from hers.

I can only hope that the remaining incongruities in her memory are as easy to identify.

MindMap Anomaly #2 of 3
Day of Their Marital Union
4 January 2187

Clouds cast a gray pall over our wedding day; pinpricks of winter numb with a biting chill. Cassie's world lies still, tense as a held breath that fears escape, as if the slightest sigh could crack the icy veneer that lacquers her mindscape.

Cassie's construct of this day—our happiest—misaligns with my own. I recall the majestic windows of the judge's chambers, a warm hearth, soft snow glistening through a filter of pillowed sunlight.

But as I've learned, the landscape—the *feeling*—can never be the Anomaly; the discrepancy lies in some twisted nuance. And this new moment presented in my wife's mindscape is foreign to my experience—that first precious connection shared between my mother and Cassie as her new daughter-in-law. It's a favorite story Mother has relayed countless times—one that makes Cassie smile.

I pray I can find the glitch.

Sixty seconds, the vitalBot reminds me, and I enter the scene.

Cassie clutches wildflowers tied with a white ribbon, the ornate bouquet selected by Mother tossed aside, much to her chagrin.

"A Caste-Alpha bride should be regal. A queen among peasants!" Mother says. Her lithe form towers over Cassie, nose and chin chiseled sharp and precise as an ice carving. The room shrinks as Mother fusses over my wife's simple cotton dress. "This most certainly will *not* do. Malcom deserves... more."

Gooseflesh rises defiantly on Cassie's bare arms.

"Is there anything *more* than true love?" Cassie challenges.

"Nonsense." Mother tsks. "As a little girl, did you not dream of this day? Flowing tulle trailing your steps, your body lost in a sea of white satin? Didn't your mother—" She stops, her crimson fingernails clicking as her fingertips steeple. "Oh. I understand."

"Oh, do you?" Cassie straightens. The air crackles with her glare.

"The grandfather who raised you, he never did teach you the societal value of proper fashion. How could he? Old men, from

New Maine, no less, know nothing of style." Leaning in, Mother whispers, "Malcom told me of your unfortunate family predicament, dear."

The room shivers with rage.

Reaching inside her gold-studded handbag, Mother retrieves a diamond brooch. Cassie steps back; Mother moves forward and clutches the neckline of Cassie's wedding dress, securing the oversized pin. It pulls the soft fabric, like a frown.

"There. Now you almost look like a proper bride," Mother says.

"Proper?" Cassie says. "You Caste-Alpha matriarchs are all the same, thinking you know what is proper. What is just."

"Feisty. Irreverent." Mother scowls. "Malcom never mentioned this side of you. Rushing into marriage, love at first sight. Nonsense."

I watch Groom-Me enter the room, my gray topcoat shining and stiff. A suit of armor.

Melting ice drips from the ceiling, like the tear cascading down Cassie's cheek. Her features soften as she sees me; her world breathes again at my presence. Mother's form dissipates in an irrelevant cloud of smoke.

I hear my voice through Cassie's mind, deep and melodious as a saxophone solo.

"My love."

Mother's brooch burns red on Cassie's chest, an enraged serpent. It slithers, hissing and fighting for release from the dress.

"Mother's gift to Cassie," I whisper. "The pin was a peacock, not a serpent."

Anomaly confirmed.

I long to kiss my bride, to thaw the frost that embellishes her vision of this day, and retreat from Cassie's mindscape, relieved yet unnerved by the additional "glitch" I've discovered. This moment, it's not the story Mother told.

MindMap Anomaly #3 of 3
Their First Meeting
27 May 2186

The sweet vibrato of Cassie's song stretches like tendrils of ribbon toward the sky, each sweet note swirling into heaven. Her guitar's tone—hopeful, mournful, yearning—voices an accompaniment that paints the world with splashes of sound. She closes her eyes, losing herself, finding herself, simple yet complex in the moment—in *that* moment—when I first saw her sitting in the park outside my favorite café. Cross-legged on the grass, she cradles that familiar old wooden guitar with reverence, as if she's holding an instrument of the gods. A satin periwinkle shawl—once fashionable among middle-aged Caste-Alpha women—drapes across her shoulders like the embrace of an old friend; her simple yellow sundress, kissed by the florets of admiring dandelions, channels sunshine.

Cassie glows with confidence. Her song lights a beacon for the weary. For a man like me.

Before Cassie, I'd never realized how lonely I was, how empty and shallow my days. Squashed beneath the gilded stamp of society's expectations—stature, propriety, wealth—I'd worn blinders to the wonder of a world my peers deemed mundane. I'd never thought to ponder the taste of rain, or dance in the shadow of moonlight. I'd never counted the veins on a leaf or searched for the fortune told in their pattern. Cassie had given me hope for a life where my bucket would always be filled, not with riches, but with love.

I can only hope I've offered her the same.

Now in her final, faulted mindscape, I loll in the warmth of the possibilities she's painted—a park filled with rolling hills, a chorus of songbirds swaying in the trees. A sky as vast as the ocean, as deep and as blue; errant clouds drifting like captain-less ships overhead.

Sixty seconds, the vitalBot reminds.

I land in the moment that changes everything.

"Hello," I hear myself say. I stand between Cassie and the sun, casting a shadow over her.

"Do you make a habit out of stealing the sunshine?" she asks.

"Oh," I stammer. "I'm sorry. Your singing, it's lovely. I haven't heard music like this in a long time."

"Interesting," she says, squinting. Sizing me up. "Music is everywhere. Perhaps you haven't been listening."

I recall the clamminess oozing through my palms with her glance, the shiver of the temperate spring breeze—of unexpected anticipation—rippling across my skin.

"I'm—"

"Filthy," she replies with a laugh. She gestures toward my paint-soaked pants, my sweaty T-shirt. Self-consciously, I run my hands through my hair and end up with fingers full of blue.

Her laughter washes over me like an unexpected tickle, and I can't help but laugh as well.

"This isn't how I usually look."

"Hmm." She raises a finger to her chin; a fine line of scrutiny etches in her forehead as she furrows her brow in a gesture of exaggerated thought. "Painting yourself incognito?"

Heat flashes across my cheeks. I'm suddenly dizzy, acutely aware of the spectacle I'm making of myself. I can only hope no one in this park recognizes me. If Mother had an inkling of my appearance...

"Incognito, yes. Something like that," I say, swallowing past the crack in my voice. "I'm Malcom. Covert painter of walls, and apparently, myself. Stealer of sunlight. And you are..."

"Cassie. Maker of music. Singer of songs."

"Beautiful ...songs."

I reach for her with my painted hand. I long to feel the softness of her palm, to secure this moment of our meeting with a touch, clasping skin to skin as if sealing a promise, so I know it is real.

She hesitates. Holding her hand back for a few seconds, *a few eternities*, she reaches toward me tentatively, as if taking a first step on wobbly legs, in an unfirm terrain. The warmth of our connection envelops me like a midsummer tide. The blue pigment smears over our skin. She smiles.

"You've definitely made an impression. Malcom."

I watch myself leave her—my steps spry and warmed with hope. After that moment, I would never leave her again.

The Anomaly, Malcom.

The vitalBot! I've almost forgotten.

This moment is exactly as I recall—her words, her touch, her smile even more dazzling inside her mindscape. Fear seizes my gut; if I cannot find the Anomaly to repair, I risk losing Cassie forever.

From a distance, I watch as Cassie stands, grinning at her painted palm. Errant blades of grass slide down her skirt and her shawl slips from her shoulders. The breeze lifts it; it flutters about like the wings of a fledgling butterfly.

Clouds creep across the sky, predators of the sun. As they pounce, the radiant hues dissipate from the park, evaporating into a sepia fog. It falls as a dull, heavy mist over Cassie's mindscape.

Sluggishly, she retrieves the limp shawl from the dried-out lawn, its periwinkle shimmer withered brown, much like the deadened grass upon which it had laid. Cassie shivers as she wraps the coarse, ratty shawl around herself like a blanket.

"There," I say to the vitalBot. "The Anomaly."

Negative, the vitalBot responds.

"But Cassie's shawl, it's Alpha Blue. It's always been—"

I gasp at the realization—the truth I am seeing for the first time. My wife wears the garments of Caste-Theta.

Cassie is Caste-Theta.

Ten seconds until interlinking commences, the vitalBot warns.

Contracting Blight was not an oddity, but a certainty that day, given the true nature of my wife's lineage. And the specificity of her corrupted memories? Perhaps it was she who'd resisted the MindMap algorithm's repair mechanism. To protect her secret.

Nine.

Our life had been a lie. The woman I loved, an impostor.

Eight.

"Wait," I instruct the vitalBot.

Seven.

I need more time.

Six.

"No! Not yet!"

Five seconds.

"Cassie!" my voice escapes me. I cannot stop myself. I cry out into Cassie's mindscape. The sound of her name thunders; the realm of her subconscious quakes at my forbidden intrusion. She falls, her knees landing hard against her guitar.

Violation! The vitalBot shrills an alarm in my brain.

"I don't care!" I shout.

Then there's silence.

Pain sears through me, hot coals explode through my cells as I push my present self to materialize inside my wife's mind.

I run toward her. "Cassie, why didn't you tell me?"

She gazes at me, her expression as soft and as heavy as a child-in-arms drifting into slumber.

"You never would have laid eyes on me if I hadn't been wearing that dreadful Caste-Alpha shawl."

"And you would have run from me if I wasn't covered in paint like some Caste-Beta working man."

"Incognito. Like me. The only way a Caste-Theta girl could play guitar in that park." She offers a weak smile. "Such a wondrous, forbidden place."

I take Cassie's hand, running my fingers over a palm I'd once painted blue, wincing at the irony. "We would have made it work, without the lie," I whisper. "Together."

She looks away; I cup my hand beneath her chin.

"What is an anomaly, if not just a twist of truth?" I say. "Your memory, it's whole, and it's real. Come back with me."

"They know, Malcom. The data is here. In the eyes of the law, *we* are the aberration." She shakes her head. "I'll be arrested, perhaps even executed. And you—? I can't bear the thought of them punishing you for my untruths."

"Then let's stay here," I say. "Safe, inside your mind."

"You'd sacrifice yourself for me? Even after I—"

Time has expired. Interlink commencing.

The vitalBot's voice warbles; a sharp pulse slices through my head.

Cassie reaches for me as I feel my subconscious tearing from my body. Her world spirals around me, inside me, a vortex of color and song.

I'm light as a feather drifting in the breeze.

"We're soulmates, Cassie. Now, in the most literal sense."

I motion toward the sunlight swirling above—red, gold, and pink weaving a tapestry in the sky. A new dawn. Our new story.

"I loved you then. I love you now."

"I'll love you always," Cassie says.

Until our dying breath.

In the Image of Evie

A PURPLE UNICORN STANDS sentinel in the poster above Zoe's bed, its hoofs planted in clouds that linger at the edge of a rainbow. Its golden horn shimmers, a hint of magic beneath the glass casing. I wonder why it hangs here, in this place beyond miracles, where patients come to die.

I take Zoe's small hand. Blood seeps through the bandages covering her head; she shrinks into a shroud of sheets. The warmth of her palm fills mine; my pulse thrums against her limp fingertips.

A single chip mars the metallic blue polish that Evie painted shakily across Zoe's nails last night. They'd played with my manicure kit before bedtime, singing along to the theme of their favorite TV show. I'd walked in on their game, gripping two sweating glasses, my knuckles as white as the milk within. Evie finished hers in a few gulps, a mustache staining her upper lip. Zoe sipped delicately, watching me wide-eyed over the rim of her glass. I lowered myself to the edge of the couch, grasping its arm to steady myself against a wave of vertigo brought on by nail polish fumes, that silly droning song, and the numbing pinch of my own guilt.

When Zoe was harvested, genetic corrections made her a slightly more perfect version of my Evie. Zoe walked while Evie crawled. Zoe spoke in polite sentences before she was two; Evie still flung her cup across the room, struggling to find words to tell us what she needed.

But we knew what Evie needed from the time we first heard her heartbeat, when I still nurtured her within my body.

Evie needed Zoe.

Zoe's breathing is so soft it's nearly imperceptible as a nurse-bot approaches, an artificial smile plastered on its almost-human features. Programmed to appear compassionate, it fluffs Zoe's pillow. "I'm sure you'd prefer to be with your daughter upstairs in recovery," it says, adjusting the thick, plastic yellow armband that rests just above Zoe's elbow. "Happy to expedite this process, if you'd like."

I glance at Zoe, her eyes dormant beneath closed lids. "I need more time."

"Very well." The bot turns away, moving toward a small form lying in the next bed, bandaged like Zoe and wearing the same yellow armband. The bot presses a red button on the child's band and hovers for a moment, taking a pulse before pulling the sheet over the still body.

Choking back a sob, I scan the row of beds lined up against the wall, the small inhabitants wrapped in cotton and linen with no one at their side. They are left to die here alone, with only the cold touch of a nurse-bot for comfort.

Children born of necessity, just like Zoe.

The doctors said Evie would begin showing signs of dementia by the time she entered first grade. Like many children conceived too close to the blast zone, Evie had a mutation that would rob her of her memories.

We began the cloning process as Evie grew in utero, making the same decision as so many others around us. Though double-strollers cluttered the local parks and daycares, no one smiled with amusement at this multitude of multiples. Instead, we looked to each other with a solemn, shared understanding as we balanced our children on a teeter-totter, knowing that one day we'd be forced to choose between them.

Evie's tremors started just after her sixth birthday. A month later, when she forgot the name of her beloved stuffed bunny, we scheduled the transfer. The quicker we acted, the better the chance to save both girls.

Zoe should have had the opportunity to live a happy, yet simple, life after the procedure. But I could tell by the slump in the surgeon's shoulders, by the way he evaded my eyes that something had gone wrong. Evie's damage had spread from the hippocampus to the frontal lobe, and they'd needed to extract far more from Zoe than anticipated.

We created Zoe in the image of Evie—raised to share the same experiences so when the time came for transfer, Evie could resume her life seamlessly, as if waking from a dream. I'd tried to remain detached from Zoe, focused on Evie's needs. But somewhere in that collection of moments that mold the foundation of a life, I'd discovered little things about Zoe that made her distinct: the way her brow furrowed in confusion at my jokes, and how she whined about the importance of keeping toys in their proper place. As I watched her fall asleep each night, holding hands with Evie, I discovered that I loved Zoe, too.

Zoe's death looms with the same heaviness I felt as I awaited her creation. She withers in the bed just as she grew in the laboratory, slow and resolute, while Evie thrives two floors above, eyes fluttering beneath closed lids as synapses fire and connect, the gift of memory restored through Zoe's sacrifice. I wonder if Evie will adopt Zoe's love of chocolates, of lilacs, if she'll marvel at the complex structures of falling snowflakes, like Zoe did.

I wonder if I'll still see Zoe in Evie's eyes.

The nurse-bot returns, a clipboard tucked under its arm. "Mrs. Williamson, your daughter is awake."

I stand, raising my hand to my mouth to stop my lower lip from quivering.

"I'm not ready." I lay my hand on Zoe's arm. Still warm. "Please."

"Sorry." The nurse-bot shakes its head. "We need the bed."

The bot grasps Zoe's armband and pushes a red button, plunging a needle into her skin.

"No!"

My legs collapse. I fall, dazed, like I'm peering through a cloud.

The purple unicorn still stands watch at the edge of the rainbow, its shimmering horn a betrayal.

The nurse-bot pulls the sheet over Zoe.

My breath catches. I can't stop shaking.

I swallow hard.

PASSAGEWAYS

Time to pull myself together.

There's no hope here. But two floors up, Evie waits.

And she needs me, now more than ever.

ON THE CANVAS OF DREAMS

FOR NINETY-SIX YEARS, I'VE resided inside the recesses of Anna's mind, the tempo of her firing synapses guiding my hand over the canvas of her dreams. I paint for her the landscape, the pleasure and the ache, of her subconscious journey lived in parallel to her waking world.

My artistry flows, deft and deliberate, aligned with emotions Anna shares when she closes her eyes and opens her world to me. On the day of her birth, her dreams were but a series of abstract images hovering on a fissure of light. Over time, the scenes sharpened with her growth, the canvas expanding with her intellect.

My smooth pastel brushstrokes complement Anna's invoked symbols of joy, images prancing across a lifetime of memories and hopes.

A puppy's bark.

Monarch butterflies.

A daffodil swaying in the breeze.

On these nights, she breathes easy, as do I.

When the staccato beat of her anxiety guides me toward brisk stiff-bristled strokes of red and black, the manic display confines her in chaotic paralysis. Her raging heartbeat commands motion; her numbed legs betray her.

Sometimes she falls. Sometimes she flies. On her worst nights, I stand ready to catch her, though I remain an enigma she will never know.

She locks her pain inside darkened corners. I attempt to mend the shattered fragments that spill into my view:

A tarnished gold ring.

Empty photo frames, blank albums.

Wilted flowers hanging from shriveled vines.

And always, a faceless man who hovers in shadow.

Each time these pieces take shape, she thrusts a cauldron of black paint in my hands, willing me to splash a dark veil over the canvas. Rare is it for a charge to commandeer her dreams with such vigor. By duty, I oblige, yet I seek only to help her.

A NEAR CENTURY OF sunsets begets a litany of losses—parents and siblings, nieces and nephews, friends. Anna is alone, the last of her family. The day her mother died, I painted Anna a portal to the spirit world, where she might reunite with the souls of those passed, should they come knocking. Should she allow them in.

Spirits queued outside, waiting. Her mother and father wrung their hands at the threshold of their daughter's dreams, begging me for entry. But only Anna could invite a spirit inside, and she kept the door shut tight, its seal as hardened as her aging mind. She relented only when Jack, her beloved childhood dog, barreled through the portal, barking and wagging. She ran her fingers over his fur; his tail thumped in time with her heartbeat. *So real,* she whispered, before succumbing to daylight.

The desolation of Anna's waking hours resonates in her nighttime murmurs, shivering over the surface of my paint wells. Though Jack's presence encouraged Anna to open the portal to her parents, too, an inexplicable longing echoes, heavy as footfalls in an empty room.

NOW THAT HER BREATHS come short and the cadence of her synapses weakens, I prepare to paint Anna's final portrait—the last image her closed eyes will see. It will be my final tribute to a lifetime spent rendering the divinations of her heart. When her light fades, I will be assigned to a newborn brain, left with fleeting images of Anna's psyche, phantom feelings of our connection. But my love for her, that will persist. Always.

I paint with broad strokes on the blank page as she drifts. I offer rolling waves over a sandy shore and the pink hues of sunset cradling the fading light. I sketch her footprints, forever embedded in the earth, yearning for them to be strong and bold as she walks on.

Anna's breath falters. She summons storm clouds over the sea. The waves crash. The wind wails. An empty picture frame rises through the sand, protruding like a lone tombstone. The faceless man materializes and drops to his knees in a glow of adoration. He reaches for her; she turns away. Sea mist, rain, and tears wash over Anna's youthful face. Dark grey splotches of despair stain her flowing white dress—inkblots marring a masterpiece.

Lightning sizzles. A flashbulb pops from an old-fashioned Polaroid camera that rests on a tripod made of shriveled vines.

An empty square flutters down—a photograph never taken.

Anna's fingers graze the paper. It crumbles, whisked into the sand along with the faceless man, whose disintegration falls like the curve of her endless frown.

"William." Anna's voice echoes into nothingness. "I should have stayed."

William—his name, a distant sigh drowned at the edges of her consciousness; his spirit, blocked from the threshold of Anna's dreams.

No brush I select, no hue I blend will alter this landscape, this scene Anna has hidden from herself—from me—for decades. But now it repeats, an endless loop of regret tainting her final dreamscape.

I cannot leave her to die with this image.

I cannot move on if she is not at peace.

Abandoning my brushes and paints, I extricate myself from Anna's subconscious and step through the portal into the spirit world. The rush of a million zooming souls stings me as I do the unthinkable. The forbidden.

I cry out for the faceless man.

William.

He approaches in a glowing orb, his features taking shape. Deep-set green eyes under a shock of black curls. Strong chin. Shy smile.

"Please, come," I say. "She needs you."

He nods, a quiver tugging at his lips. "I've been waiting for her."

William glides through the portal toward the beachfront. He whispers her name in the breeze, and Anna's storm clouds retreat.

I paint a vibrant sunbeam over Caribbean-blue water. The waves undulate, steady as a heartbeat. Daffodils sprout in the seafoam: they burst into butterflies, flitting through the sky. It's a landscape befitting paradise.

William takes Anna's hand and softly kisses it.

"I will," she whispers. He leads her toward the portal.

A flashbulb pops.

Synapses silence.

Light fades.

I detach, drifting through darkness. Onward.

Unfinished Business

An Alterative History of the Titanic

20 April 1912

Walter Harrigan's legs wobbled as he walked down the gangplank at Pier 60, rucksack slung over the shoulder of his topcoat, violin case in hand. Though the RMS Titanic was safely moored in the dock, he still felt its motion, his body confused by the pull of his inner ear.

He breathed in the unique smell of America—the salty air of the Hudson, cherry blossoms blooming along the shoreline, intermingled with rotting rubbish and the odor of steerage passengers who milled about on the dock.

"Three days late. Fastest ship in the world, aye?" A grimy dockhand tugged at a rope securing the gangplank to the pier.

Walter nodded. "Better three days late than three days dead. We nearly clipped an iceberg up north."

"Your Cap'n steered that ship with angels at the helm." The dockhand nodded toward the ship's main deck; Captain Smith stood tall and stoic, overlooking the cityscape.

The dockhand wiped his hands on his trousers. He gestured toward Walter's violin case. "You one of those great musicians folks keep talking about?"

"Something like that."

He grinned at Walter through broken, blackened teeth. "Then I'll be seeing you in a fortnight. Just got a job swabbing the decks on the return to Liverpool."

Walter straightened. He had no intention of ever returning to England.

15 May 1912

Kenneth Campbell was a name Walter would never forget, and he found the man sitting at the edge of a bar, the stale, sticky air of the pub heavy against his crisp tuxedo. Campbell's long fingers—the fingers of a cellist—caressed a sweating mug of Guinness. His stature conveyed the relaxed confidence of one better than those around him; his expensive attire a shimmer of moonlight over a muted sea of filth-covered workingmen. He lifted the glass to his lips and took a long, gentlemanly drink, then dabbed the foam from his moustache with a linen handkerchief.

It hadn't been difficult for Walter to find Campbell. Violin in tow, Walter appeared to be just another musician seeking to breathe life into the Great White Way. He knew just the right questions to ask, leading him to this pub in the middle of Hell's Kitchen. It was a pity; Broadway might have been enjoyable had Walter not ventured to New York for other reasons. It had been as easy to track Campbell in America as it had been in England, this redheaded Scotsman who favored his pint as much as he did his

Mozart—perhaps even as much as he favored Walter's sweetheart, Victoria Leighton.

Walter removed his hat and overcoat and strode toward the empty seat next to him. He sat, gesturing toward the barkeep.

"A pint."

The bartender slid a mug toward Walter; he took a bold sip before resting it back on the bar. He glanced toward Campbell, who continued to stare ahead, lost in his own reverie.

"Square peg too, eh?"

Campbell turned, brow furrowed.

"Excuse me?"

"Square peg, round hole. Don't exactly fit with this crowd."

Campbell grinned. "Cheapest pub near the theatre," he said. "And on a musician's salary..."

Walter nodded, forcing a smile.

"Besides," Campbell continued. "I need to save up every bloody cent. Got a wee babe on the way."

Walter's breath caught as he fought the heat building in his body. "I see." He took another sip and swallowed hard to calm his roiling stomach. "Are you happy about it?"

"Wouldn't you be happy if you'd just fathered a child with the most beautiful girl in the world?" Campbell winked. "Sure, I'm glad to be a papa. But the path to get there? Like heaven."

Chortling, the man slapped Walter on the back.

Jaw set, Walter dropped his eyes. He swirled his glass, the beer within rising and falling like an angry sea.

"So enough about me. What brings you to these parts? Bring your shovel to get your share of gold in the streets?"

Walter looked up. He took in the man's slick hair, his pockmarked skin, green eyes that twinkled under the spell of Guinness in the dim pub lighting. He hated Campbell, now scores more than the first time he saw him with Victoria that night in Liverpool. The night she'd left Walter behind.

"Good lad, I asked you a question."

Walter surrendered to the sneer that curled from his lips.

"I've got some unfinished business."

16 May 1912

Walter stood on the street corner; his face warm under the spring sun. Violin at his chin, he found comfort in the long, melancholic notes he drew with his bow. "Nearer My God to Thee" seemed appropriate. City folk stopped intermittently to watch him play, oblivious to the scene unfolding down the street outside a quiet brownstone, where paddy wagons blocked the road and police-men stood, waiting.

As the last sweet notes drifted into the morning air, a team of medics carried a sheet-covered body down the brownstone's stairs. Though he couldn't see it, Walter envisioned the spot on the fabric where the blood seeped from Victoria's chest, from the center of the heart that had broken his. He frowned, considering the two heartbeats silenced in the twilight.

He hadn't intended to harm his Victoria. But he couldn't raise Campbell's baby; he'd always see that man's eyes, every time he looked upon the redheaded child that was not his own.

Walter did enjoy killing Campbell, the man who'd taken his beloved across the sea. How he'd cackled in a drunken stupor, flinging the body into the river. Walter swore he heard the man singing about lust and gold-paved streets as the water overtook him.

Amid the murmuring crowd, Walter bent down and placed his violin back in its case.

"Whatcha doin' here, pal?"

He looked up. A red-faced detective glowered at him, tapping a nightstick into his palm.

Walter secured the clasps and stood. He nodded; his expression grim.

"Music brings such comfort in times of tragedy."

Here, There, Everywhere

A Journey to the Middle of Nowhere

Avvy sat *Here*, on her favorite thinking rock. It was translucent pink, a flawless circle that pulled light inside, twisting and turning it until the perfect rainbow swirled within. A cotton-candy sky flourished above her, and magenta birds flitted in and out of blushing clouds. Their tailfeathers trailed behind them, shiny as curled ribbon. Silver-capped trees stretched out their branches, their long arms intertwined. They swayed to the sweet melody of birdsong, embracing like old friends. Avvy rocked back and forth, entranced by their tune. She sang along, too.

A great calm lapped at her. She closed her eyes, rooted yet floating. Still, though in motion. Something like the tide at sunset.

The tide! Avvy remembered cotton-soft foam upon clear waters that rolled in and out, chilling the tips of her toes. It filled the momentary imprints she'd left with each step, clearing them away before anyone could see they'd existed at all.

Avvy wished she could recall more about where she came from.

Someplace Else.

Memories flashed, lightning quick, random snapshots whose images melted away as quickly as they were formed. Flickering lights. Seven flames. Vivid and real for an instant; whooshed away with a puff of smoke. What had she wanted? She tried to grab on tight, but as hard as she squeezed, the memories always slid away, washing over her hands, dripping cool and slick through her fingers, leaving nothing but an unfamiliar remnant of something she thought she knew.

Was she in a dream? Avvy didn't know. But she knew she liked it *Here.*

The ground quivered beneath her thinking rock as a sharp noise echoed all around. It sounded something like *"Hark, hark!"* Avvy jolted, wobbling atop the rock until she steadied herself, holding her breath, still. Watching. Listening. Thinking. Even the birds ceased chirping. She exhaled, smoothing her hand over the stone as it quieted *Here.*

The scent of vanilla tickled her nose. Avvy fought a sneeze as the sweetness shivered through her. She turned toward the source of fragrance; a brook that had sprung up, spontaneous, between the blades of teal grass surrounding her rock. It streamed beside her; its liquid bubbling a melodic jingle. Like tinkling bells, tiny crystals coalesced on the surface and danced in the rays of the chartreuse sun. They rose, floating before landing on her skin, light as summer drizzle. Avvy squinted in the light around and above her and stuck out her tongue, desperate to catch a taste.

She savored each drop of candy that melted in her mouth. Avvy closed her eyes, giggling in harmony with the song of her surroundings—a pleasing sound she'd heard *Before...*

"You're *Here*."

Avvy's eyes popped open. A portly man with enormous green eyes and a shock of sparse, graying hair materialized beside the brook. His ample gut strained the buttons of a white jacket painted with pink and blue pinstripes. He removed his polka-dotted hat and wrung it in his hands as if apologizing for something.

What could he be sorry for?

"I am. *Here*. Who are you?

"My name is Hoff," he said.

Hoff was the first person she'd seen since she arrived *Here*. Avvy failed to suppress her grin. She supposed it was alright to talk to him, even if he was a stranger. What a funny idea, she thought, strangers. Everyone starts out as a stranger. If you don't talk to the people you don't know, you'll never meet anyone.

"I'm Avvy." She extended her hand. It was different from Hoff's. Hers was small and smooth, swallowed in the man's grasp—his hand large and rough, cold and pale.

She bit her lip.

Avvy couldn't remember when she'd last touched another living thing. Until that moment, she hadn't realized how lonely she was.

Here.

"Where did you come from, Hoff?"

His eyes darted from side to side, and he glanced over his shoulder, exhaling. Hoff pointed toward the murky haze in the distance, so thick it blurred the line between land and sky.

"*There*," he said.

"*There*?" Avvy wasn't sure exactly where *There* was.

"I didn't like it. *There.* I bumped shoulders with my own shadow—at least, I think it was my shadow." Vanilla crystal dust settled on Hoff's jacket; he breathed in deep as he brushed it aside with a trembling hand. "So many others milling around. They just looked straight ahead, like their eyes were stuck in place. And they never stopped humming, not even to take a breath."

Hoff shuddered. "That vibration... it rattled through my bones."

Avvy's brown eyes widened. "That sounds dreadful. How did you end up *Here*?"

"I'm not sure. One minute I was marching along with the rest of them and the next thing I knew, I was on my hands and knees. All I saw were legs, all around. Like bars on a prison cell, but when I moved, they did, too."

Avvy hugged her arms across her chest. She was glad Hoff was *Here*, now.

"Then this snaggle-toothed old man showed up. He picked me up from the floor. And he said something... odd." Hoff shook his head. "He told me I needed to find *it*, if I wanted to get *Out*."

"What's the *it* you need to find?"

"A pinprick. Of light." Hoff shrugged. Glancing past Avvy, his gaze fixed on the horizon. "At least, I think that's what he said."

"Is getting *Out* like going *Someplace Else*?"

As beautiful as *Here* was, Avvy carried a pinch inside her gut. She didn't know why, but pinches never lied, and they always hurt enough not to be ignored. And her pinch squeezed, hard, every time she thought about *Someplace Else.*

"Perhaps." Hoff rubbed his chin. "Though I can't be sure."

"What else did the snaggle-toothed man say?" Avvy asked. She bit her thumb to stop the line of questions that tap-danced on her tongue. Happy for the company, she feared she would scare Hoff away if she talked too much.

"I couldn't make it out. His voice sounded like it was trapped in a bubble. I asked him to repeat his words, but then, he just screamed, like I've never heard anyone scream before." Hoff leaned in toward Avvy, his voice surrendering to a whisper. "It was as if he was trying to push that scream inside of me."

Avvy felt her lips shape into an O. She was careful not to open her mouth too wide. It wasn't polite to gape.

"What did you do?" she asked.

"I yelled back, as loud as I could. And before I knew it, I wasn't *There* anymore. I was *Here*, with you."

❖

THE TOPS OF THEIR heads touching, Avvy and Hoff lay cushioned by the blue grass. Birds performed acrobatics against the unchanging sky, poking holes in the clouds as they darted in and out. The creatures cawed and screeched, cheering each other as they dipped, and tumbled, and twirled.

Avvy patted her full belly. Together, she and Hoff had slurped thick liquid from the vanilla brook. When she'd dipped her hand inside and let the syrup pass between her lips, it expanded and solidified—spongy and moist, like a sugary cake. Quite by accident they discovered if they whistled in unison, the vanilla crystals froze in the air, able to be spun with the wave of a hand into a crunchy, candy cocoon.

Avvy ran her tongue over the sticky coating on her teeth. *Here*, she had everything she wanted—unlimited sweets, pastel colors and soothing sounds, and a good friend. Yet, Hoff seemed sad.

"How long have we been *Here*, Avvy?" Hoff pushed himself up on his elbow.

Avvy shook her head. She had no idea of time, whatever that was.

"We may need to start looking now," Hoff said, "for the Pinprick of Light. Nice as it is *Here*, nothing ever changes."

"But it did change," Avvy said. "You found me. Maybe the Pinprick of Light will, too."

"No," he said. "It won't be *Here*. And it wasn't *There*." Hoff furrowed his brow. Avvy stifled a giggle; Hoff's face scrunched like an old raisin. "I wish I knew what else the snaggle-toothed man said."

A wish... Flickering lights. Candles? Lingering smoke.

"Can you pull it out of your head, Hoff? What if you think really hard?"

Reaching up, Avvy tapped at Hoff's forehead to try to jar his brain.

"His words were garbled, like we were underwater," Hoff said. He reached up, resting his hand on Avvy's, her palm stretched across his forehead. "Help me, Avvy."

"I'm making a wish, now. That you remember. Look around your brain, Hoff. Maybe his words are hiding. Maybe they're scared to come out."

"All around my brain." Hoff squinted, pulling his skin taut with concentration. "Coaxing out the words..." After a moment, his face relaxed, brightened.

"*Everywhere.* He said to look *Everywhere* until I find it."

Avvy sat upright, grimacing under the strain of an overly full belly. "But how would we go *Everywhere?* It's—"

—*Impossible?* She finished the sentence in her mind. Her thumbnail found her lips again; she tugged at blond curls with her opposite hand.

"It's simple," Hoff said. "We do what I did, to get *Here* from *There.*"

Avvy cocked her head, wiping her thumb on the grass. "We yell?"

Hoff nodded. "We yell."

❖

It was loud *Everywhere.*

Avvy pushed her palms into her ears so hard, she heard her hands pulsating. Sirens wailed, their shrills competing to see which one could outlast the other. Motors roared and big machines drilled into the ground. And the hammering, it was an endless *bam! bam! bam!* as metal slammed against metal. Avvy clenched her jaw to stop her teeth from chattering in the din. She could barely see Hoff through the flashing strobes, at once mesmerizing and disorienting. Bulbs clung to pencil-thin skyscrapers that scratched the sky, reds and yellows and blues and greens flaring, broadcasting some indecipherable code. The sun and the moon crossed over each other in a game of double-dutch and gumdrops fell, steady as rain, plopping into puddles at Avvy's feet.

Dark creatures flapped massive wings as they circled overhead, watching.

"Look around!" Hoff shouted. "We have to find it!"

But there was no searching *Everywhere*. Avvy knew that. She suspected Hoff knew it, too. *Everywhere* was too much for anyone to manage at once. There would be no way to find the Pinprick of Light in this chaos. Avvy feared she'd lose her mind, or worse.

The endlessness constricted around Avvy in a coffin of sound and light. Her arms and legs trembled. Avvy felt herself shrinking in the cacophony.

"We have to go!" Avvy screamed, though she knew Hoff couldn't hear her. Avvy watched as he removed his hands from his ears and pushed his palms against the chaotic lights and dissonant racket that inched in to trap them.

"Hoff!" Avvy's screaming melded with the sirens. Her heart thudded in time with the hammering—*bam, bam, bam*. She felt herself swoon and her legs give out beneath her as her eyes twitched and the lights swirled and the creatures circled, staring—eyes red, beaks open and sharp.

❖

Coughing, Avvy rolled to her side, the ground beneath like stone. She rubbed grit from her eyes and opened them to a dusty haze. Orange sand clung to the insides of her mouth; her tongue rubbed rough against its roof. She pushed herself up, resting on her elbows, and stared into a sepia sky. A red tumbleweed rolled past a weather-beaten sign that read "The Outskirts."

"Hoff?" Avvy's voice croaked in the stale air. Around her, a faint echo resounded, her own voice calling out. "Hoff?"

"You got *Nowhere* fast, young lady."

Avvy blinked and rubbed her eyes again. An old man appeared, hunched beneath the sign. With deft fingers, he rolled a red paper, igniting the tip with a puff of his breath. He lifted the unlit side to his lips and inhaled, deep, closing his eyes. A halo of smoke curled around his head as he exhaled.

Choking on dust is bad enough, Avvy thought. She held her breath to stop the smoke from infiltrating her nose.

"Where's Hoff?"

"Patience, child, he'll arrive soon," the man said, taking another drag. "Perhaps... now."

Avvy glanced down as Hoff's form took shape through the dust. He peeked up at her, blinking; his wan complexion paled as he turned to the man, jaw twitching as he glowered.

"You," Hoff said.

"Me," the man replied, grinning. A large tooth protruded from the center of his mouth, sentinel among the others.

The snaggle-toothed man.

"You said I needed to look *Everywhere* to find the Pinprick of Light," Hoff said, heat blustering over his face.

"I did. And did you look *Everywhere*?"

"Being *Everywhere* almost tore us apart!" Hoff shouted. "I'm an old man, but she's just a…" Hoff shook his head with a violence that startled Avvy. "How could you expect us to find anything in that mess?"

I was right, Avvy thought. It is impossible to be *Everywhere* all at once.

"Aye," the man said, taking another drag.

For a moment it seemed Hoff's eyes glowed as red as the man's cigarette. He pushed himself up, towering over the snaggle-toothed man who chuckled under Hoff's hazy shadow.

"Where are we?" Hoff demanded.

The snaggle-toothed man took a final drag of his cigarette and extinguished it in the sand. With a crooked finger, he drew a circle and two Xs—one large, one small, on the perimeter.

"*Nowhere*," the snaggle-toothed man said.

Avvy cleared her throat. "*Nowhere*?"

"*Nowhere*," the man repeated. "It's what remains when you're neither *Here* nor *There*. When you've already been *Everywhere*."

Avvy didn't think she'd ever been *Nowhere* before.

"This is ridiculous," Hoff said. "You told me if I looked *Everywhere*, I'd find the Pinprick of Light—the way *Out*! And Avvy needs to be *Someplace Else*." He threw his hands up, then rested them on his hips, pacing. Small canyons formed where he dragged his feet, filling themselves with each step.

"You are both exactly where you are meant to be." The snaggle-toothed man ran his finger over the circle he'd drawn on the ground.

Avvy felt Hoff's frustration rising like heat from the baking sand.

"How do you know?" Avvy asked, her voice hinging between a croak and a whisper. Being around the snaggle-toothed man made her belly flop; it stole her voice away.

He grinned again, the skin on his cheeks taut as tanned leather. Another tumbleweed tufted by, this one light green with pale yellow flowers. Pretty, she thought.

"Trust the process." He drew a line from the Xs in the sand to the circle's center. "Find the *Middle*."

Hoff ran his hands through his hair, tugging. "You mean to say the Pinprick of Light is in the *Middle*. Of *Nowhere*?"

"Aye."

"And we're supposed to go looking for the *Middle of Nowhere*?"

"Aye."

Hoff beat his fist into his palm. Avvy bit her lower lip to stop it quivering. She didn't understand why Hoff was so angry.

Hoff continued his rant. "No one goes looking for the *Middle of Nowhere*. You just... end up there. Somehow!" The rivulets in the sand beneath his feet deepened. Avvy worried that Hoff would dig so deep he'd get stuck in the sand.

"Do they greet you with a sign?" he shouted. "'Congratulations! You've reached the *Middle of Nowhere*?'"

The man pointed at the weathered wood above his head. "Perhaps."

Hoff yelled so loud Avvy feared he'd be knocked out of *Nowhere*, all by himself.

The snaggle-toothed man snickered as he lit another cigarette. "You'd better get a move on, Hoff. That light," he paused, flicking away newborn ashes. "It waits for no one."

❖

THEY'D BEEN WALKING SO long, Avvy's legs could no longer carry her. Hoff had lifted her onto his back, and she felt herself weigh him down as he pushed forward. Avvy was grateful for the warmth radiating from Hoff's back, for his salty scent that reminded her of *Someplace Else*. For their synchronized breaths. They were two nomads traveling as one, sharing a sole mission.

"What do you think you'll find? When you're *Out*?" Avvy said.

Hoff stopped, letting Avvy slide off his back. Her feet hit the dirt with a soft thud, and as she turned toward him, she saw a glaze overtake his parched eyes. It dropped like a damp veil, resembling tears, but different—the luster of memory sealing cracks in the haze.

"*Out*. There were tastes, mostly," he said. "Bitter liquid burning hot into my stomach when I swallow it. It always smells even better than it tastes." He laughed. "I used to drink it to keep my insides warm. My fingers, too."

Hoff scratched his head. "There's a song that plays, over and over again. Somehow it wormed its way into my brain. Loud, too. A bit like *Everywhere.*"

Avvy smiled at Hoff's vision. Had she not met him, had he not wanted to find the way *Out*, Avvy would have stayed *Here*, the pinching reminder of *Someplace Else* ignored until the knot released and faded. Avvy and Hoff were like that sun and moon they saw *Everywhere,* journeying together in an accidentally purposeful, yet random sort of way. She had a good feeling about finding the *Middle of Nowhere* and hoped the snaggle-toothed old man was right: that when they finally found themselves in the *Middle of Nowhere*, it would lead... somewhere.

Someplace Else for Avvy. A way *Out* for Hoff.

"There was water, *Someplace Else,*" Avvy said. "Clear and cold, rolling in and out, kind of like breathing. And..." She frowned. The memory slipped through her fingers. Again.

"We should keep moving," Hoff said. "It'd be a damn shame if we reached the *Middle* and walked right on through it. Besides, old Snaggletooth seems to think there's an hourglass hanging over our heads." He leaned down, extending a hand to Avvy. As she was about to again climb onto his back, she stopped, pointing ahead.

"Look."

In the distance, two spires, shimmering gold, rose from the sand to the sky, the cornerstones of a latticed fence that enclosed the space within. Silky white vines wrapped around the spires—yellow, red, and orange blooms burst from their skin like cottony thorns.

Avvy took Hoff's hand and they sprinted forward. A sign hovered between the spires; glowing infrared letters proclaimed: "Welcome to the *Middle of Nowhere*."

"Ha! I knew it," Hoff said.

Hoff squeezed Avvy's hand and kissed it as they passed under the threshold. As they walked through, Avvy thought she heard the blossoms whispering—chanting, even—words she didn't recognize. Their voices lilted around her in a soft lullaby.

The Middle of Nowhere was like *Here*, but better.

The same blue grass blanketed the ground and Avvy breathed in the sweet aroma of vanilla emanating from a brook that ran parallel with the fence. A pink bird swooped down and landed on her shoulder. Hoff laughed as Avvy squirmed before reaching up to pet its satin wings. It emitted a bark-like caw, and as quickly as it landed, it fluttered away, shuffling its feathers, settling to bathe in the cool water.

The ground beneath them quivered as they approached the center of the garden. Like a puddle of black ice, a large portal opened, and Avvy and Hoff glanced into its reflection. The surface swirled, a centrifuge in slow motion. Looking down, Avvy scrutinized her face—wide-set brown eyes, long eyelashes, freckles peppering her cheeks and her nose. And her curls, those blond curls that bounced in time with her every step. She smiled. It had been so long since she'd seen herself.

The longer she stared into the portal, the more her appearance morphed; her chin elongated, eyes sunken, until her face warped to the point of being unrecognizable. Avvy turned away, shaking her head to rattle the odd picture from her brain, and glanced up at Hoff. Mesmerized, he wept as he beheld his own image, opaque to Avvy but raw and real for him.

Then, in the center of the circle, a tiny gold dot appeared. Through it, a beam of light shot upward, piercing the sky.

Avvy squealed, squeezing Hoff's hand as she leapt. "Do you see it, Hoff?"

Hoff stared dully into the portal.

"See what, Avvy?"

"The Pinprick of Light! We found it, Hoff, we found it!"

He shook his head, frown lines etched deep into his skin, pulled by his downturned lips. Everything about Hoff suddenly seemed deeper, heavier—the bags beneath his eyes darker, his shoulders so rounded Avvy feared he'd cave in upon himself. That pinch in Avvy's gut resurfaced, twisting and squeezing as it never had before.

"Hoff? Don't you see it?"

"I see nothing." Hoff dropped her hand and turned away.

Avvy shoved her thumb between her teeth and bit down, hard. They'd come so far, and Hoff, he deserved his way *Out*. Why couldn't he see the Pinprick of Light?

Could the Light have waited only for her?

Avvy shuddered, remembering the snaggle-toothed man's words.

"What if you look again? Look harder," Avvy whispered. "Please." But as the words floated from her lips, the pinprick widened. Avvy squinted, then raised a hand to shield her eyes from its brilliance.

The chanting of the blooms intensified, their words indistinguishable but their sound an audible motion, filling the space around them. With a rustling of the vines, the flowers plucked themselves away, one by one, rooting in the thick grass. The stems shifted in Hoff's direction, leaning into him as if pushed by a curt wind, though the air remained still.

"You need to go, now, while you have the chance." Hoff rested a heavy hand on Avvy's cheek.

A fat tear streamed down Avvy's face and through Hoff's fingers, lingering before it splashed onto the portal. The drop sizzled, then evaporated in the growing light. Hoff kissed her forehead gently, reminding her of someone she thought she knew, *Someplace Else*.

"You needn't worry about me." Hoff said, the thin-lipped smile of the resolute pulling his skin taut. "I won't be alone. He'll come for me soon."

"Who?" Avvy asked, her eyes round as orbs. "Who's coming for you?"

Hoff lifted Avvy and placed her on the portal. With a swift nudge, he pushed her upward until her feet left the ground. The Light wrapped itself around her, swaddling her in warmth. Avvy watched the stems of the flowers grow taller and thicker and darker. Like dandelions puffed away in the breeze, the blooms disintegrated, leaving behind empty casings. The stems writhed and strained until each one sprouted arms and legs and featureless faces.

"Hoff!" Avvy's lower lip quivered. "I don't want to go without you."

"It's your time, child," he whispered.

She raised a hand toward Hoff and wriggled her fingers in a final goodbye. The shadows slithered around him, wrapping his body in a dark, tight embrace.

Hoff was gone.

Avvy knew she'd never forget him, no matter what.

❖

THE LIGHT UNRAVELED. IT detached and retreated. Avvy was alone. Cold.

She tumbled in the dark. She kicked and she flailed. She pushed and she squirmed.

She opened her eyes to a blur that stung, worse than tears. She could neither see, nor hear, nor speak within the nothingness that consumed her.

But she remembered, now.

The tide. How the water glided over her feet, receding and returning. The foam covered her toes, tickling like soap bubbles that popped over her skin. Avvy had wanted to chase it, catch it, hold it in her hands.

But her mother said *"No,"* her expression stiff as stone. *"And that's final."*

Sea mist had turned to drizzle, chilly as ice crystals on her cheeks. An old man walked his big, fluffy dog along the beach. She wanted to pet it, to feel its soft fur curled between her fingers. But the jingle of the ice cream truck sang in the distance. Avvy wanted a vanilla cone with crunchy sugar sprinkles. And she wanted to splash, too, one last time before nightfall.

Cupcake icing stuck to the corners of her mouth. It was her birthday; there was so much Avvy wanted. She bit her thumb. It was impossible to be everywhere all at once.

Her mother wasn't watching, but the seagulls were, spying on Avvy as they circled and squawked in the pink-tinged sky.

Avvy ran into the sea for just a moment. No one would know.

Seaweed grazed her ankles; its cold fingers grabbing, dragging her into shadow. She tumbled in the dark. She kicked and she flailed. She pushed and she wiggled.

Hoff's body floated past, tangled in dark plants sprouted from the *Middle of Nowhere.*

The snaggle-toothed man chuckled, the tip of his cigarette burning in a fiery sunset.

Sunset. A pinprick of light.

Avvy landed with a thud.

She screamed, soundless. Sodden, slimy tendrils twisted down her throat, stealing her voice. Avvy strained to release breaths held captive by uncooperative lungs. The glow stung her eyelids—the pinprick exploded, planet-large and hovering. Heat grazed her forehead in close whispers—*it's okay, it's okay*—breathless platitudes gave way to shouts that shivered across her skin.

Breathe. Breathe.

Avvy's lungs ignited, the tendrils shoved from her throat. The slime streamed from the corners of her lips, down her cheeks, like tears. Her eyes fluttered open. A circle of faces surrounded her; their smiles half-moons, moist eyes leaking warm rain on her skin.

A dog barked, wagging with joy beside her. She reached up, clenching its soft fur between her fingers.

So familiar.

"Avvy." Her mother's fingertips on her cheeks, the stony mask crumbled. "You came back. You came back!"

Avvy was *Someplace Else.*

She was home again.

❖

THE MAN LEANED AGAINST the truck; his smooth cheeks flushed by the seaside air. Thin shoulders rested against pastel-colored stickers advertising ice cream cones, cotton candy, and gumdrops. His expression twisted in a curious scowl; he tugged at an over-sized pink and blue pinstriped jacket that hung from his wiry frame like a windless sail. Its hues matched the hand-painted sign atop the vehicle: "Hoffman's Sweet Treats." The tinny jingle from the truck's speakers echoed at the edge of the beachfront, as they did each night, its pull on the children mesmerizing, like the sea itself.

Vacationing parents rarely said no to their children's pleas—weepy eyes and protruding lips compelled them to reach for their wallets and their purses, and a wad of napkins to blot chocolate beards and vanilla mustaches that dripped down sunburned faces. It was an honest living, every day the same as the last.

Except for today.

Wrapping his hands around a Styrofoam cup of steaming black coffee, Hoff shivered in the August night. The snaggle-toothed old man next to him took a long drag of his cigarette and together, they surveyed the scene on the beach.

Hoff's gaze rested on the young girl washed up from the surf, tangled in seaweed, on the barking dog that ran toward her, and the crowd that surged around them. Farther down the beach, the body of a gray-haired, portly man, clad in an ill-fitting pinstriped jacket, rolled in, alone and unnoticed amid the melee.

"Why'd you lie to her? Tell her you didn't see it?" The old man's wrinkles burned deeper into his skin with each pull of his cigarette. "That was your way *Out*." He thwacked Hoff on the chest. "Back to your truck. To your grandkids. Your wife. A comfortable life."

Hoff's glance rested on Avvy, reaching for her mother. The girl's long, blond curls wrapped around the trembling woman who held her close. "Those flowers, in the *Middle of Nowhere*. I heard it in their chanting, clear as I saw Avvy sucked down by those waves when I ran down the beach after her. 'Only one will pass,' they said."

"Aye."

"I saw the light, long before we reached the Middle. That's how we found it so easily. But I couldn't leave her to be swallowed up by..."

Hoff's voice trailed off as the snaggle-toothed man took a deep drag. Ashes scattered in the sea breeze and fluttered to the pavement as the sun drowned in the horizon and starlight twinkled through the newborn night. Shouts from the beach melded in a macabre harmony with the truck's jingle—someone had discovered Hoff's earthly body, cradled in the sand.

As the snaggle-toothed man flicked away the deadened cigarette butt, another materialized between his fingers, bearing a white flame. He raised a bony hand to Hoff's face; it shone in the pulsing glow.

"This light, it's different. It's yours, pal. Whenever you're ready."

Hoff lifted the cup to his lips, the steamy remnants of his coffee wafting past his face and encircling his hair, halo-like. Cup emptied, he crumbled the Styrofoam in his hand; it dissolved like sand through his fingers. Hoff stared at Avvy's mother, trudging up the beach, the living child in her arms. He watched Avvy's eyes widen, entranced by the tune from his ice cream truck. The girl's gaze fixed on the truck as she raised her hand and wriggled her fingers in his direction.

Does she see me? Hoff wondered. And if she did, would she recognize him, as young and skinny as he was now? He turned toward the snaggle-toothed man.

"Where to next?" Hoff said.

The snaggle-toothed man raised his eyes skyward. The glimmer of his cigarette swirled into a cyclone, growing and morphing around them and above them into a shimmering dome that prickled every one of Hoff's senses. He squinted into its brilliance—its light a million pinpricks converged into something...

"Beyond."

There's a Monster in Jacob's Bedroom

Monsters liked the taste of little boy breath. They lapped it up like ice cream melting from a cone.

At least that was what Jacob's big brother Marcus had told him. Mom and Dad were still out to dinner and Jacob was stuck with the useless babysitter. She sat on the couch taking selfies—the stupid duck-lip ones—and posting on Tik-Tok, ignoring the slasher film that Marcus had on the TV.

Jacob hated that movie. It was the one with the rotting guy in a hockey mask who carried a knife bigger than any Jacob had ever seen. It was 'R' rated, too. Mom and Dad would not have approved.

How Jacob wished he hadn't spied on his brother and his stupid movie. How he wished Marcus hadn't caught him hiding behind the reclining chair, eyes big as gumballs as he watched that half-dead, half-living slasher cut down one person after another. And the blood. Oh, so much blood. Jacob had gagged, clasping a hand over his mouth to stop the vomit that threatened to burn up his throat.

That's when Marcus noticed him sitting there.

"You little shit," Marcus had said, grabbing Jacob by the hair. "You tell Mom and Dad and you'll be deader than those corpses on the TV."

Jacob gulped once, then nodded. When you were eight and scrawny and your twelve-year-old brother threatened you over a secret that could get him grounded for a week, you listened. Even though you wanted to beat the crap out of him for being such a jerk. Even though you knew you couldn't.

Marcus had pushed him to the carpet. "Good. 'Cause if I don't get ya, the monster will!" Marcus danced around Jacob, waving his arms and wiggling his fingers as if summoning some sort of demon. Or worse.

"Little Jacob, scared of the big bad monster!"

JACOB LAID IN HIS bed, trying hard not to breathe. Not to move. Lightning flashed a warning from outside, and the thunder rumbled with a guttural growl that rattled the windows, rattled his bed, rattled Jacob's insides, the sick tickle like pinball in his gut.

He blinked hard to fight sharp tears that pricked the corners of his eyes.

Was the Monster hungry?

"The creatures feed at night with their big teeth and poisonous tongues." Marcus had rasped as Jacob padded from the bathroom to his bedroom. His brother had opened his eyes wide and curled his fingers, claw-like, tipping his head back and howling before exploding in a cackling fit. Jacob scurried by him. The tears brimmed and flowed, a salty sting running rivulets down his cheeks.

What if the Monster smells my tears? What if tries licking them off my face?

Jacob envisioned a monster tongue, slimy as a worm yet prickly, like his mom's cactus plant that he wasn't allowed to touch.

If the Monster bit through its tongue, would it have two tongues? Like when you cut a worm in half?

"Daddy!" Jacob called. He gripped his Batman sheets, pulling them up over his nose so only his blue eyes peeked above the taut line they drew across his face. The scratchy cotton blocked the minty smell of his toothpaste and the heat of each breath he couldn't help but exhale in the darkness of his room.

A glow emanated from beneath Jacob's bedroom door as the hallway light flicked on. Footsteps. Big-shoed, booming footsteps. Not like the clack-clack of Mommy's heels or the erratic drumbeat of Marcus's feet.

Daddy.

The door creaked open, and a shadow appeared in the frame.

"What's the matter, champ?" Dad moved toward the bed and it creaked as he sat, the warmth of his thigh comforting on Jacob's leg. He threw himself at his father.

"There's a monster in here that wants to eat me," Jacob said, his voice muffled into his father's flannel pajama top. He felt a mixture of tears, snot, and thick saliva converge into a growing stain on the starched cloth, but he didn't care. He didn't think Daddy cared much about that, either.

"A monster?" Dad placed his big, strong hands on Jacob's shoulders as he pulled back to look at him. Jacob studied his father's face—squared jaw, round and intense blue eyes, lines persistently etched into his forehead like he was always puzzling over something—and wished he could be so strong and smart and brave.

Jacob nodded, gulping past the hiccups leaping from his throat; air-frogs spring boarding from the bottom of his tummy.

Maybe the Monster is a giant frog.

"Is Marcus harassing you again?"

"Please don't tell him I told you. He said I'd be dead meat. And especially if I told you about the R-rated horror movie he was watching—"

Jacob clamped a hand over his mouth. He'd said too much.

Dad's lips pursed, then stretched into a thin line, the kind the cowboys drew in the sand before a gunfight in those old westerns he liked to watch on Sundays.

"I'll deal with Marcus in the morning. But for now, you need to get to bed. It's late, Jakey. And there's no such thing as the Bogeyman, no matter what your brother tells you."

"It has a NAME?"

"What has a name?"

"The monster. You said BOGEYMAN. You called it a Bogeyman. What's a Bogeyman, Daddy?"

Jacob's dad leaned in and kissed his forehead. "Never you mind," he said. "There are no monsters in your room, in this house, or anywhere else. Except in here." He tapped between Jacob's eyebrows. "And the pre-pubescent one snoring in the next room."

"What's pre-pubescent...?"

Dad ruffled Jacob's hair. The mattress creaked again, sighing as Dad stood.

"No monsters here. Don't go looking for things that don't exist. You're a good boy. Get to sleep, kiddo."

❖

JACOB HAD NO IDEA how long he'd been staring at the ceiling. He tried counting sheep (they all had vampire teeth). He tried humming a happy tune (it always turned into that singsong one about some guy who lived in a basement and chased you with knives while you were dreaming). He tried reciting the alphabet, forward and backward, but stopped every time he landed on "B."

Bogeyman.

What is a Bogeyman?

Shadows cut irregular shapes across Jacob's ceiling with each flash of lightning—triangles with their middles carved out, squares with jagged corners. Each shape looked as if something had taken a bite out of it; each shape cried and screamed with the rain and wind that swirled outside. The thunder grumbled louder. Hungrier.

Jacob couldn't take it anymore. He had to know.

Jedi-knight Build-a-Bear tucked under his arm, Jacob slid from his bed and tiptoed over to his desk. This was an emergency, and he was sure his mom and dad would forgive him breaking the "No Electronics After 7pm Rule" for the sake of his sleep.

A boom of thunder shook the house.

Or, for the sake of his survival.

He squinted against the screen's glow and typed in the word **"Boogieman."**

"Yes!" he whispered as several hits popped on screen. He went to Wikipedia first. Mom had referred to it as the authority on anything anyone ever wanted to know about anything at all, but for some reason always rolled her eyes when she said it.

Wikipedia showed:

"The Bogeyman (/'baugimaen, bougi- also spelled boogeyman[1], bogyman[1], bogieman[1], boogie mon-ster[1], boogie man[1], or boogie woogie[1]) is a type of mythical creature used by adults to frighten children into good behavior."

So it was made up, Jacob thought. Like some make-believe monster that would take away his Xbox if he got a bad grade, or some imagined creature that would sit outside Marcus's room to make sure he 'stayed grounded' if he kept teasing Jacob.

Maybe Dad was right.

Monsters weren't real. Monsters were just ideas planted inside our heads to scare us out of our own skins so we'd behave the way someone else wanted us to—whether it was our big brother, our parents, even ourselves. Jacob clicked the tablet off and shuffled back into bed. Yawning, he clutched his bear and closed his eyes.

Oblivious to the raging storm.

JACOB WAS ON A train. The wheels rolled over the rickety track with a jolting, screeching rhythm, like a crotchety old nanny rocking a baby too fast, her voice croaking a lullaby that pulled a scream from that baby's throat. Clickety-clack, clickety clack. Jacob frowned in his slumber. He longed for sleep to soothe him but he tossed and turned, the light from the train blinding as it flashed again, the train rocking over the tracks leaning left and right, as if it were about to fall over the side of the cliff as it rounded the curve. The babysitter's face hovered above, duck-lipped for an instant until, with the flash of the cell phone's camera, it melted over her bones, the crotchety old nanny cackling over a selfie of her own skeleton. And the train rocked and rocked...

...and Jacob bolted awake, upright, in his own bed, trembling like a scared puppy.

But Jacob's bed, it trembled, too, as if someone, some *thing*, were shaking it.

The Bogeyman.

With a grit he didn't know he possessed, Jacob swallowed back the fireworks bursting in his gut. His bear tumbled over the edge of the bed; he grasped the edges of his sheet and comforter and leaned over the side until he was upside down, looking beneath the bed.

The bed silenced itself.

He stretched his arm underneath, fishing through the dust bunnies and gum wrappers for his Fortnite pickaxe—the one Marcus laughed at him for getting. '*Only losers play Fortnite,*' Marcus had said. '*Loser.*'

You're the loser, Marcus. At least I have a weapon.

Popping upright, Jacob shook his head to rid his vision of the tiny stars that surfed across his sightline. Two-fisted, he wrapped his hands around the handle of the axe. No matter what Dad said, there was a monster in Jacob's room, and as his parents always told him, the best way to rid yourself of a fear was to face it, head on.

So that's what Jacob would do. Find that monster, and get rid of it, once and for all.

Jacob slid from the bed, pickaxe in hand, and padded over to the window to scrutinize the old Oak tree outside. Its drenched leaves dangled like broken fingers under the streetlight as the rain continued to pelt the night. But nowhere, anywhere, was a monster lurking. Aside from a waterlogged squirrel, no creature clambered up the great Oak's trunk or swung from the branches to taunt him. None sat atop the tree like some maniacal devilish angel. The streets slept silent, impervious to the bullets of water that assaulted them or the tiny rivers that tickled the edges of the curb.

A bolt of lightning cracked the sky and again the thunder bellowed. Jacob jumped back from the rattling glass, fearing it, too, would crack with the light.

The monster was not under his bed. It was not outside. There was only one place left to look.

Jacob skulked toward the closet, releasing his left hand from the pickaxe long enough to turn the knob. He pulled the door open, the hinges creaking like old bones. He shoved his weapon into the line of clothing hanging from the rod, tapping against the back wall with each push. But when he knocked into the plaster, the wall knocked back at him, tap-tapping in some secret code.

The Monster... it's trying to tell me something.

"Hello," Jacob croaked. "I know you're in there. Come out... come out, come out wherever you are."

"You're a good boy, Jacob," a voice rasped. "Why do you disturb my slumber?"

Jacob froze, his jaw dropping with the toy weapon from his hand. From the top corner of his closet, behind his bin full of baseball cards, a shadow wriggled out. It was dark as smoke, its form as tangible, and as it slid down over the shirtsleeves hanging from the rod, it grew. It grew and it grew until it stood three heads taller than Jacob, its form filling in as if something had taken a silver crayon to it, coloring ragged inside the lines.

The creature had the head of a wolf, vampire teeth and claws like talons. It stood upright with the legs and feet of a bear, the tail of a scorpion curling behind it. Hunching down to regard Jacob with its beady, glowing red eyes, it cackled like the old, rotting woman from Jacob's nightmare.

"You're... you're..." Jacob couldn't stop himself from stammering. Hot liquid streamed down his leg, saturating his pajamas.

It smells my fear.

"The Bogeyman," the creature said. "And you've woken me from my nap."

"You're real."

The Bogeyman patted Jacob's head and ran its claws through his hair, ruffling it. Jacob shuddered.

"As real as what you see with your own eyes."

Jacob's legs trembled and betrayed him as he wobbled, landing on his behind with a thud. The creature bent down and knelt across from him, staring.

"I'm not going to eat you, if that's what you're worried about," the Bogeyman said. "I feast on the souls of naughty boys and girls. Not nice little children like you."

Pictures of Jacob's night flashed like a series of selfies through his mind. The babysitter. Marcus's horror movie. Lightning. Thunder. The way his mattress creaked when Dad sat on his bed. Clutching his bear as he fell asleep. Was he still dreaming? He reached out to touch the creature.

"Ow!" Jacob retracted his hand, a thorny hair from the Bogeyman's head stuck in his finger like a splinter.

"You're not dreaming, Jacob. I'm here. I'm real. And I'm not going to eat you. In fact, I'm already quite full for the night. Want to see?"

The creature wriggled his nose and opened his mouth wide, so wide Jacob thought the Bogeyman's head would crack open, right there in his room. The Bogeyman placed cold claws on the back of Jacob's head, urging him closer to its open mouth. Jacob squirmed under the Bogeyman's grasp, holding his breath as the stench of old sweat socks, moldy tuna fish sandwiches, and Cool Ranch Doritos overtook him.

It was the smell of Marcus.

"Open your eyes," the Bogeyman commanded.

There, in the belly of the beast, Jacob's older brother slept, curled in the fetal position.

The Bogeyman released his grip and Jacob scurried backward, his back slamming against his bedpost. He sat, staring, glassy-eyed at the creature, unable to twitch or breathe or scream or move.

Taking the toy pickaxe in his claws, the creature reached across the floor for Jacob's abandoned teddy bear. Pulling it into its arms, the Bogeyman settled, cross-legged, next to Jacob.

"You need to get some rest, kid," the Bogeyman said. "Why don't I tell you a bedtime story?"

Jacob blinked hard, attempting to rid the image of the Bogeyman that sat before him. Each time he opened his eyes, though, the Bogeyman was still there, watching. He closed his eyes, tight, thinking that maybe if he fell asleep, this nightmare would go away.

Jacob tried counting sheep, but all he could see was his brother's head on each wooly body and the Bogeyman biting those heads off with bloody, razor-sharp teeth. He tried humming to himself, but the Bogeyman always joined in with creepy songs about slashers who invaded people's dreams, about killer blood-drinking dolls who hid in basements, and men whose dark evil was so powerful it could not be concealed by the masks they wore.

The Bogeyman warbled in a sickly-sweet, cracking falsetto that shattered the windows in Jacob's room. The last thing Jacob heard before he finally passed out into a dreamless sleep was his father's footsteps booming down the hallway.

The Shadow of My Little Boy

The shadow of my little boy floats across the sky.

His right hand grips tightly to the string tethering him to a yellow balloon; it cuts through cerulean blue with the conviction of a sunbeam.

With his left, he waves at me with frantic joy

looky me, Mommy!

as he rises

up...

up...

up...

He sings a long-forgotten nursery rhyme about chasing rainbows on a summer's day—the one that once lulled him into dreams; he's

PASSAGEWAYS

~drifting away~

swallowing clouds like they are fresh-spun cotton candy. He smiles, his gap-toothed grin sugary, leaving me gaping in a puddle on the asphalt below—

—*I* am the puddle—

years melted by the wick of slow-burning remembrances; droplets of love and fear and hope raining from within me, a torrent

down...

down...

down...

From the child I have turned, distracted,

~drifting away~

for a millisecond's breath

failing to notice the wanderlust in his eyes,

failing to consider the finite wonder of dimpled knuckles, or the sweet stickiness of his palm as I clutch his hand,

failing, in this moment, to stop him from tugging the string of that yellow balloon, despite my cautioning

Don't touch.

It's not yours.

Not yet.

I cannot interrupt his fingers plucking it from that technicolor plume rooted in gloved hands of a faceless theme park attendant whose shoes adhere to the ground by some magic spell that freezes time, while my tiny child levitates

up...

up...

up...

~drifting away~

from me on a lonely summer's day, a shadow in the sky.

Beyond the Red Door

At the end of the cavernous alley between the American Bank building and the headquarters of Tigert's Department Store, there is a red door.

Beyond that red door resides a monster.

I'd only seen its shadow, but I had no doubt it was there. A hulking *thing,* it stole away the speckles of sunlight that danced between those massive skyscrapers.

It took my little sister Annabel, too.

Annabel disappeared from the Big City on a rank summer day. Whiffs of hot garbage overwhelmed us as we walked along the cracked sidewalk with Mom. She'd taken us shopping for those fancy National Girl dolls we'd begged for, with real-girl hair and blinking eyes, whose dresses rivaled any Instagram fashionista. Not that Mom allowed us Instagram or cell phones. We only got to peek at our favorite influencers over the shoulders of the popular girls at recess.

I held Mom's hand and hugged my doll, and as usual, Annabel lagged. Her sandals were too tight, she had big ugly blisters, and she was hungry. Annabel was always hungry. She'd asked Mom to stop for candy, for ice cream, for soda, and when Mom said no (as she usually did), Annabel threw a tantrum, stomping her feet and screeching like a rabid fox, right there in the middle of 57th Street. Even the beggars stared and tsked at her tightly closed eyes and wide-open mouth as they passed her by with their overflowing rusted shopping carts.

I felt Mom's anger rise through her tightening grip as she turned toward Annabel.

"You want to scream?" Mom said through gritted teeth. "Stay there and scream." Her face stone, Mom yanked Annabel's doll away from her, and as my sister howled, stomped off with me in tow.

"Shouldn't we get her..." I started.

"No. She needs to learn her lesson."

Mom sighed when I gazed up at her, and her expression softened. "Don't worry, Lizzie, she'll catch up once she's calm."

But Annabel didn't catch up. As I turned back toward my sister, the last thing I saw was that massive shadow bursting from between the buildings, a tsunami of smoke that pulled her inside that alleyway.

The air screeched.

The ground shook with an echoing boom, the clanking of a massive vault sealing.

"Mom?" My voice cracked.

I glanced back. A large red rectangle floated in the alley. Then it vanished.

"Mom! Annabel's gone!"

"For heaven's sake," Mom said, turning on her heel to the empty sidewalk behind us. Her face paled through her makeup; her features fell like melting wax.

"Annabel!"

❖

THEY NEVER FOUND MY sister.

Nobody wanted to hear about the shadow in the alleyway or the red slamming door—not my parents, not the police. They'd rounded up some of the homeless who had been in the area that day; interviewed the shop keeps and apartment dwellers above them, but typical of the Big City, *nobody saw nothin'.*

Mom stopped talking. Dad stopped looking at her, other than to glare. Before long, she left us, and for the next several years, Dad didn't let me out of his sight.

But he couldn't always be there, watching me.

❖

IT'S EASY TO SLIP away from the class mothers chaperoning our middle school trip to the City Museum, so busy prattling on about hair dye and micro-blading. Taking bus selfies together, they don't notice one missing from the herd.

Funny how that works.

Since the day Annabel disappeared, I've studied maps of the city, memorizing its footprint. For four years, I've thought about nothing but my sister's too-tight shoes and the way she'd slapped the soles to the pavement when she walked, as if trying to awaken the earth. When I close my eyes, I can still see her gap-toothed smile, the secret stash of chocolates she'd kept in her room, even the way she ate an ice cream cone, always from the bottom up.

Time has moved on, but I haven't.

I need to bring Annabel home.

A curt breeze thwacks me in the face as I approach that all-too-familiar alleyway. Clouds circle like vultures above the tips of the skyscrapers and a chill sidles up my leg with the first steps I take into the shade of those buildings. All around, the detritus of children's favorite things—Annabel's favorite things—swirl on the gritty pavement. Faded and tattered candy wrappers, filthy and dented pint-sized ice cream containers drift amid a sea of shredded coloring books and broken crayons. Fast food containers, sad and stained plush animals, a headless doll—much like the one Mom had taken from Annabel that day.

She needs to learn her lesson.

I wonder how those words must haunt my mother now. Wherever she is.

I wonder if I'll ever see either of them again.

As I wade through the trash, the tickle of a shadow brushes against my neck, and I flinch. That monster could be anywhere.

The alleyway stretches, an endless tunnel, and a red light pulses ahead through the fallen darkness of midday. I reach for it, my hand pushing through the gloom with a slow-motion stroke as if I'm swimming through a sea of warm taffy.

The light radiates outward, morphing into a square, and then a rectangle.

A door.

A red door.

With that nauseating screech I've heard only once before, the hinges turn. The door inches open. My breath catches as dark tentacles of smoke stretch from its recesses.

The monster.

Annabel stands, framed in the doorway like a faded photograph.

Smiling and waving. Wide-eyed and pale.

Gap-toothed.

My baby sister, eternally seven.

"Annabel!" I shriek.

As I reach for her, I feel a punch to my gut, silenced as the alley steals my voice and the shadow rips air from my lungs. It wraps itself around me and pulls me through the door. My bones quake when it slams shut, like a casket closing.

Annabel grasps my hand, her fingers icy in the darkness.

"Lizzie?" she whispers. "Did you bring my doll?"

The Victory Garden

Luana's gnarled hands bonded with the handle of her broomstick, their roughened knots indistinguishable from the old wood. A hunchbacked and bone-thin relic of days long forgotten, she dragged the bristles over her crumbling doorstep, its timeworn brokenness not unlike her own body. She wiped moisture from her brow, her wrist grazing the wiry gray sprouting from her scalp where soft locks used to flow.

She gazed over the horizon with the forlorn wistfulness attired only by those in mourning. Deep indigo displaced the light hues of lavender and pink that once draped the land of Timeron, before the Grand Tyrant and his beasts infiltrated, bursting from the Nether Realm on wings of leather and steel.

Prior to the invasion, her tiny cottage had nestled into a hamlet so green and lush that the land seemed to breathe of its own volition. Now, it lingered a fossil in the parched forest, listless, flanked by trees on the precipice of death; they leaned into each other lest they fall and crumble to ash. The grass had shriveled, dry as a corpse. In its stead, black nixotweeds, blemished with bubbling green rot, grew in abundance, the reeds so tall they touched the tops of her window sills.

In the quiet of night, Luana swore she could hear those reeds chanting the dull drone of the Grand Tyrant as they drained the last vestiges of color from the once-verdant land.

No matter how dark the days and the nights, though, Luana busied herself by keeping a tidy home. She swept as if she were expecting company, grasping tight to the broomstick to hold on to some semblance of the life she once knew, the life she hoped she'd see again one day. Her home was her refuge in a chaotic world, the flame on the hearth inextinguishable even as the death winds swirled to devour any trace of beauty that remained.

Luana had cut a path, almost indistinguishable through the weeds, from the dirt road to her door, and from her door to the back garden. The warping wooden trellis where her aeroses once clung, painting the threshold in yellow, red, and white blooms, stood aged and defiant, perhaps a bit like Luana herself. Past the trellis, rows of branches that once sprouted lylack flowers inter-twined, bridging themselves together in a barren fortress, hollow yet thick, and prickly as a bed of thorns. Her marble bench was cracked and wrought with decay, strangled by yvivines that wound through the dirt, desperate for a last gasp of air.

Luana missed the sweet, crisp perfume of the yisminbuds in the mornings, and the song of the wood nymph as it nestled within the blooms for its nightly slumber. She could almost hear them sing each time she tiptoed into her ruined garden, braving the sting of the nixotweeds as they leeched blood from the skin of her ankles. Her fingertips remembered the touch of newborn blossoms that once cascaded over her, their satin skin as soft as air. And when she breathed in deep, it was not the sour stench of the nixotweed that prickled her nostrils, but the sweet perfume of the lylack tree that transported her back to the garden as it once was, before darkness cut through Timeron with its bloody scythe, sucking the life from the paradise she had known.

She stilled her mind; closed her eyes until she could feel the garden flowing through her, unyielding as a new leaf unfurling under the summer sun. Luana had lived long enough to know that hope was not something for humans to possess. Only fools sought to grasp its light with their bare hands, and when they neglected to capture it, they wallowed in the muck of their own failure. No, hope was a living thing to nourish, that would grow in its own time. And through the parched ruins of her garden, she'd planted its seeds, willing them to thrive, if only in her own heart.

The Grand Tyrant had taken the menfolk from the villages and the hamlets first, the cries of their wives and children as raw as a tree skinned alive by the blade of an arbor hunter. Some men were morphed into soldiers; the Tyrant's mind-twisting enchantments so painful that horns protruded from their skulls, white as bone but tainted with the crimson stain of bloodlust. And their bodies fell away from their human form, grown into massive beasts designed to serve a master who nourished them with fear and hatred for the living. Others were dragged to the mines, thrust into the belly of the Eroll Mountains. Man and machinery melded into an infernal automaton, intended to suck the marrow from Timeron—for without joy and color and verve, their world was nothing.

To Luana's knowledge, none of the taken men resisted or questioned their fate, genuflecting to a darkness they didn't understand—the fear of death eclipsing the dread of damnation. The Grand Tyrant's magic was far too powerful for overt revolution. Sadness seized Luana's gut as she thought of those men, burdened by shackles of despair that pulled them down, flailing and prostrate, feeling they had no choice but to acquiesce.

Luana's broom bristles scraped the ground, scratching the earth with slow, yet resolute strokes. Dust rose over the hem of her tattered robe like clouds in a rising storm. There was always a choice, she thought. Luana mourned the decline of her world with every bit of her soul, and in her own infinitesimal way, she wanted her withered world to know that she'd be there, clutching its hand until it somehow revived—or until it breathed its last. So on she swept, confident that with each turn of dust, the land of Timeron would know it was not alone in the dark.

The motion was interrupted by a crunching, faint like distant footsteps over gravel. Luana stopped to listen. She craned her neck in the direction of the road, watching the empty landscape with eyes as large as those of the wildebirds that once hovered over the forest, their golden wings ethereal, the light from the sun and the sky reflecting pools of shimmering shadow below. But the wildebirds had long since flown off or died, along with all the animals of Timeron—the blue bucks that galloped with their long striped legs and twin tails, even the tiny nubs that nibbled on the purple elefruit that grew outside Luana's garden.

Still eyeing the road, Luana crouched down, her old bones creaking like the trees around her. A strand of brittle hair fell from the tight bun she wore at the nape of her neck; she tucked it behind her ear as she felt around the dirt, careful to avoid the venom of the nixot weeds. With a tremor, her hand closed around three round pebbles and as she rose, she dropped them into the pocket of her apron. It was too soon for a visit from the soldiers who'd traveled the road each fortnight for the monthly tithe, but one could never be too careful.

With the effort of the aged, Luana pulled herself up, leaning on her broomstick for support. She wiped her hands on her dress as she stared ahead.

She heard his breathing before his small head emerged over the clearing. The boy stumbled as he ran, gasping like a man on his deathbed, unwilling to take the hand of the reaper. Blond curls stuck to his forehead, his cheeks radiated heat, and his eyes darted from side to side, watching for the shadow of a predator.

The deep wrinkles on Luana's cheeks smoothed; years dripped from her skin as her lips pulled back into a smile.

It had been so long since a child had passed by Luana's cottage, she'd feared they'd become extinct. When the supply of men had dwindled and the Grand Tyrant began plucking children from their homes like fruit from the vine, Luana had offered the grieving mothers a haven for their young—a place where they could grow and thrive and blossom, outside the reach of the Tyrant or his minions.

She'd collected countless children over the years. Time would tell if Luana had saved enough of them.

"Young man!" she called.

The boy froze, his expression feral. He couldn't have been more than a decade old, though his sunken eyes and deep-set frown belied his age. Even in the dim Timeron sky, the boy's tears shimmered like sunset on the Gunsam Lake—before the Tyrant and his herd had drained it.

"They're after you?" Luana asked.

Shoulders slumped, the boy nodded. "They killed my mum. And my baby sister..." He covered his face, his sobs electric. "They ripped her apart, sucked the flesh from her bones."

Luana felt a dagger through her bosom, she placed a hand over her heart to quell the pain that radiated within her—for that mother, that baby. For this boy who stood, helpless and hopeless before her. She left her broom standing upright, attentive and waiting, its bristles floating just above the ground. The boy glanced at it hovering there, his furrowed brow staunching his tears.

Padding down the pathway to the road, Luana reached out for the boy, longing for him to feel the love of his own mother, the love of all the mothers in Timeron, in her embrace. The Grand Tyrant had taken so much from them all, Luana thought.

"There isn't much time," she whispered. "You must hide."

"But where?" he said. Breaking free of Luana, he glanced around, frowning. "They're sure to find me. And they'll kill me. Or worse."

Draping her arm across his back, Luana pointed toward her garden. "There."

"Through those old trees?"

The distinct clopping of a Tyrant's soldier echoed in the distance.

"Do you know what defeats the darkness?" Luana brushed the boy's hair from his forehead and felt his skin shiver beneath her own. Her breath caught as he looked up at her, wordlessly. "Hope does. Now I promise, if you go hide in that garden, not only will you be safe, you will be strong. Stronger than you ever thought possible."

"But what if—"

Luana hushed him, kissing his forehead. Some of the children she had hidden had gone willingly. Others, like this boy, required greater convincing. But with the Tyrant's minions approaching, there was little time for hope to grow within him. Faith alone would lead the boy into Luana's garden. Their future depended on his readiness.

A flicker of hesitation clouded his eyes but then, with a quick nod, the boy bolted through the nixot weeds. Rustling in his wake, they cackled as he disappeared through the garden's threshold.

Luana retrieved her broom from where she'd left it hovering, returning to her work as if a young boy hadn't just been swallowed beneath her yard's decaying foliage.

Moments later, a vast shadow eclipsed Luana's home.

"You there!"

Luana looked up from her sweeping to the glare of a centaur soldier. Its chin was squared in an over-exaggerated masculinity; long black hairs hung from its ears to its chest. It clicked its hooves about and puffed out a muscled torso while tilting its head to expose two horns. A bloodied sickle hung from the leather strap across its chest.

"Good day, soldier," Luana said, her lips pulled into a thin line. As many times as Luana had encountered the centaur soldiers, she struggled to reconcile their former humanity with the beastliness their metamorphosis yielded—the fear and helplessness of man incarnate.

She rested the broom against the door and curtsied. "How may I be of service to you, and to his Eminence?"

"I am searching for a traitor." The soldier huffed, a cloud of steam emanating from its nostrils.

Luana shook her head. "I'm sorry, sir, but you will find no traitor here."

The centaur scowled. "It was a boy. A defector from his destiny. The Grand Tyrant had marked him with the honor and dignity of armed service. Yet, he ran." The centaur clopped close to Luana, sniffing the air around her. "In this direction."

"I saw no boy," Luana said. "In fact, I've seen no one since your colleague last rode by to collect the tithe."

"Hmm." The centaur grunted. "I will take your tithe, old woman."

"Of course." Luana reached into the pocket of her apron. She squeezed the pebbles hard into her palm, the heat of her skin transforming them into silver coins. The centaur opened its large mouth; Luana placed the coins on its scaly blue tongue. The centaur swallowed the coins whole. Its eyes glowed red.

"I will search the premises," the soldier said. "You are aware of the penalty for disobeying the Grand Tyrant."

Luana nodded. "You will find no traitor here, I assure you," she repeated. "Fulfill your duty, as the Grand Tyrant expects." With a grand, sweeping gesture, Luana bowed as she opened the door. She hoped her grandiose motion was enough to mask the tremor in her hands, that the calm timbre of her voice was enough to quell the cracking that settled in her throat.

It was the first time the Grand Tyrant's minions had ever darkened the threshold of her home. This violation of the hearth served as a harbinger—not of death, but of a force far more powerful.

Luana pressed her lips together. She stifled her breath, hoping the silence of her feigned surrender was plausible enough for the soldier to move through quickly.

The centaur stomped past her, its hooves clopping over Luana's creaking wood floors. The beast ravaged the tiny rooms of her cottage. Ceramics smashed. Furniture crashed and cracked, upended. Windows shattered. Hinges cried out as the doors were ripped from their frames. The centaur would not rest until the cottage was nothing but a hollow shell of the miniscule life Luana was deigned to live. She had no choice but to stay quiet and lower her head.

As an old woman, Luana was of no use to the Grand Tyrant or his mission. The centaur needed to believe she would be grateful to die with the world around her.

Galloping through the front door, the centaur raced past Luana and on to the path leading to the road. The beast turned its torso left and right, hooves stamping about, and with a mighty whack of its tail, it turned back to her.

"I will search the full premises," the soldier said. "You are fortunate that the Grand Tyrant allows you to stay. It is only the tithe that saves your kind."

The soldier raced toward Luana's shriveled garden at the back of the property. Bolting through the trellis, the beast kicked at the arid grass. Luana watched it raise its face toward the ceiling of branches, snorting and sniffling as if it intended to consume the garden into its cavernous nostrils. She cringed as it stamped down the marble bench, hooves crushing it like bone into dust. The beast raged, flying from the empty garden. Heat emanated from its body, blurring the air around it in a smoky haze. Its roars reverberated over the deadened landscape; the arid trees, bushes, and grass smoldered when touched by its breath. And as swiftly as it had arrived, the beast left, without a glance toward Luana or the disarray it left within her home.

When the silence had once again settled, Luana picked up her broom, marveling at the nature of evil, and how a momentary storm could twist and tatter and pulverize the things that are held most dear. Dragging the bristles across the earth, she scrubbed away the dust left by the centaur's rant. Faster and faster she brushed, the friction rising a cloud of powdery earth that enshrouded her. On unsteady legs, she pivoted toward the interior of her house in a swirl of white. Luana pursed her lips and blew, whistling sweeter than the wood nymph's song, and the mist lifted from her body, reaching into every corner of her dwelling. It raised the broken ceramic dishes, racing in a cyclone around them until they shined, polished and clean, not even a chip marring their surface. It righted the broken furniture, bending the cracked wood as it smoothed fractures and splinters, leaving the pieces sturdy, secure. With the rush of a waterfall, broken glass melted and flowed over the window frames, the panes restored to clarity.

Luana breathed in deep, inhaling the remnants of the veil of earth dust that she'd blown into her dwelling. It warmed and filled her, rich like the nectar of the elefruit. Her skin glowed, the deep, sagging lines of her aged complexion filled in with light. Her fingers straightened, the knots fading as if they were never there. Luana stood tall, long snowy hair released from its bun, flowing freely behind her. Her eyes sparkled, lavender as the skies of her childhood.

While evil feasted at the table of despair and drank from the font of destruction, Luana drew sustenance from a wellspring laden with sunrise.

Restored to her true self, there was one thing left for Luana to do.

She needed to check on the children.

Luana thrust the broomstick forward and released it into the path. With wide, pendulum-like strokes, it sliced through the nixot weeds leading from the house to the garden. The weeds shrieked as they desiccated, then liquefied into inky pools that were swallowed into the earth. Luana laughed as she followed it down the cleared path, her sound as light as the breeze that once kissed the treetops. As she approached the garden, reds and blues and violets and yellows glowed against the shining trellis; light burst through the threshold of the victory garden she'd tended and loved through the darkest times.

The lylack blooms cascaded down upon Luana, sweet as rain. She stroked the softness of their small, delicate petals, her fingers glistening with the life oozing from them. Rainbows disguised as budding plumes burst from lush, emerald leaves. Technicolor twinkled in a kaleidoscope of wonder as it reflected from the stretching vines and the foliage that breathed around them.

Luana glanced up. Hundreds of silver chrysalises shimmered through the flowers, giggling like sicaydabugs.

The children lived, tiny clouds dotting the lavender sky that would once again be restored to Timeron. The garden was but a single microcosm of the world that once was, the world that would be again.

Hope was the one thing that could grow, unfettered by evil. And it was almost time for Luana's angel army to burst forth from their cocoons, winged and ready to take on the night.

83

I Know About the Dragon

"Tell me about the dragon, Edgar."

Fucking red-faced, fat-ass cop's got some nerve grilling me. If it wasn't for me, that little fire breather would've imprinted on Old Man Petersen the minute it crawled out of that egg we found in the old misanthrope's backyard.

Which would have been an epic disaster.

"I don't know what you're talking about."

Cop slams his coffee cup down, pushes those sweaty, meaty palms against the table and leans in. He's so close I can see the goddamn pock marks on his face. I hold my breath to ward off the spittle spewing from his disgusting pie hole—stale coffee and last night's garlic and god knows what else.

"Don't you bullshit me, son!"

I shake my head, pressing my lips together in a tight line. Nobody's getting nothing out of me. Definitely not that smelly cop. And Old Man Petersen can go fuck himself if he thinks he's ever gonna find that baby dragon.

Drew and Alice better keep their mouths shut. If they know what's good for them.

❖

"Is this your first time in a police station, Alice?"

I can't look at him. I won't look at him. I squeeze my hands together—they're wet and squishy. Kind of like the inside of that dragon egg when we found it. Poor little creature all by himself in a world he doesn't belong in. Maybe if I close my eyes tight enough this will all be just some weird bad dream that Drew, Edgar, and I can laugh about later—well, not Edgar. He doesn't laugh at anything.

"Alice?"

I shake my head.

"Sweetheart, you've got to talk to me."

I crack my eyes open, slowly—*like that egg cracking open before the little guy poked his head out, shivering and lonely and afraid*—and see the cop leaning in. He's soft and pudgy with these big puppy dog eyes and red cheeks, a bit like Santa Claus, if Santa had shaved his beard.

"No."

"No?"

"I've never been in a police station before. Except when I got my Good Citizen patch in the Girl Scouts when I was thirteen."

"That's nice," he says. "You know why you're here, right?"

I hang my head, staring at my mud caked Keds. They were new, perfect white canvas, before we'd gone traipsing through Mr. Petersen's backyard. All the "No Trespassing" signs in the world wouldn't keep the locals off his property—especially the local kids. Ever since Josh Bowman stole those old hubcaps from Petersen's trash pile and he claimed his car... flew... after he'd installed them on his Jeep, there'd been an irresistible fascination with the junk in Mr. Petersen's yard.

Especially for Edgar.

But that egg, it wasn't junk. It was a tiny miracle.

"Alice, answer me."

"No, I don't know why I'm here." I bite my lower lip to stop it quivering. Edgar, Drew, and I, we'd made a pact. I look up at the cop and feel sorry for him. He seems like a nice enough guy, and I'm making his job much harder than it needs to be. "And I'd like to go home. I have an AP Calculus exam tomorrow, and I need time to study."

"DREW, YOUR FRIENDS HAVE already told me everything. I just need your side of the story to validate." The cop hovers over me, big as—no, bigger than!—the Incredible Hulk. Gooseflesh prickles through my skin as I grow cold in his shadow. "Tell me the truth and you can go home, like none of this ever happened."

Did they tell? Maybe Alice cracked. It had to be Alice. She's never broken a rule in her life and there's no way she'd be able to lie under pressure. It's one of the things I love most about her, in fact, there's a lot I love about Alice that I've never had the guts to tell her. Too late now. If I get hauled off to juvie—*juvie!*— maybe even Death Row, I'll never have a chance to say it before they give me my last meal and send me to the chair.

Will they send me to the chair for this?

"Drew, I'm waiting for your statement."

Nah, there's no way Alice said anything. She may be a bad liar, but she's also loyal to a fault. The best friend anyone could ask for. But Edgar? Ehh. He can be shifty. Send you down the river if it suits him. Like the time he blamed me for breaking Old Man Petersen's window when we were playing Wiffle Ball in the street when we were twelve. Wiffle balls don't crack glass, but thrown rocks do. My mom didn't believe me when I told her what happened. Neither did Mr. Petersen, or the cops he'd called when he caught me trying to clean up the glass outside his house. Edgar had promised to help, but somehow, he'd managed to disappear—*poof!* as if he'd vanished into thin air. So much for the truth setting you free! I'd been grounded for a month, missed out on half my summer. No bikes, no pool, no camping trip. And yet, once I had my get-out-of-jail free card, who was the first person I called?

Edgar.

Because days with Edgar are exciting. He's the kind of kid your mother warns you about, and her admonitions make you want to hang out with him even more. He's the candle to your moth. The flower to your bee. The crumbs to your ants.

Edgar is a lot of things, but he isn't a snitch.

He wouldn't have snitched. Couldn't. As tough as he makes himself out to be, I saw the way he looked at that little creature when it crawled out of its egg and climbed up into his arms. It was as if he'd found his life's purpose.

And when you find your life's purpose, you hang on to it as tight as you can.

"Drew?"

The cop's voice bounces in my brain. My mouth goes cotton dry.

"I..."

"Spit it out, kid. We don't have all day here."

"I... I have nothing to corroborate. There's no side of my story because there is no story. Petersen's out to get us. He's crazy. He made the whole thing up."

The cop raises his eyebrows.

"Oh? And what is it that he supposedly made up?"

I gulp back my non-existent saliva. I may have said too much.

"TELL ME WHY WE'RE here again?" Alice scowled, her pale face reflecting the moonlight. She pulled her black hoodie tighter over her head.

"Petersen's up to something, and I'm gonna bust that sono-fabitch. Expose him for the freak he is. Make him pay." Edgar cracked his knuckles, his expression stone.

"Pay? For what? I'm the one who was grounded for the window incident, remember? Not you." Drew fidgeted. "Dude's a cur-mudgeonly old weirdo, yeah, but maybe we should just go. Leave him be."

Alice nodded. "I agree with Drew."

"You *always* agree with Drew. And Drew..." Edgar clenched his fists. "This bastard's up to something and I'm gonna find out what. I'm gonna stop him, before it's too late."

"What's gotten into you, Edgar? Why the obsession with Pe-tersen?" Alice reached for his arm, and he shrugged her off, glar-ing.

"You wouldn't understand."

"Try me," Alice said.

"Yeah, try us," Drew repeated. "If you can't trust your friends..."

"Look, this isn't about you. This isn't about any of us. It's much... bigger." Edgar's expression darkened and an eerie chill drifted over the night. "Petersen... that fucker is... Never mind. I can't explain it. Why don't you two just go the hell home. This is my score to settle, not yours."

Alice and Drew exchanged concerned glances.

"Whatever it is you need to do, we're not going to let you go alone," Drew said. "Right, Alice?"

Alice nodded, her eyes wide.

A slow, uncharacteristic grin spread across Edgar's features as he stepped from the shadows. "I knew I could count on you."

That darkness, it clung to him, Edgar wore it like a cloak as he marched into Old Man Petersen's yard. Alice and Drew trailed, their steps short but quick, as if afraid their footfalls would land in Edgar's wake.

❖

"I repeat, what is it that Mr. Petersen supposedly made up?" The cop takes a swig of his coffee and thunks the empty cup on the table. "Drew, we know about the dragon."

"The... dragon?"

"Mr. Petersen's rare exotic pet that you and your friends stole from his backyard."

Oh, that dragon is rare, alright, but it's far from any pet I've ever seen. It's no reptile—even an illegal one whose venom can kill you within hours!—I'd learned all about komodo dragons in sophomore year biology. This dragon, it's mystical, magical, like something out of a fairytale.

"We didn't steal anything from Old Man Petersen. He... he..."

"I know, he made it all up. You kids trespassing on his property, absconding with his personal belongings. Just fess up, Drew, and this will be all over."

But it will never be over. I'll never forget what I saw that night, the shimmering gold of the dragon's egg hidden in a nest beneath piles of junk—candelabras and moldy old books and cracked clay pots. A fortress of overgrown weeds, big as cornstalks, or... *beanstalks?* shielding it in the back of the yard. Edgar, on a mission, dashing straight for it like some crazy homing pigeon. Edgar, slashing through the overgrown plants with a switchblade knife that seemed to grow longer with each cut. I could swear he had sheathed a sword by the time we'd reached the egg.

But that's crazy talk. Seventeen-year-old tough guys do not carry swords. And baby dragon eggs don't simply appear in the yards of eccentric, grumpy old men.

Maybe I'm losing my mind. Maybe it's all some crazy hallucination and I'm experiencing some sort of psychotic break.

Is this cop even real? *Am I?*

I wish I could talk to Alice. About what we saw. What we did. She's the smartest person I know, and if anyone can make sense of any of this, she can.

Sweat pools on my brow and a wipe it away with the back of my hand.

"Can I have some water?" I croak.

"Can you tell me the truth?" The cop mocks me, his voice an exaggerated gravel.

I shake my head.

I have nothing to say.

"AP Calculus," the cop repeats. "Impressive. I failed algebra, twice. You have a scholarship for next year, don't you, Alice? Rumor has it Columbia's giving you a full ride."

I can't help but smile. Every time anyone says *Columbia University* a happy shiver runs through me. I've worked hard, *really* hard, to get into my dream school. In a few more months, I'll be settled into my dorm—crisp sheets on the bed, posters with quotes from my favorite sci-fi authors plastered to the walls. I'll have a super-cool roommate, brilliant professors, and a brand-new start outside this small town.

I feel a twinge when I think of Drew, though. He's staying here, headed for community college.

"They offered me a full scholarship, yes."

"Your parents must be proud."

I nod, recalling my mom's shrieks when I'd showed her the letter, my dad's warm bearhug.

"You know," the cop says, "Kids with a record don't get to go Ivy league. You go to juvie, no scholarship for you."

My insides run hot as sunburn, then cold. Frostbite. I'm not sure which sensation is worse. But my scholarship? There's no way they can retract it, can they?

"Now, you want to tell me why you're here?"

I glance down at my Keds again. The right foot is almost entirely caked in mud, but on the left the dirt leaves a dark halo around the rubber sole. Mom's not going to be happy with me; I'd begged her for new sneakers, and she treated me with a visit to Foot Locker—rather than our usual trip to Goodwill—to celebrate my scholarship.

Shrugging my shoulders, I continue to stare at the floor. I wonder how many criminals have sat in this chair before me; how many of them had committed worthwhile and justifiable crimes.

Or crimes they *thought* were worthwhile and justifiable.

When we'd found the egg, it felt as if the ground surrounding it was trying to swallow us whole, something like the cartoon quicksand we'd all been conditioned to fear when we were children, even though deep inside we knew it wasn't real. Drew had grabbed me and pulled me out just as my shoe had started to sink.

Fast and sure-footed, Edgar had swiped the golden egg; its veneer rumbling with each step he took, a massive crack blemishing the outside as he sprinted toward the woods behind Mr. Petersen's property. Edgar fell to the ground, and the tiniest, most adorable little creature poked his head out of the shell. It was purple—no, more violet—with eyes like giant blueberries. It had a tiny little snout and some orange fuzz on its head; and its little wings, how they shimmered like the golden shell from which it had emerged.

And Edgar. I'd never seen a person transform so quickly. All his rough edges melted away as the baby dragon nestled in his arms. *"Beithir"* Edgar had whispered, cooing to the dragon in a strange tongue. Norse, perhaps? Celtic? It was difficult to say, but in that moment, Edgar—our Edgar—had become someone else.

"Hurry," he'd said, leading us through the dark woods behind Mr. Petersen's home with only moonlight to guide our steps. Without knowing why, Drew and I obliged. A mythic tug pulled at my gut as we ambled through the woods toward the river, running—soaring—led by this little creature who'd somehow entered our world.

And what of old Mr. Petersen? I'd never questioned why or how he'd acquired that egg, or Edgar's motives in seizing the dragon from his property. I knew, without knowing, it was the right thing to do.

"Alice." I glance up, and the cop's expression morphs from friendly to fierce. "I know about the dragon."

I bite my lip. Hold my breath. Weigh my scholarship—my future—against that of a tiny little life. And pray that my friends don't crack under the pressure of interrogation.

"GODDAMIT, EDGAR," THE COP rages. "Where is that dragon?"

He reaches for the holster at his hip, and instead of a gun or a taser, he pulls out a wand. Grabbing the back of my hair, he presses the cold metal to my throat and his pudge melts away to reveal a skeletal, yet glowing, old man. The police uniform morphs into wizard's robes.

"Clever, Petersen, clever. I never took you for a shapeshifter."

"And you're the sorriest excuse for a wizard I've ever met. Did you think you could scare me away with a rock through my window?" He presses the wand harder; I try to gulp past it.

"It was an enchanted rock, you asshole. Or did you forget about all those pus-filled boils that sprouted on your face after it crashed through your window?"

Petersen sneers. "Boils. Dead rats on my stoop. Snakes in my garden. Enchanting those old hubcaps in my yard."

"Can't lay low when the world thinks you're some crazy hoarder, can you?" I say. "The eyes on you were good for me. Must've enjoyed talking to the board of health!"

"Wiseass punk!" He flings me against the wall, the metal chair flipping over as I fly into the cinderblocks. My body slides up, up, until it almost touches the ceiling. "Where is he?"

I smile through the pain. "Long gone. On his way back home to his family, where he belongs. Did you really think you'd get away with kidnapping him?"

"That dragon was my ticket to acquiring yet another world! Lest we forget my dominion over yours."

I stiffen at the memory. Petersen—otherwise known as Zelguis Vigil—on the back of a dragon. The flames consuming my village. My parents' screams as they engage in their final act of magic; opening a portal for me to escape, to wait and to watch, to ensure that Zelguis Vigil never finds a path to power again, on any world.

"It's over," I say. Zelguis Vigil cackles, and a grey haze falls over the room as the old wizard flicks his wand toward my throat. The air is yanked from my lungs as his spell tightens its grip on my windpipe.

As my world starts to go dark, the cinderblock walls quake. With a flash of flame, daylight explodes into the room. I fall, gasping, as the baby dragon hovers, incinerating Zelguis Vigil in an instant.

Wide eyed and pale, Drew and Alice race through the rubble. Each grabbing an arm, they lift me to my feet. The baby dragon flits about, resting on my shoulder. He sneezes out a puff of smoke and sidles up against me.

"Edgar, are you ok?" Alice asks. Drew takes her hand as she reaches out to stroke the dragon's head and he purrs.

I glance at the two of them. It's impossible to contain my smirk. "You know, you'd make a good couple."

Drew gulps, his face turning as purple as the dragon.

"Thanks for keeping your mouths shut in there," I say. "You might not realize it, but you just saved the world."

Muttering my parents' incantation, I raise my hand, moving my arm in an exaggerated circle. The familiar portal opens, and I turn toward my human friends. "I knew I could count on you." I hold the dragon's feet against my shoulder and together we rise, sucked into the vortex.

❖

ALICE GLANCES AT DREW's hand, his fingers still entwined in hers.

"This is real, isn't it?" he asks. "I'm not dreaming."

She shakes her head and lifts her chin. "Not dreaming."

"How do I know?"

Alice giggles. "Are dragons purple?"

"Violet," Drew says. "I believe they are violet."

He leans in for a kiss.

A group of police officers burst through the doors into the interrogation room, which is now very much intact.

"What the hell do you think you kids are doing in here?" a pinch-faced cop asks.

Drew coughs through a laugh as Alice turns away, staring at her feet. "Kissing?" he says.

"Very funny." The cop sighs. "We're looking for a kid named Edgar. Got a call that he's been trespassing on private property. Seen him around?"

Drew and Alice glance at each other, brows furrowed with confusion.

"Edgar?" Alice says. "I don't know anyone named Edgar."

"Me either." Drew shrugs his shoulders. "Sorry. Can't help you, officer."

Self-Actualization

MY KNUCKLES WHITENED AS I squeezed the arms of the examination chair. The DentaBot regarded me with thin lips and empty eyes, its movements swift and cold as it plugged a wire into a port behind my ear. The light bore down with an intensity that would have stung my eyes, had they not been synthetic.

The office door whooshed open, and a stout human with a grin as bright as the exam room hustled in, humming. He stopped, silenced by my presence.

"NahNee."

"Dr. Smiles." My grip relaxed.

It had been fifteen years since I'd first met the dentist. His hair had been darker, his girth less pronounced, but his eyes retained a kindness uncommon among adult humans. Together we'd soothed a squirming Felicity through her first exam. Three years old and kicking, she refused to open her mouth, other than to bite the dentist. I'd held her hand and stroked her curly blond locks, singing the lullaby about twinkling stars that came with my programming.

I was encoded to nurture, not to care. But my love for the child overrode design logic.

"Here without Felicity?" he said, peering at me over wire-rimmed glasses.

"Yes. But I'm not sure why." I offered a halfhearted grin. "Bots don't require routine dental care."

"Indeed. How is Felicity? Must be almost grown."

"Off to University last week. And feisty as ever." I recalled her impatience as I fussed over her graduation cap. And the hug that lingered long after she'd gone.

The DentaBot tugged at the lead behind my ear. I winced as my pain sensors activated. "Pleasantries exceed protocol, Doctor. Her orders are ready."

He sighed. "Very well."

The DentaBot projected an image of me—the NahNee-721. Petite, with shoulder length chestnut hair, blue eyes, and a dimple gracing each cheek, I was built to delight children and engender parental trust—the manual described my model as a cross between a 1950s mom and a teenage best friend. Like millions of ServeBots, I was charged with taking on mundane and undesirable tasks to allow humans to achieve self-actualization.

I'd often pondered the meaning of self-actualization—the terminology exceeded my programming—but it seemed to be something that generated happiness. For Dr. Smiles, I supposed it manifested by helping and healing. Felicity's parents were like most humans; they found their joy in golf and Pilates, in wine and chocolate.

I wondered what Felicity's self-actualization would be.

Dr. Smiles frowned at code that flashed over the displayed image.

"Rest back," he instructed. An aroma of garlic and after-shave tickled my nostrils. My olfactory processing was advanced, detecting everything from a soiled diaper to an errant match-strike to an illness brewing beneath a child's skin. All three were tested by Felicity before she was six years old.

"Open."

Obliging, I saw my teeth reflected in his head mirror; shining pearls unblemished by time. At the back of my mouth, red and green sensors pulsed from the interior of my top right wisdom tooth. Dr. Smiles prodded it; each poke emitted a beep.

"Hard drive is fully functional," he said, wiping his hands. "It'll make the process easier."

"Process?"

"NahNee, do you know what *re-purposing* is?"

The DentaBot interrupted. "Explanation violates protocol."

The doctor scowled, waving a hand to quiet it.

Re-purposing—a word I'd heard spoken in hushed tones. From time to time, ServeBots vanished, replaced by newer technology. I never gave it much thought, but after Felicity left for University, the word lingered in whispers, intermingled with her parents' rumblings about a European holiday, the expense of a new valet droid, and the need to dispose of "it."

I shook my head, eyes widening.

"It's why you're here." Dr. Smiles placed a hand on my arm, his expression dour. "Re-purposing entails removal of the wisdom tooth where your hard drive resides. After I've extracted it, the memory is erased."

My simulated breathing caught like a bullet in my throat.

"The drive is reformatted, ready for new assignment programming. The tooth is re-implanted. Then," he paused, his eyes misting beneath his thick lenses, "you're sent to Central Processing Internment, where you'll be sold to a new owner."

I jumped up. "No! Felicity needs me!"

The DentaBot flew toward me, shoving me into the seat.

"Doctor! This outburst violates—"

Dr. Smiles glared at the Bot. It slinked away, and he turned toward me.

"I suspect Felicity knows nothing of this," he said.

She couldn't. The last time we spoke, we'd made plans for her Christmastime return—days spent baking and shopping...

"Help me?" I whispered.

He pinched the bridge of his nose. "I'm sorry." He eyed the DentaBot. "I'd be reported to the authorities."

Dr. Smiles had already risked so much by sharing this information. I couldn't dare place him in further danger.

"Well, let's get on with things," I said with the false cheerfulness I'd used to ease Felicity's childhood disappointments.

Dr. Smiles squared his shoulders and nodded, grim. The DentaBot zoomed to his side, pushing my chair back until I was lying flat. I laid trembling hands onto my lap and opened my mouth.

"This may pinch."

He yanked my tooth free. My vision pixelated into black, white, and gray; color reduced to the flashing lights of my extracted tooth laying on the tray. Though my hard drive pulsed with life, its removal triggered my body to initiate a three-minute emergency power backup before my senses shut down.

Dr. Smiles addressed the DentaBot. "We're out of silicone. It's needed for implantation." She nodded, gliding from the room.

Through a haze, I watched as Dr. Smiles switched my extracted tooth with another concealed in his sleeve. He swiftly pocketed *my* hard drive, humming a lullaby. Something about stars.

The DentaBot returned. Dr. Smiles fitted the decoy tooth into a device that emitted a loud buzz. Upon its silence, he squeezed silicone onto my gum and, with some difficulty, wedged in the new tooth.

"This ServeBot is ready for shipment," he said. "Re-purposing. Per protocol."

FALSE HOPE

THE QUEUE OF VEHICLES leading to the Mobile Apothecary snaked through the hills of the Ganymede Moon. Aside from the amber-hued gas spewing from the Oleg Mine accident site, the convoy seemed the only sign of life in the colony.

From the service window, Malven Roberts peered outside. "They just keep coming. Ants to a picnic."

Bumper-to-bumper, drivers waited hours for a ration of elixir to counter effects of the contamination. The air was thick with the dust of a moon that crumbled beneath them. With his classification, Malven was only told so much, but he'd lived long enough to know disaster when he saw it. And bullshit when he heard it.

The floor vibrated with another aftershock as Ilya Kruz, the Chemist-at-Large, crushed green and black granules with a mortar and pestle.

"Mostly Tan autos, now," Malven said. "Some Blues and Greens."

"Mmm-hmm. Reds are long gone." Ilya doled the antidote into vials aligned on the counter near the window. Vials on the left were reserved for the government, military, and healthcare workers who had not yet been evacuated. Those on the right were for the Tans—non-essentials who comprised most of the colony's population.

"Better get moving if we want to get this line down before closing," she said.

Malven pursed his lips. He bagged three vials from the right side and placed the package in the suction chamber; it traveled through a tube into the waiting vehicle.

Malven mostly avoided looking at the Tans—their sunken eyes, their sagging, mottled flesh that hung like cobwebs from protruding bones. A few days after the blast, he was unable to recognize even the most familiar customers, those souls whose names and lives he once knew obscured by waxen masks.

He glanced over to Ilya's backpack, resting by the door. A blue boarding pass jutted from the half-zippered bag. "Your last shift," he said. Chemists were Blue Class C; Ilya's shuttle to the space station was scheduled to leave that evening. As a Tech, Malven was Blue Class H, with 48 hours until his evacuation.

"You'll be fine," Ilya said. Malven noticed a new streak of white in Ilya's black hair and the hint of a boil rising on her neck. "Just keep the line moving."

The ground rumbled. Horns blared a wail of desperation as Malven and Ilya steadied themselves. A red light flared beneath the window like a pustule—a customer request for Chemist counsel.

Ilya sighed. "Another Tan."

Malven busied himself, assembling vials as Ilya pressed the intercom.

"Your question?"

The woman's words sputtered in a wave of hysteria. "Help! He's stopped breathing!"

Malven peered into the car. In the passenger seat, a man sat, rigid. Blood trickled like errant tears from beneath closed eyelids. In the back, a little girl snuggled under a blanket, a pool of black seeping into the upholstery beneath her blond curls.

The child was as old as Malven's granddaughter, who anxiously awaited his return to Earth at the end of his contract. Malven bit his lip to restrain the sob rising in his throat.

"Ma'am. Calm down." Ilya seized the vials from Malven's hands and thrust them into the airlock. "Go directly to the hospital."

"I tried!" the woman shrieked. "I couldn't get past the bodies! Couldn't get to the door!"

Horns blasted; the car behind the woman accelerated, nudging it forward.

"Ma'am. You need to drive. Go now," Ilya said.

Malven shook his head. They couldn't risk another crash at the service window—last time, The Guard arrived just before the angry mob broke through. Now, The Guard was gone.

The woman screamed and slammed on the accelerator. Tires squealed, protesting the hot pavement.

Ilya exhaled as the next car approached.

"Tans are getting worse," Malven said. "Upper echelon's responding a lot better to the treatment." He rolled up his sleeves, revealing few blemishes. "Us included."

Ilya reached past him, pulling vials from the left. The next driver was a Blue.

"We're almost out of serum," she whispered. "Tans get placebo."

Malven's eyes opened wide. "You mean, they get nothing?"

With a massive bang, the ground rocked. Ilya and Malven fell.

Ilya pushed herself up, her expression hardened. "We give them hope." She brushed her hands on her lab coat.

Malven scrambled to his feet, glaring at Ilya. She'd betrayed him, betrayed all of them. Amid the chaos, she'd forsaken her oath to heal, drawing Malven into a lie that served no purpose other than crowd management via a well-contained queue.

"False hope," Malven said.

"Better than no hope at all."

"What about Charles?" Malven pressed, recalling the way Ilya's palm lingered on the glass as she passed rations to the mining foreman who'd struck her fancy. "You gave him the real thing, didn't you?"

She turned away. "I needed him to live."

More false hope.

"Why do you get to choose?" Malven challenged.

She shook her head. "Does anyone, really?"

An alarm boomed, loud as a foghorn. The cacophony of vehicles, shouts, and cries outside rivaled its volume as metal shades dropped over the window.

Curfew.

Ilya squared her shoulders, her gaze fixed on a supply shelf. She retrieved the mortar and pestle. "You'll need more vials for tomorrow's rush. I've got some time before my flight."

Malven scowled. What was the point? Tomorrow wasn't guaranteed. Hell, tomorrow wasn't even likely. Here they stood, waiting for the moon to implode.

His silence an admonishment, Malven stormed toward the door. Ilya's boarding pass still poked through her bag, tempting as forbidden fruit. Malven glanced over his shoulder at the chemist occupied by crushing granules, the sound like grinding bone. He knew he was no better than Ilya—no better than any of them, Red, Green, Blue or Tan.

But he needed to live. His granddaughter was waiting.

Malven inhaled, his breath deep and deliberate. From his pocket, he retrieved his Blue Class H pass, slid it into Ilya's bag, and pilfered his ticket to salvation.

Aunt Tessa's Special Blanket

The box from Great Aunt Tessa's house smelled like old mothballs.

Then again, so had Aunt Tessa. I got a good whiff every summer when Mom forced me to go visit her mother's sister, a couple hours from us out in the middle of nowhere. Aunt Tessa lived alone in a tiny brick house that looked like it was built by the smartest little pig. Not a huff nor a puff nor a breeze would penetrate it; no matter how hot it got inside, Auntie kept the windows locked up tight and the shades drawn.

That house always felt like it was holding its breath, waiting for something to happen.

I was twelve the last time I saw her on a brutally hot August afternoon. Aunt Tessa's tea had been weaker and more bitter than usual, her cheese sandwiches a stale and mushy mess on those frilly, ugly flower-petal plates she pulled out for "company." Auntie scowled and said I ate like a barbarian when I tried scraping the bread and liquid cheese goop off the roof of my mouth with my index finger. But it was stuck there and she tsked at me, as if

I were supposed to be grateful that her sandwich was making a papier-mâché mold of my teeth while choking me to death.

I wiped the ooze from my chin with the back of my hand and Mom kicked me under the table, a painful reminder to watch my manners. I could almost hear Mom yelling, inside my head, not a second before Aunt Tessa chimed in with her high-pitched, old-lady whinge:

"My word! Keep those filthy, dirty hands off my lace tablecloth! It's an heirloom!"

But as many times as I wanted to laugh or cry or pass out in old Auntie's living room, I never did. I'd even smiled and nodded politely when she showed me her rotting antique books, her teacup collection, and the rows of good little ceramic boys and girls standing at attention on her knick-knack shelves.

"See this, young man?" Aunt Tessa never referred to me by name. I was always 'young man,' or 'sonny' or 'dear.' I wasn't sure she even knew my name was Jeremy. Mom never corrected her.

She pointed toward a glass figurine. I think she called it a Hubbel. Or was it a Hummel? "The turtle is following the little redheaded girl to school. Isn't that so special, dear?"

"Yes, yes," I said. "So special." My mother glared at me; from my tone she sensed the eye roll that threatened.

But it wasn't any more special than Aunt Tessa's lace doilies or her multi-colored knitted blankets. She called them afghans, like they were something exotic. Yarn was strewn everywhere, as if the house had been decorated by a gang of mischievous cats. Auntie always walked around wearing one of her hand-made sweaters, complaining she was cold—even in the middle of summer.

Every year, my aunt made us each a pair of knitted mittens for Christmas. Mom took a family picture in front of our tree; we waved at the camera with our hands swallowed up by that thick, scratchy wool. My fingers always felt like they would suffocate, and my hands emerged red and sweaty after just a few minutes in those hateful things. After Mom took the photo, I'd stash them in the back of the closet behind my old jigsaw puzzles. Mom thought those mittens were just wonderful. To me, they smelled like stinky old lady breath. And they felt like death on my skin.

I'd reached my breaking point on visiting Aunt Tessa the day I noticed that toilet-paper-holding doll in her bathroom. It was the kind with the beady eyes that watched you while you did your business. Aunt Tessa had knitted the skirt in puke green. It stretched out over the roll of paper and was supposed to be clever and cute. I just thought it was creepy. I didn't need some crazy-ass doll scrutinizing me while I wiped my behind. No, thank you.

When I'd told Mom that I wasn't going with her the next time she visited, she nodded, smiling with thin lips. "I was about your age when I stopped visiting Auntie, too," she said. "But she's a lonely little old lady. She's not getting any younger."

Mom encouraged me to join her, saying I'd *rue* the day when it was "too late" to visit. ("Rue" was an Aunt Tessa word, some-how Mom picked it up along the way). She said that I'd come to appreciate Aunt Tessa and all her quirks, just as she had. But the decision was mine, and my answer was always no. After a while, Mom stopped asking. Maybe she finally realized my summers were better spent bike riding and playing video games than sitting in some stuffy little house with an old lady who raised her eyebrows if I breathed on her precious trinkets or spent more than two minutes in the bathroom.

Two years later, Great Aunt Tessa died. All that was left was a big old cardboard box of stuff Mom and Dad dragged in through our front door, after the burial. Dad had loosened his tie and tossed his jacket to the side and Mom was still wearing her funeral dress when they hefted the box onto the dining room table.

I had stayed home, even though Mom asked me to go. Aunt Tessa creeped me out enough when she was alive.

"Cousin Leigh is handling Tessa's estate," Mom said. "She told us to take whatever we wanted."

I felt my nose scrunch up as I eyed the worn cardboard.

"Please tell me Toilet-Time Dolly isn't in that box."

"A little respect for the dead, please," Dad said, wagging a finger at me. He could be such a hypocrite. Sure, he went to the funeral, but only because Mom made him. He'd stopped visiting Aunt Tessa long before I did, making excuses like he had too much work. And of course, someone needed to stay behind to walk the dog. But I knew better. What Dad really wanted was a cold beer and the Yankees on TV. Old Aunt Tessa and her army of glass figurines would have staged a revolt over that.

"But Mom," I asked. "What would Aunt Tessa have that we'd actually want? I mean—"

"Memories, Jeremy. Memories." Mom scowled at me as Pepper, our golden retriever, came padding in, yawning. She stopped, stiffening as she sniffed the air around the box. She raised her front paw, her tail pointed straight. She howled.

"Pepper?" Mom said, reaching for the dog.

Tail between her legs, Pepper scuttled away into the living room without looking at any of us.

"See, Mom? Even Pepper gets it."

"Tessa never liked dogs," Dad mused. "She thought they were dirty. And smelled like mulch."

Dad and I exchanged knowing looks. Ignoring us, Mom leaned over the box. Her long pearl necklace raked over the cardboard like baby teeth. Gooseflesh raised the hairs on my arms; the sound of anything rubbing against cardboard cut through me with such a chill that I felt like my legs were going to fall off.

"Can you do that a little quieter, Mom?" I asked.

"You don't have to stay here. Especially if you're not going to appreciate—"

"No, I'll stay," I said. I did have a morbid curiosity about the contents of that box and sat next to Mom, leaning in closer. Taking stuff from a dead person's house was the opposite of burying them in the ground. Old things became new. And at least if you didn't like what you got; you could always sell it on eBay. I wondered how much we could get for one of those Hubbels. Hummels. Whatever.

A blast of heat, attic-hot, burst from the box as Mom opened it. I squinted as I peeked inside. My eyes stung with salty sweat; I wrinkled my nose at the hovering stench of moldy cheese.

Mom held up each item for us to see. She turned the objects slowly, ogling them like they were some sort of buried treasure. The first piece was that figurine of the little girl and the turtle. Despite being trapped on Aunt Tessa's shelf for, well, eternity, there wasn't a speck of dust on it.

Next, Mom revealed one of Auntie's famous flowery plates, this one gold-rimmed, with yellow blobs painted on the shiny white china.

"They look like dandelions," I said. "Who has a dish with dandelions on it? Aren't dandelions just a bunch of scraggly weeds?"

Dad nodded his agreement.

"They are NOT dandelions." Mom scowled. "Look closer and you'll see. They are roses in full bloom."

I didn't want to look closer. I wanted to get out of there, maybe go bike riding before dark. I tried to get up, but a sensation I couldn't fully grasp kept me sitting in the dining room with my parents, as if someone had attached weights to my ankles, rooting me to the chair to watch this weird unveiling of stuff I didn't care about. It was like Christmas morning, but boring. No lights, no tree, no stockings. No gifts for me. But the same flutter of anticipation tickled my gut.

"Wait until you see this," Mom said. I flinched as her pearls skated over the cardboard. Mom dipped her head so far into the box that only the tops of her shoulders poked out, upside down. She looked like one of those beheaded people they talked about in my history class—Anne Bowling something-or-other.

Mom's voice was muffled through the box. "Remember how Aunt Tessa never let anyone inside her bedroom? Well, I couldn't resist a quick look-see. It was just as I expected, pink and pristine, like the inside of a little gingerbread house…"

Mom emerged, breathless. She grinned in triumph, as if she had just won the mothball lottery. "Cousin Leigh said we could take whatever we wanted… so…"

Mom raised a woolen blanket over her head. Peach and ivory intertwined in a tight pattern, seamless and smooth.

I'd never seen anything like it in all my years of torture at Aunt Tessa's house.

I'd never seen anything like it in my lifetime.

It was the color of flesh, with the perfect, imperfect, consistency of human skin.

Bile rose in my throat.

"Tessa kept all her best work in her bedroom. Such a shame that she never shared it with us," Mom said. "I found this throw lying at the foot of her bed. I had to have it. These muted tones, and the pattern—why, they make the intricacies of this blanket come alive!"

"You found that on her bed?" I said, my voice cracking. "Didn't they find Aunt Tessa in her bed… dead?"

"Don't blame me," Dad said. "I waited outside. In the fresh air, while your mother went rummaging."

"Stop talking nonsense," Mom said, still cradling the blanket. "This may be the most beautiful thing Tessa ever created. With her own hands." Mom stifled a sniffle. "We'll always have a little bit of Tessa here with us now, don't you think?"

I didn't want to think about it. I didn't want to look at it. I tugged at the damp collar of my shirt; sweat dripped into my ears. The air was stifling, even though I was sitting directly beneath the air conditioning vent. It was as hot as it had been in Aunt Tessa's house that last time I'd visited.

Mom rubbed the blanket against her skin. It looked like it was eating her face.

Dad moved toward her, entranced, and reached out to pet the blanket.

"Come touch it, Jeremy! It feels as soft as a baby's bottom," Dad said.

"Are you crazy?" I bolted from the chair. The fuzz emanating from the blanket clouded around my parents' skin, radiating like sunlight baking over pavement. "That... thing. There's something not right about it."

Dad chuckled, his laugh deep and dark, like some deranged Santa Claus. "It's an afghan," he said. "A blanket."

"And a very well-crafted one," Mom said. "I was lucky to find it."

I felt myself turn green as nausea overtook my gut.

Dad glanced at Mom with a smirk. "Must be his hormones bubbling."

"Teenagers," Mom said. "Odd, oversized toddlers."

"Scared of the big, bad blanket?" Dad opened his eyes wide and wriggled his fingers at me. And they both giggled.

Somewhere in the space where breathing interrupted their laughter, I heard Aunt Tessa's voice, as raspy as a shovel digging into the earth.

Isn't it special, dear?

The heat from the open box swirled around my head like a blast from the oven; ridiculous and stifling. As I stared at the blanket, red dots seemed to ooze from the tiny spaces between the stitching, spreading like blood.

I AWOKE IN THE darkness of my room, sheets damp and wrinkled against my skin. I didn't remember how, or when, I'd come upstairs. Turning toward my nightstand, the clock flickered 3:33 a.m., the red LED warped through a glass of water that had been left for me, presumably by Mom or Dad. A plate of stale toast rested next to it.

I rolled over and stared at the ceiling. Finger-like shadows hovered above me, moving with the breeze. They were curled like a pianist's hands ready to play.

Or like finger puppets.

Or an old woman knitting.

Funny how our eyes paint pictures of what we want to see. Or of things we don't want to see.

I rubbed my eyes, hard. Maybe my imagination had simply run amok when Mom removed Aunt Tessa's things from the box. Or maybe now that she was dead, I felt guilty that I'd stopped visiting her, as painful and suffocating as those visits had been.

Aunt Tessa used to say I was a quiet child and that was a good thing, because, '*After all, Mary, children should be seen and not heard.*' I was sure Mom and Dad got a good chuckle out of that.

Turning to my side, I closed my eyes again, pulling my sheets tight to my body. And just as I felt the lapping waves of sleep begin to wash over my mind, I heard it.

Creeeak!

I bolted up, wide awake.

Creeeak!

Jumping from bed, I grabbed a flashlight from the dresser and crept toward the door. The sound came from somewhere inside the house. Quietly, I turned the knob. I clicked on the flashlight and shone it up and down the hallway. I heard my father's snores, subtle as a chainsaw, emanating from their bedroom.

Creeeak!

Whatever it was, was downstairs.

The noise was getting louder, rhythmic almost, like a heartbeat.

Creeeak, creeeak!

Creeeak, creeeak!

I glanced at the floor. The flashlight winked up at me, a glowing eyeball leading the way.

Creeeak, creeeak!

I followed.

I descended the stairs, my feet moving in time with the eerie groan.

Step, step.

Creeeak, creeeak!

I shuddered as I passed the cardboard box holding the remains of Aunt Tessa's life.

And then, I saw Pepper, lying atop Aunt Tessa's blanket on the floor. Her paws rested over her nose; her eyes, unblinking, as she stared ahead. Body stiff, she didn't react to my approach, not even to twitch her tail. She neither whimpered nor barked, just stayed eerily still.

It was as if she were afraid to move.

I followed her blank stare toward Mom's rocking chair, flowing in its own rhythmic dance against the floorboards.

Creeeak, creeeak!

"Pepper!" I whispered. I licked my lips with a sandpaper tongue. "Come here, girl!"

But the dog didn't move. Her soft, golden-white fur seemed to have become part of the afghan.

"Pepper, please," I begged. "Get away from that."

But she was paralyzed. Her glance flickered toward me, deep and sad. *'Help me,'* her eyes seemed to say as she sank deeper into the belly of that knitted abomination.

I crept around it, and her, wondering what to do. I needed to get Pepper away from this *thing* that wanted to eat her. This *thing* woven by an old woman who'd once called the cops on a neighbor's dog for barking too loudly in its own yard. This *thing* that Mom brought home from that old woman's death bed.

Mom and Dad were wrong. It wasn't *just a blanket*.

"Hold on, girl," I whispered.

I knelt beside Pepper, my bare knee grazing the corner of the blanket. Raw heat seared my skin like rug burn as the floor slid beneath me and the afghan pulled us toward the center of the room, its intricate stitching rising and falling in a silent staccato rhythm.

The room spun; my vision fizzled. I fell atop Pepper, landing on her ample belly. She yelped as I wrapped her in a bear hug. Her paws flailed, claws poking through the blanket and scratching the hardwood so deep it seemed she was trying to dig through to the basement. I tugged and pulled at the blanket, but it wouldn't release, folding her tight in a womb-like cocoon.

We three wriggled and thrashed and crashed and in that moment, I realized the true horror contained in Aunt Tessa's creation.

A piece of her soul was ingrained in each woolen stitch; she, and it, were getting their revenge on me.

For every face I made when chewing one of her rubbery cheese sandwiches.

For every eye roll that flitted over her knick-knacks, and every not-quite-stifled sigh.

For every doily I sat on, every crease made in her perfectly fluffed couch pillows.

For every sarcastic comment I muttered under my breath that I didn't think she'd heard.

For every day I never saw her again while she was still alive.

I yanked on the blanket that was swallowing my dog and fell back against the rocking chair. It crashed with a bang, forcing me to release my grip. The fabric cinched around Pepper's throat, pulling the dog toward me with such force that her tags were nearly in my mouth.

And then, the light clicked on.

"What the hell is going on?" Dad's voice boomed as loud as his footsteps marching down the stairs. Clutching her robe to her chest, Mom followed.

"Dad! Mom!" I shrieked, holding tight to Pepper's collar. "Aunt Tessa... Aunt Tessa's blanket... it's trying to kill the dog! And me!" My breaths heaved, though I tried to breathe through my nose so Pepper's dog-slobber wouldn't drip into my mouth.

"There is something seriously wrong with you." Dad stomped over and peered down at us. He glanced at the afghan coiled around me and Pepper, and with a deft swipe of his hand, released the hook from Pepper's collar, which had become stuck on the fabric. Finally free, she bolted from my chest, stepping with a heavy paw into my stomach before retreating to a dark corner of the room and curling into a tight ball. She stared at me, her eyes accusing.

"But, Dad..." I said. "Mom!" Still lying flat on the hardwood, I turned from one parent to the next, hoping they'd understand. Hoping they'd finally see what I saw and recognize what I'd felt from the moment Mom had first pulled that blanket from the box.

But all I got were headshakes, finger-wags, and those stony looks that invariably led to a lock-down of my cell phone and Xbox. Not to mention a week's worth of extra chores.

"I don't know what kind of stunt this is, but I don't appreciate it." Mom pulled her robe close. "I drove four hours round trip today, said goodbye to a dear member of the family, and visited her home for the last time, ever. It's been a heck of a day and I have no patience for your shenanigans."

"Shenanigans?" I pushed myself up, flailing as I realized the blanket was still strewn over me. "This blanket is haunted! It's possessed! And it wants revenge! How can you not see that?"

"There will be no more of this talk." Dad pointed toward the stairs. "Get back to bed."

"Back to bed?" Yowling, I tugged at my hair. "How do you expect me to sleep?"

I turned toward my mother, her expression blank.

"You took a blanket from a dead woman's bed," I said. "I bet it sucked up her soul when she died, and now she's stuck. Here!"

"Now," Dad said, his arm and finger unwavering. Mom turned away, shaking her head.

I stomped toward the staircase. "You just don't get it," I said. Two at a time, I leapt up the steps, leaving my parents murmuring downstairs, oblivious to the terror that poor Pepper and I had just endured.

I woke up the next morning to the sound of Pepper barking outside my door. My eyes were heavy from lack of sleep and the oppressive sunlight pushing against my tired lids. I dreamt that I'd been running through a teacup factory in a pair of knitted baby booties, slip-sliding across a floor of ice and smashing every cup and saucer I touched. My arms and legs throbbed, hands numb from the gigantic mittens that choked my wrists. Every time I removed one set of mittens, a new pair emerged in their place, each one tighter than the last. They squeezed and squeezed until my hands finally popped from my body, leaving two bloody stumps in their place. And on my head, the knitted dress of Toilet-Time Dolly gripped me like an ill-fitting cap.

I was happy to be awake.

"Pepper!" I said. "Be quiet!"

She howled outside the door.

I sat up.

And I screamed.

The blanket lay folded at the foot of my bed.

As I scrambled up toward the headboard, crouching into a fetal position, the door swung open and Dad plodded in, a cat-like grin plastered on his face. His coffee sloshed over the edge of his oversized mug.

Pepper barreled toward me and with one giant leap, flung herself on to the bed. She danced across the blanket, paw pads triumphing over her nighttime captor.

"Sleep okay?" Dad asked.

"That blanket. IT FOLLOWED ME UPSTAIRS."

"It didn't follow you. I put it on your bed, after you fell asleep."

"But... why would you do that?" I asked. I clenched my teeth to fight the tears that threatened. He could be such a jerk sometimes.

"So you'd stop being afraid of it."

Dad glanced toward the open door and leaned in toward me.

"Listen," he said, lowering his voice. "I always thought Aunt Tessa's knitting was a little... much. But that blanket isn't possessed, Jeremy. It's just ugly."

He took a sip of coffee.

"It didn't kill you, did it?"

I shook my head.

"And neither did the boogeyman in the closet. Or the shadow beast under your bed. Or that clown statue from the carnival that you swore was growling at you." Dad squeezed my shoulder. "You're getting too old for this kind of thing, son."

I glanced at Dad, and at the blanket. It glowed white as a shroud in the morning sunlight. Tiny hair-like fibers reached up to touch the dust motes floating in the air. The closer I looked at it, the more the afghan appeared to breathe on its own.

"You don't get it!" I yelled. "Why won't you listen to me?"

I grabbed the blanket, bumping against Dad as I ran from the room. I heard the coffee mug clatter and Dad cursing behind me. I flew down the stairs, shoved my feet into flip flops, and bolted out the front door.

I'd had enough of that old handcrafted rag. Enough of Aunt Tessa. It was time to put them both to rest.

Balling up the afghan beneath my arm, I hopped on my bike and pedaled toward Main Street. The air whipped against my face; I welcomed its cool biting strokes.

I knew exactly where to toss this creepy throw, and finally put myself out of my own misery.

Familiar storefronts rushed past me in a blur. I ignored the calls from friends and neighbors as I rode past the toy store and thrift shop, the chocolate store and the movie theatre, toward my favorite place to stash things I never wanted to see again—bad report cards, love notes from girls I had no interest in, leftover meatloaf Mom packed me for lunch. That stupid clown statue from the carnival all those years ago.

The dumpster behind the local fast-food joint. It was perfect.

My brakes squealed and I hopped off my bike. It crashed to the pavement, and I inhaled the sweaty smell of greasy burgers wafting from inside the restaurant all the way to the curb. Clutching Aunt Tessa's blanket, I crept through a narrow alleyway where the dumpster was waiting. I creaked the lid open just enough to stuff the blanket inside and watched as it floated down among the rotting chicken nuggets, squished ketchup packets, and moldy vegetables at the bottom. For a moment, I felt a twinge as I thought of Aunt Tessa's gnarly old fingers clacking her knitting needles at that blanket, and how her hands would never weave colors and shapes and textures to take on a different form, ever again.

But it was for the best. That afghan, and Aunt Tessa, needed to rest in peace, and so did I.

I brought down the dumpster lid with the reverence of a funeral director closing a casket.

I STAYED OUT UNTIL sunset, stuffing myself with French fries and fresh air. Mom was waiting as I walked my bike up the driveway. We locked eyes as I rested the bike against the garage and approached the porch.

Mom had "that look" where her eyes sunk smaller in her head and her brows pulled tight, straight as arrows. Whenever she looked at me that way, she always managed to pull the thoughts straight out of my head no matter how deep I tried to bury them.

"Productive day?" she asked.

I eyed her curiously before responding. Mom was wearing a hoodie and her fuzzy slippers, even though it was 90 degrees outside.

"I guess. Aren't you hot?"

Mom waved off my question. "Hungry?" she asked. "I can make us some nice cheese sandwiches."

"No, thank you." The last thing I wanted to eat—ever again—was a cheese sandwich.

"Well, at least you have your manners. Children without manners are simply insufferable—barbarians! A reflection of the parents."

Insufferable? Barbarians?

She rested her arm across my shoulders. Her face shifted, and I caught a glimpse of a deep laugh line, or was it a frown line, etched into her features. Mom looked tired. "I'll make some tea."

She pursed her lips, as if deep in thought. "I've got the perfect little cup," she said. "It's Lennox, dear. The one you like, with the pattern of yellow roses."

She ruffled my hair, her touch planting a shiver inside me.

"Are you mad?" I asked.

She tsked, wagging a finger at me. "Dogs are mad. The insane are mad. Mind your words, young man."

"Mom? Are you okay?"

Maybe she was still sad about Aunt Tessa. Or just messing with me. But Mom was acting strange.

"That blanket was special, dear," she said, her voice a whisper.

"I can get you some of Aunt Tessa's mittens...?" I offered. "From my closet? To make up for the—"

"—It's quite alright," she said. As we were about to walk through the front door, I noticed a small cardboard box on the porch. It had been opened; packaging tape stuck curled around the edges.

"What's that?" I asked.

"A special delivery! It arrived just before you did. Take a look inside, dear."

Mom smiled as I moved toward the box with tingling, wobbly legs; the air had become thick as Jell-O.

A wave of molten angst washed over me as I recognized the familiar stench bursting from the box, worsened with the remnants of rotten dumpster food. My hand trembling, I reached inside. The fibers of Aunt Tessa's blanket pricked at my skin like tiny teeth; I felt my blood seeping into the fabric as I touched it.

I glanced at Mom. She lifted the afghan from my hands, cradling it into her neck. The image of Aunt Tessa flitted across Mom's face—lips scrunched in a scowl, nose pinched and eyes beady. Mom's skin shriveled up like a prune. Opening her mouth to speak, her thin lips pulled back to reveal rotten, gritty teeth.

Liquified cheese dripped from her gums.

Red dots—*my blood*—swam over the blanket, over Mom. I grasped the doorframe and blinked hard, desperate to squeeze away the heat baking behind my eyes, to quell the throb that pulsed my brain.

"Dad, where are you?" my voice cracked. Maybe he would know what to do, how to make Mom normal again. I reached for the doorknob and screamed as the metal scalded my palm. Mom—*Aunt Tessa*—planted a crooked, knobby finger over my trembling lips. I tasted wet salt.

And mothballs.

"Young man, I've been looking for this blanket all day long," she said. "Isn't it so special?"

Special.

"I created it just for you, dear."

I held my breath.

"My word, the least you can say is thank you."

I nodded, my eyes widening as the blanket slithered down her shoulder.

"Thanks," I whispered.

"Thank you, *Auntie Tessa*," she corrected.

The Ugly Vampire

Archibald Rollinstern never thought his life would end like this.

The straitjacket pinned Archibald's arms across his chest, the numbness in his limbs matching that of his soul. He rested on a lumpy cot, staring at the ceiling of a white room. A tiny square window cut into the seamless wall, a lidless eye, watching.

Archibald had seen enough movies to know that white padded rooms weren't supposed to have windows. In fact, Archibald knew much about things that were not supposed to be. He still lived, even as he waited to die—*again*—in some godforsaken psych ward. He adored Amethyst, even though she'd abandoned him more than once. And although the Reaper would soon extend its shimmering reach through that small window, Archibald was not afraid. Archibald knew that he was not meant to be.

He was the *One Who Never Should Have Been Made.*

Blessed and cursed with the simultaneous gift of life and of death, Archibald was an abomination among monsters. A freak, forsaken by fiends.

An *ugly* vampire.

It wouldn't matter for long. Hues breaking through that small opening painted the walls with the tint of a fresh bruise. Dawn marched forward, brandishing the torch that would burn immortality off the undead. Soon, Archibald would become nothing more than a pile of ash, buried in the folds of cotton fabric starched one too many times.

Archibald had never been a morning person, even when human. *The early bird catches the worm*, his parents had said. A mediocre late bloomer, he was last in line for everything, much to his parents' disappointment. Archibald was never the bird, but always the worm.

Worms, like Archibald, were grateful to be plucked from the earth, chosen from the writhing bugs and vermin, waiting for something—anything—to happen. The worm nestled in the night creature's claws was special, for it could take flight.

By human standards, Archibald was ugly. He stood five feet two with a belly that showcased his favor for cheap beer and fried foods. Frizzy graying hair barely hid his greasy scalp. Yet, Amethyst chose *him* on that night all those months before, when the full moon rose in a star-filled sky.

Archibald wriggled against his restraints. He wasn't insane. His love for Amethyst, that wasn't insane either.

But this barren cell was the worst place imaginable. A basement full of rotting, musty coffins might have been a preferable final resting place—not this asylum, this farce of a room designed to protect Archibald from himself. Laughter would fit a moment like this, as would tears. But Archibald didn't have the energy for either. Archibald held life in one hand and death in the other, his body weary of their tug-of-war.

Because of Amethyst, his life had ended once. Now that it was about to end again, all he wanted was to see her one last time.

To thank her for everything.

❖

ARCHIBALD HAD JUST DOWNED his fourth lager, lining the sweaty bottle next to its empty counterparts on the bar. One drink for the lady who'd cut him off on the freeway that morning. Another for his bastard boss at the megastore who'd droned about Archibald's surly expression—*friendly faces are selling aces!* The third was for the pimply-faced kid who put anchovies on his salami and provolone hero sandwich. Who does that? And the last was for Sally, who broke up with him in a meme. It wasn't that he really liked her but announcing to her thousands of Instagram followers that she was tired of dating *little men* was a bit much.

Hate. Love. Indifference. The same heavy drink, with a different aftertaste.

Hunched forward, he'd wrapped his hands around the cold bottle when, in the corner of his eye, a quick flash popped, brilliant and fleeting as lightning. Archibald turned. Perched on the stool next to him—empty, only a second prior—was the most beautiful woman he'd ever seen. Her ivory skin glimmered under the dim lights, shining and marble smooth. Ebony hair cascaded down her back, deep as nighttime waters. Her violet eyes sparkled like gemstones in sunlight; Archibald lost himself within each facet. An icy cold droplet trickled down her glass—a Bloody Mary, curious given the hour as they approached last call. She gazed at him with the hunger of a starving waif at a banquet and raised a manicured finger to trace her lush, red lips.

Archibald rubbed his eyes and blinked, hard. I must be intoxicated, he thought.

"Intoxicating," she whispered. She leaned in. Archibald's eyes widened and his brows rose, cheeks aflame as she rested her hand on his thigh.

Archibald opened his mouth and abruptly closed it. He took another swig for bravery before he spoke. "Do I know you?" Beer-tinged spittle stuck to his lips. "I'm..."

"Intoxicating," she repeated. She was close enough for Archibald to breathe her scent—fresh snow and lilacs and vanilla. He closed his eyes and inhaled, her name a whisper flitting across his mind.

Amethyst.

"Amethyst," he repeated.

Laughter rumbled in the woman's throat, a low growl, like nothing he'd ever heard before. He opened his eyes to the tip of her icy tongue trailing over his lips. He leaned in to return her kiss. She turned away, her smile playful. Coy.

"Do you want to...?" Archibald's question trailed as he found himself in an unfamiliar circumstance. He'd never been so close to a woman this beautiful, at least, without needing to leave money on the nightstand. One and done, he swore that he'd never do that again.

Could someone like her want someone like me?

"I want to," she said, smiling with brilliant white teeth, chiseled, like exquisitely crafted porcelain. With a whoosh, she cloaked herself in a red velvet cape. She gripped Archibald's hand with fingers long and powerful as talons.

No sooner did he look up at her to ask "Where...?" than the barroom faded and Archibald found his back pressed against a brick wall in a dark alley. It was as if he and this mysterious woman had flown from the bar to this quiet place, hidden from the world among the rats and rotting garbage.

She pressed her body against his. Archibald's heart thrummed into Amethyst's unyielding form. He moaned as she yanked open his shirt collar, ripping the first few buttons away. She tore at the fabric with her mouth and pushed her cold, hard lips against his neck.

Lightheaded bliss overtook him as her teeth—*fangs*—pierced his skin. Lights flashed beneath his closed eyes. City sounds gurgled to a noisy silence, as if Archibald were suspended beneath the surface of water, cocooned yet floating. He surrendered to the moment. Time and memory marched by in an instant; his life played before him like a black and white film—childhood dreams and the disappointments of adulthood danced like shadows.

The homerun he'd always yearned to hit.

Placing third in the school spelling bee.

Being stood up at the prom.

Dropping out of community college.

Saying goodbye to his parents as they traded his childhood home for a condo in the Bahamas.

Sally cackling as she scrolled through her phone, counting likes.

All interspersed with images of Amethyst.

Amethyst.

She pulled back, studying him. Her eyes morphed from violet to crimson. She licked her lips, slick with blood. His blood. Archibald closed his eyes, content to let his mind and body drift somewhere beyond.

He jolted as a voice boomed through the alleyway.

"Amethyst!"

That voice, more lion than man, echoed through Archibald's gut.

Amethyst let go, leaving Archibald to slump onto the damp pavement. Through the haze, Archibald saw him. A massive caped man with blond locks swept back into a long braid. *A prince? A god?* Like Amethyst, his skin shimmered in the moonlight. Closed fists situated upon his slender hips. Glitter emanated from his skin.

"Another drunk, Amethyst?"

"He wasn't *drunk*, Mario." Her voice purred. "Just... buzzed... when we met."

"Will you never respect the Code of Merciful Death?" Mario demanded.

"Oh, but I showed him mercy," Amethyst said. "What's wrong with giving a lonely middle-aged guy a night he'll never forget?"

"By killing him?" The man—the being—threw his hands up in exasperation.

"Spiked blood is the sweetest, isn't it, Mario? That's what you said the night you made me, remember?" She batted her eyelashes.

Mario turned from her. "That was a long time ago."

"We never escape that which we truly are, Mario, despite our best intentions. Why don't you join me for a nightcap, for old time's sake?" Amethyst turned from Mario, grinning as she crouched next to Archibald.

Amethyst sank into him again. Archibald's body shuddered at the endless twinge of pleasurable pain.

Mario swooped down next to Archibald. "Stop this! The Council forbids it!"

Sprawled between the two most beautiful beings he'd ever seen, Archibald's insides fluttered. Every vein in his body tingled as Amethyst pressed her mouth into his skin.

"I will not let you take him!" Mario said. "It's not his time!"

Archibald felt stone pressed into his cheeks, then a tug on his jaw. His mouth forced open, cool night air coated his lips and his tongue. A moan escaped him. The feel of chilled, rigid skin pressing over his open mouth silenced him. The warm tang of sweetened metal—like a candy-coated penny—awakened each taste bud.

"Drink," Mario urged Archibald, "or you'll die."

Archibald suckled the man's wrist as if by instinct, desperate as an infant plucked from the womb. Though his mind glided across a sea of stars as he fell deeper into Amethyst's allure, a fire awoke in him as he drank from the font that Mario offered.

Blood. There was no drink more potent.

In all his days, Archibald had never felt better. He'd never felt worse.

As Amethyst tugged him away, Archibald pulled from the well-spring Mario offered. With each gulp, Archibald's limbs softened, relaxing in a state of numbed delight. Archibald envisaged his body morphing into something else. Something not him. Something not human.

His arms and legs stretched like warmed taffy. Amethyst took from him as Mario gave, and Archibald lurched with the stops and starts, in a place where supple ended and rigid began. His right leg retracted, shriveling until his heel lay even with his left calf. The skin on his back bubbled; golf-ball sized boils effervesced across his muscles, violent as boiling water. A massive hump rose beneath his shoulder blades. His right eye pulsated, optic fluid sloshing and foaming as thick as the head on Archibald's favorite beer until it exploded, a waterfall rushing down his cheek.

Push. Pull. Push. Pull.

"Amethyst, stop!" Mario yelled.

Archibald slumped onto the filthy alley. His throat constricted, he lapped at the honey-sweet air. Choked by the night, Archibald gasped as the deities released him. His head hit the asphalt. Through Archibald's left eye, the world illuminated in a hazy brilliance. The shadow of Amethyst hovered.

Like an angel.

"Mario, what have you done?"

"What have *I* done? *You* violated the Code. *We* are the bridge between human life and human death. *We* live by feeding on the blood of the dying *only*. Easing their suffering sustains us! But you preyed on a healthy, innocent man! And for what, Amethyst? A fleeting high?"

"I liked him, Mario," she said. "Everyone falls off the wagon sometimes."

"*We* do not," he said. "Ever."

"I just wanted to taste his desire. If you saw the way he looked at me..."

"Remember what you are," Mario snapped.

Bright lights obliterated midnight darkness. With his intact eye, Archibald watched hands darting toward him, quick as arrows, reaching beneath his armpits, pulling him upright. He stood, off-kilter, one leg shorter than the other, his newly formed humpback pushing him forward. His voice emerged low, gravelly. He cleared dirt from his windpipe.

"What's happening?" Archibald mumbled, staring at the two figures. His beautiful Amethyst. And this man. This Mario.

Amethyst's hand raced to cover her lovely, gaping mouth. Blood—Archibald's blood—seeped between her fingers.

"Look at him, Amethyst! Look. At. Him." Mario grabbed her by the scruff of the neck, pushing her face toward Archibald's. Archibald craned his neck toward her, desperate for another kiss. "Your indiscretions led to this... mutant!"

Archibald would soon learn that he was the ugliest vampire ever created. And vampires were vain, shallow creatures.

❖

ARCHIBALD SECURED HIS EYE patch and straightened his new velvet cape. It hung, crooked, over his hump-back, one side grazing the floor, the other hanging at his knee. He pulled back the thick, velvet curtain of the sleeping chamber. Archibald could barely see the night outside through the tinted glass, yet the darkness weighed heavy as a mantle over his new world. He glanced at his reflection in the windowpane. Though mostly shadow, Archibald could still see himself, or rather, what he'd become when Mario had given him this gift, this curse of anomalous immortality.

Archibald's life was mundane at best when he was human. At least he'd blended into the retail backdrop with his nondescript blue work smock, into the crowded freeway with his crummy old Toyota. Even at the bar, he was nothing more than another fixture—no more interesting than the grease-caked lights hanging over the threadbare pool table.

But now Archibald stood out—a painter's errant brushstroke disfiguring a masterpiece. Vampire blood enhanced the looks of all those who drank it; fledglings were among the most gorgeous creatures on Earth. All except Archibald, for something had gone horribly askew in the push-and-pull fight between Mario and Amethyst.

Archibald would never forget the cool heat blazing from Amethyst's eyes when the Council had cast her out for hunting him at the bar. For seducing him. She wore her pain in her gaze, imparting it with every glare she tossed over the dozens of vampires occupying the Council chambers. Sentenced to exile for committing the ultimate immortal flesh-sin with him—with Archibald!

He'd heard the slurs they whispered about Amethyst as she turned toward the long hallway leading to the wide and lonely world beyond. They called her a lush, an addict. Reckless and wild. Unworthy. But without the favor of Amethyst's sweet kiss, Archibald would never have dared stand among beings of their stature—whether mortal or immortal. He existed; a bastard child steeped in the riches of royals. For that he was both thankful and horrified.

Amethyst was his one remaining link to the man he once was, to the imperfect life that was his. Most women delighted in Archibald's lack of confidence, burrowing into it firm as a parasite. Yet with a whisper, Amethyst blew all Archibald's in-adequacies away, blind to his dead-end job, his excess girth, his awkward blushing and sweaty palms. In her arms, Archibald felt like a person of worth. With Amethyst, Archibald had teetered in that netherworld where the most vivid dreams stand palpable. He'd dropped his shields and allowed her a glimpse of his soul. Although Amethyst was the most beautiful creature he ever beheld, there was something more to her—something that superseded words or rational thought. Comprehending his feelings was like grasping smoke, an enigma never to be harnessed.

Then again, so was love.

Before Amethyst left, she glanced at Archibald, the fury in her eyes tempered to soft embers. She embraced him with her stare.

"Rare is the flawed creature in the sea of false righteousness," she said.

"Please." Archibald clasped his hands as he turned to Mario. "Don't send her away." He couldn't bear the thought of beginning this journey without Amethyst.

Mario scowled. "Would you prefer to join her? This Coven offers shelter from the heat of the rising sun. Out there..." His voice trailed off.

"I do not fear the sunlight. And I do not need this coven to save me." Amethyst turned toward Archibald and winked at him. "Until we meet again, my friend."

Before Mario could open the door to escort Amethyst out, she vanished in a dazzling puff of mist.

Archibald lingered on Amethyst's words and stared hard at his reflection. *She chose me for my flaws?*

"Ready?" Mario's hands grazed Archibald's shoulders. Mario's beauty, and the beauty of all others in the Coven, defied reflection. Yet, Archibald could still look at his mangled self with his one remaining eye. Ironic, Archibald thought, how it remained possible for him to see the eternal ugly while the splendor of his counterparts was impossible to mirror.

"Yes." Archibald nodded, though he was not ready at all. Archibald was living as an unwanted child; he sensed Mario's regret overtake his guilt with every test and trial Archibald failed.

Archibald lacked the supernatural speed of the others, standing still as the Coven raced past him in a windy blur. It was Mario who grabbed him by the collar, pulling him along, lest they leave him behind. Mario supplied him with rats and squirrels so he would not die of thirst; Archibald was unable to pounce on his prey with the precision expected of any vampire worth his fangs. And his fangs; how they hung flaccid and thin from his gums, his mortal teeth receded, leaving him gap-toothed with a smile more laughable than charming, a sneer more fatuous than formidable.

Despite Archibald's obvious vampiric shortcomings, Mario wanted him to experience the divine joy of drinking human blood. He wanted Archibald to commit to the Coven's vow—to provide human victims already on their deathbeds a quiet, peaceful passing for a taste of their life-sustaining elixir.

Archibald thought it seemed a fair and altruistic exchange, and likely far more appetizing than drinking the blood of vermin, in a macabre sort of way.

On this night, when the full moon was high and the Coven set out on their Mercy Mission, Archibald would feed for the first time, as Mario's apprentice.

"Do not disappoint me," Mario admonished.

Before Archibald could respond, he found himself standing behind Mario at the bedside of an elderly woman, so shriveled in her blankets that her body was indistinguishable from the material enshrouding her. Her breaths came shallow, the rise and fall of her chest rapid, nearly imperceptible. Mario's body glimmered as he laid his hand on her forehead, his glow penetrating through her feeble skin. The woman pulled in a deeper breath, turning slowly toward him. Archibald peered around Mario's side, gaping, as Mario leaned in and kissed the woman's cheek, her wrinkles smoothing at his touch.

"Merciful Death," Mario whispered.

Archibald nodded. If he still had a beating heart, he'd have imagined it pounding in his chest. He would have surrendered to the surreal floating-fuzzy sensation that comes with those life moments that define years and give meaning to decades. But for one of his kind, the physical thrill of anticipation was like a phantom limb—feelings remembered, not real.

He wondered if that was how Amethyst felt when she'd carried him to the place where this world and the netherworld entwined. How she must have longed to remember what it was like to feel wanted, needed, punch-drunk with adrenaline and alcohol and lust.

Human lust, or something like it, at least for him.

And now, he wondered about this dying stranger, what type of life she'd lived. If she'd experienced love. If her family had left her behind, just as Archibald's parents had when they moved away, leaving him to shoulder the disappointments of his young adult life with no support.

But it comforted Archibald to know that this woman wouldn't pass alone, that his touch would lead her beyond this bed, beyond the pain of this world, to someplace better.

Mario took Archibald's hand, guiding him toward the woman. His cape grazed the sheets, velvet kissing hospital-grade cotton. Through half-closed blinds, he saw a young nurse sitting at a desk outside the room. He froze, glancing over his shoulder at Mario.

"What if she sees us?" Archibald asked.

"Do this right, and no one will ever know we were here."

Mario rested his hand on Archibald's hunched back. "Now," he said, "lean in, gently."

Archibald lowered himself toward the woman. Through the bitter tinge of morphine, he smelled summer: sea salt and coconut, with a hint of jasmine. Then, the metallic aroma of her blood, pulsing thick through her carotid artery.

"Careful," Mario cautioned. "Careful..."

The woman's eyelids fluttered as Archibald's face hovered over her.

Archibald wiped his brow. Dull vampire sweat, slick as blood, covered his sleeve. He leaned in, his canines twinging as they extended. He kissed the woman's cheek as he'd watched Mario do. Archibald's body jolted as his lips connected with her skin.

"Merciful death," he whispered, lowering his face to her neck.

Steadying himself, he opened his mouth wide. His fangs wobbled in his gums; his canines made contact but did not penetrate her flesh.

"Archibald," Mario said. "Do it, now."

Archibald hesitated for a moment. He took a deep breath, tilted his head back, and with the motion of a swift headbutt, thrust his fangs into the woman's neck.

Blood spurted into his mouth.

Sweet, sweet blood.

The woman bolted up, screaming.

"No!" Mario grabbed Archibald's shoulders, pulling him from the woman. Her eyes were wide and white as the moon as she stared at him. She cried and shrieked, before collapsing, dead, into her pillow. As the doorknob turned, Mario waved his hand over the woman's neck to close the ugly wounds Archibald had left. Before the nurse stormed into the room, Mario swirled his cape around Archibald. Archibald closed his eyes, and they both disappeared from the room, trailing on a shadow of a shadow, left in the wake of moonlight through the window.

AFTER THE DEBACLE AT the nursing home, the Vampire Council unanimously voted to cast Archibald *out*. His misshapen vampire form was too much of a liability; his inability to feed without inspiring terror made it impossible for him to adhere to the vow of Merciful Death to which they'd all committed. They suspected he wasn't bold enough to go rogue, yet they feared another blunder would lead to their discovery and ultimate demise.

Archibald was too heavy a burden for the group to carry.

Yet they wouldn't kill him *outright*. Murder among vampires was forbidden under the Code. So, they sent him away, leaving his fate to the elements, in a perverse twist of natural selection.

Archibald understood. In his job at the megastore, he'd applauded every time his bosses dispensed with the lazy and the riffraff who weren't worthy of their nametag. Last thing he'd ever wanted was some deadbeat making his job harder. Archibald never won trophies or awards; but he'd never considered himself dead weight.

Now, he was nothing more than *undead* weight.

Mario draped his arm over Archibald's shoulder as they walked from the Sanctuary, passing by the others lined up to watch him go. Some had wept golden tears at his departure, sad for the demise of the vampire who should never have been. Others hid their faces as they giggled beneath their fangs, whispering *"monster"* under their breath as he walked by. Yet, despite his limp and his hunch, Archibald held his head high. Amethyst had seen something special in him, special enough to pick him among a pool of men more handsome than he, with a swagger he'd never possess. If only he could find her again, he'd show her the man—the immortal—he was always meant to be.

He didn't need the Coven. He needed her.

"Merciful death," Mario whispered, turning to avoid Archibald's eye as he left him on the doorstep, closing the Sanctuary's massive iron door behind him.

But Archibald was grateful. When the Coven released him, Archibald was free to seek his beloved; banished, just as he was. And although his days were challenging, he managed to survive.

Archibald wrapped himself in refuse, seeking shelter from the sun beneath the lids of alleyway dumpsters, or in the private enclaves of unlocked basement doors. He fed on the blood of roadkill, sucking the remnants of dead and decaying animals, a vampire incapable of enchanting any living beast. He'd never mastered the art of the pounce, no matter how hard he tried. The rats laughed him off, as if he were no fiercer than a field mouse.

By night he took to the rooftops, following harried and busy humans into offices and apartment buildings as they held the door, inviting him inside. (It was, indeed, true that a vampire could only enter one's home if invited). He sought solace in the moonlight and counted the stars, wondering if Amethyst clung to their shine, just as he did, two lonely outcasts in the night. He wondered if she thought of him, waited for him, just as he longed for her. Archibald had never been in love until that moment he looked into Amethyst's eyes twinkling through the smoky air of that dive bar. He'd never felt the waves of ecstasy that crested over him until she'd connected to his lifeline. That night skated cold and eternal at the edges of his memory, while lingering warm, its imprint an embrace.

They were similar beings, he and Amethyst—an escape from a mundane, lonely existence their primary endgame.

Children out past their bedtimes occasionally pointed at Archibald and gawked, leading their parents to rush them on by, lest his ugliness taint them, too. Most people were as likely to ignore Archibald in his undead state as they had during his life as a human. But it was good for a vampire to fade into the background, especially one as unskilled as Archibald. He was fortunate to have mastered the art of being unobtrusive in his human days. No one spoke to him; few offered even a glance. He preferred it that way.

The more Archibald embraced his virtual invisibility, the braver he became on his nighttime jaunts. As he slunk through the darkness, his view of the world sharpened from a dull blur to a clear focus. He was alone and ignored. But for the first time in his existence, he felt like something. Someone.

Vampire, a child of the night.

Hear me roar, he thought.

One night, when Archibald was feeling particularly dauntless, he decided to perch on the rooftop ledge of the Public Library building. He sat and dangled his legs over the edge, wading in the warm summer air as if it were a clear, sparkling pool, like the one he'd had as a child. Archibald remembered how he loved that feeling of anticipation, jumping from the backyard deck and pulling his knees into a cannonball just before he hit the water.

Archibald dug his fangs into a flattened squirrel he'd retrieved from a side road, one whose unfortunate brain had seeped through its crushed skull. He ignored the voices on the street below as he sucked bitterness from the small creature's veins. Car engines, sirens, voices—they were nothing more than a running soundtrack for Archibald; as insignificant to him as he was to the world.

From somewhere on the roof behind him, a long-forgotten aroma arose that, in his human days, had made his mouth water with desire, but now filled him with bile. He lowered his meal and turned, the odor of garlic burning into his nostrils, setting his throat and tongue aflame. Bloody saliva gushed from the corners of his lips as he found himself staring at a fresh-faced police officer.

Great, Archibald thought. A rookie cop.

"Hey, pal," the cop said, spittle spreading garlic drops like a cloud of acid. The officer looked down at the squirrel and back up at Archibald. Brows raised, the cop swallowed twice, as if digesting his disgust.

"Stay back," Archibald muttered. "Please."

The cop reached a hand toward Archibald. "There's no reason to jump," he said. "Life's worth living, you know."

Jump?

All Archibald wanted to do was enjoy his meal and dream about his girl in peace.

"No, officer, there's some mistake," Archibald said. "I'm fine."

The cop frowned, shaking his head. "You're not fine, buddy, not if you're up here. You look like you've had a rough go. Now if you'll just come down with me…"

"No," Archibald said. Panic rose in his gut, fluttering like a bat in a cage. The more the cop spoke with that awful garlic breath, the more the flames ignited inside Archibald's nose. He reached up, feeling his nostrils to be sure that they hadn't melted down his face. His throat seared; his eye spilled rancid tears.

"Are you a praying man?" The cop reached inside the collar of his shirt, retrieving a solid gold cross.

"No… No." Archibald stammered, his feet scrambling for ground in the air below. He dropped the squirrel; the growing crowd screamed as it splattered on the pavement. "Please. Please, put that away."

"Find your faith, man." The cop gripped tight to the cross. Archibald closed his eye. Every nerve in his undead body tingled, electrified. He trembled as the cop continued. "I've been in that lowest of low," the cop said. "I know what it is to feel like being dead is better than being alive…"

"You have no idea," Archibald said. Paralyzed by the garlic cloud and the weight of the golden cross, he toppled from the building. *Can vampires fly?* Archibald wondered as the chorus of voices below sang a requiem to his life, his death, his undeath. *Will I bounce when I hit the ground?* The Council had never warned against falling—it wasn't one of those aspects of life to be avoided, like a summer day at the beach or the choir loft during Christmas Eve services. Or garlic bulbs. Or crosses.

Arms and legs flailing, Archibald swam in the warm night air.

With his nose an inch from the pavement, Archibald stopped, as if lassoed. He glanced at the crowd of wild eyes and covered mouths. In its midst, Amethyst stood, hands raised like the conductor of a grand orchestra. She grinned with those wide, blood-red lips he saw every day in his dreams and blew him a kiss.

Amethyst came back. She saved him.

Archibald scrambled to his feet, unscathed. His eye patch had flown off during his descent, and the crowd recoiled in horror as he gazed over them, one eye wild and the other a twitching empty socket.

"Amethyst!" he yelled, reaching for her.

With a wink and a nod, she dissipated into the night. Where she belonged.

"It's ok, Buddy. You're going to be okay. I'm going to bring you someplace safe."

Damn rookie cop.

Archibald swooned as the stench of garlic swirled around him. The last thing he remembered before blacking out was the click of handcuffs, the cut of cold steel into his wrists.

❖

Archibald squirmed on the cot, struggling against the restraints as a sunbeam reached through the tiny window in the white padded room. *Merciful death*, he thought, as he squeezed his eye shut, waiting.

Warmth enveloped him like hot sand, rough and grainy against his skin. Oddly, the sensation was comfortable, reminiscent of a worn sweatshirt or a well-loved blanket. Though dawn burst into the room, Archibald was still breathing. He cracked open his eye and for the first time since he'd been converted, he laughed. He thought of the rows of coffins lining the Sanctuary, of Mario and the Coven curled up and sleeping through their days— immortals fearing their own mortality—the pointlessness of it all.

The sunlight didn't kill him.

In fact, as Archibald beheld the sunrise stealing through the room, the heat infused his veins, peaceful as hot springs in the snow, calming as a shot of whiskey on a brisk February night. The pressure from the hump on his back released like a balloon deflating. Archibald sat straighter, taller. He hadn't felt this way since that long-ago night when Amethyst sidled up on the barstool next to him, whispering a promise of immortality into his ear.

If he were still human, this would have been Archibald's *moment*. The day he would have quit the bar scene. The day he would have asked his boss for a long-overdue promotion; or at the very least, a path toward middle management. The day he would have confronted his parents about their decision to leave him behind, when he would have asked for a plane ticket to visit, to talk things through.

He'd faced down the dawn, awake and alive. No longer the worm, but somehow, a glorious bird whose wings glistened in the sun.

For Archibald, life now was even better. He was immortal, unbound by the shackles of night.

Now if only he could find a way out of this straitjacket.

"Good morning," a voice called, as the door creaked open.

Raven hair, violet eyes. And those lips, pursed, scarlet, and perfect. Amethyst entered, clad in a crisp lab coat. She tapped a pen against a clipboard, her pearlescent fangs gleaming as she smiled at him. She'd come back for him—again.

Archibald's soul exploded with joy.

"Someone told me there was a vampire in this room," she said, her voice a purr. "How crazy is that?"

"Insane," Archibald mumbled.

"And a handsome one, too."

"Handsome?" Archibald laughed. "Neither the living nor the undead would describe me as handsome. There must be a good-looking vampire hiding somewhere in here."

"Outward appearances are but a shell," Amethyst said. "The plainest, most unassuming stones yield the brightest gems. Those in the know keep that secret tightly guarded." She gestured toward the window and the sunburst that captured the room. "You are a rare find, Archibald. You didn't crumble. You didn't quit."

"I don't understand," Archibald said. He fidgeted against his restraints.

"It's why I chose you," Amethyst said. "Your heart was open that night. You had nothing to lose. And you wanted me. In fact, you needed me."

"But Mario is the one who…" Archibald swallowed hard. "You, um. You tried to kill me."

Amethyst chuckled, her laughter rich as syrup. Thick, like blood.

"Mario always had eyes on me when I was part of the Coven. I knew he'd come. I knew he'd turn you, since I am incapable of doing so." She sighed. "We are mutants for reasons that transcend our looks."

"You? A mutant?" Archibald furrowed his brow and shook his head. "You're perfect."

"You're a sweet man, Archibald. I have my flaws. Maybe in time, I'll share them with you." Amethyst moved toward Archibald and ran her fingers through his hair.

Archibald glanced up to meet her gaze. "How are we not ashes?" He tilted his head, gesturing toward the window.

"Mutants are immune to the sunlight. We need not dwell in the darkness."

Amethyst leaned in and kissed Archibald softly. A sweet shiver rippled over him.

She tugged at his restraints.

"Now, why don't you slip into something a little more comfortable? Perhaps we can talk over a drink? It's the perfect hour for a Bloody Mary."

Entranced, Archibald nodded, abandoning all thought about things that were not supposed to be. He had never been more alive than he was in that moment, with her.

And the Light Faded

Rosa Santos focused on the road ahead as she ran. Her feet ached, pounding heavy on the cracked pavement, her strides as labored as her breathing in the icy air. She ignored the clouds of dust billowing through the woods around her and the trees swaying in violent protest against the advancing swarm.

Rosa had looked forward to ringing in the new year quietly—Netflix, popcorn, and a warm blanket. She clicked on the television; it painted her living room in a soft glow. The light cast shadows in the empty corner. Dust collected in the space where her Christmas tree usually stood. It flitted over a mantle devoid of decoration—not a card, a holiday stocking, nor a candy cane hung from the fireplace. She hadn't seen the point of displaying her Nativity scene, either. Baby Jesus still lay sleeping in a cardboard box stacked at the top of her closet.

This year, Santa Claus was not a symbol of giving. He was a reminder of all that had been taken from her.

Rosa hadn't felt like celebrating—she wanted it to be over.

◈

AN EARTH-SHAKING BOOM HAD jolted Rosa awake. It sent the popcorn bowl skittering off the coffee table and a photo frame crashing from the wall to the floor, the face of the child in the photograph distorted by the broken glass. A siren screeched outside, piercing through the flash of heat and gooseflesh that washed over her body. Rosa leapt from the couch and ran toward the window.

Graffiti covering the walls of the bodega across from her apartment glowed a sickly green. An odd radiance painted the sky, it was as if midnight were dueling with dawn. She turned away as the floor rumbled beneath her and cracked. Through a massive fissure, the face of her downstairs neighbor stared up at her.

Rosa grabbed her coat and raced outside, greeted by a street full of stunned neighbors staring at the sky. The invaders descended like giant hailstones; the hulking multi-legged creatures crashed down with such fury, Rosa felt as if the Earth had been knocked from its orbit.

2043 arrived not with bursts of confetti or popping champagne corks, but with a firestorm from space. The aliens invaded just as the Times Square Ball began to drop. The world counted down its final moments, and a thousand fireworks exploded simultaneously in a grand finale gone horribly wrong.

And there was nothing to do but run. Or die.

⬖

Three days had passed since New Year's Eve.

Rosa needed rest and shelter, and her options were limited. Few structures remained intact after the onslaught. When the aliens swarmed, they devoured everything in their path, like cockroaches on stray crumbs.

She pushed forward, her focus on breathing and moving one foot in front of the other. Through eyes blurred by tears and lack of sleep, she thought she saw a crumbling mansion in her sightline. It must be a mirage, she thought, or maybe I'm desperate. Le Château was the place to see and be seen; a threshold she had never expected to cross, unless it was through the service entrance.

Or unless it was the end of the world.

Though a section of the outer wall had collapsed, and a massive hole was blown through the roof, the building still stood. Like the few survivors she'd encountered once the sirens had stopped, it too was crooked and broken.

Rosa's legs quivered as she approached the fractured marble steps. She leapt over a body splayed between the blown-out double doors. His tuxedo was soaked in blood, his face twisted in the scowl of a man surprised by his own death. Taking two steps at a time, she raced into the building.

Shards of glass from a broken chandelier shimmered across a cracked floor strewn with tattered paintings, chunks of brick, and abandoned personal effects—high-end handbags, shattered cell phones, the keys to luxury cars mashed like tin cans in the parking lot. A tremor sent Rosa tumbling into the rubble. She landed with her cheek pressed against the face of a dead woman, fresh blood oozing from beneath perfectly coiffed hair.

Trembling, Rosa pushed the body away and stood, her foot landing on a small metal object. She looked down at the cracked face of a Rolex, its hands frozen, the links of its metal band broken and jagged. She kicked it away.

So valued by the living, so useless to the dead.

She turned and ran down the hallway, glancing into the open doorways for signs of life. The grand rooms stood like mausoleums, some with their ceilings blown away, others pulverized into twisted masses of steel and wire and plaster. Well-dressed bodies lay everywhere, gathered in their finest to usher in the end of the world. *Like civilized people.* She pushed through a metal door and found herself in a kitchen.

Dust coated the black and white floor, though the stainless-steel appliances still shone under the grayish glow of a skylight. A sliced tomato wilted on the countertop; a butcher knife lay next to it, still wet with juice. Curious, Rosa thought as she shoved the warm fruit into her mouth. She couldn't remember the last time she'd eaten.

As she chewed, Rosa heard movement in a cabinet beneath one of the kitchen's many industrial-sized sinks. She took the knife and crept toward the noise. More shuffling. Her heart thrummed in her throat as she raised the knife.

The cabinet door creaked open and banged shut just as quickly. From within, a muffled sound arose, something like a groan. With a thump, the door burst open and a woman's leg shot out, her stockings ripped, the heel of her shoe broken off. "Oof!" a voice cried. The leg retracted, the door closed.

Rosa released her breath, though she still held tight to the knife.

"Hello?" Rosa called.

After a pause, a woman's voice rasped from within the cabinet. "Are you... human?"

Rosa relaxed her grip. "The last time I checked."

The woman's feet jutted out, scrambling to find the floor, and two hands covered with liver spots and glittering jewels grasped the framing of the cabinet as the woman attempted to pull herself out. She fell back into the cabinet again with a grunt.

"My legs are all pins and needles," the woman said.

Rosa reached out a hand to help. The woman trembled as she rose, her designer dress in tatters.

"Mrs. Parker?" Rosa said.

"Rosa?" Frown lines broke through the woman's Botox-smooth skin. "How did you get in here?" She brushed off her dress, scattering a few errant sequins to the floor.

"Free trial membership." Rosa scowled and folded her arms. "Guess they'll let anyone in these days."

"I'm sorry," Mrs. Parker said. She wrung her hands, avoiding Rosa's glare. "I didn't mean it like that." Rivulets of smudged mascara streamed down her cheeks. "William is dead—they're all dead. I'm the only one left."

Rosa nodded. Mrs. Parker was the only living person Rosa had seen since the prior evening, when she and a group of strangers spent the night hiding under a highway overpass. They fled at the first rumblings of the swarm, and Rosa was on her own again.

She placed a hand on the elder woman's shoulder. Mrs. Parker shuddered, then relaxed with an audible sigh.

"I thought I might be the only one left, too," Rosa said. "But we're not alone now."

Pots and pans rattled on the walls. Rosa felt the building vibrate through her clenched teeth. She wondered how much time they had.

"The aliens are on the move again. We need to hide until they pass," Rosa said.

"Won't there be anyone to rescue us?"

Rosa shook her head. "I don't think so." In limited exchanges, other survivors had told her the National Guard was destroyed; the enemy cut through their steel wall of armor like it was paper. She gestured toward the cabinet where the elder woman had hidden. "But we'll need to find someplace bigger than that."

Mrs. Parker nodded. The women looked around the kitchen. Next to an oversized refrigerator, Rosa found a wooden door leading to a small pantry.

"Here," she said. "This should do."

"I wish I had seen this earlier." Mrs. Parker grimaced. "My knees are killing me."

Still holding the knife, Rosa opened the door. The air was damp and musty, and there was enough room for the two women to sit cross-legged, facing each other. As her eyes adjusted to the dim light, she noticed rows of shelves lined the walls; kitchen aprons and clean dish rags crisply folded amid black and white oven mitts. And stacked in the corner, almost like contraband, were a half dozen cans of fruit cocktail.

"Eureka!" Rosa grabbed two cans.

"Canned fruit at Le Château." Mrs. Parker wrinkled her nose. "I never would have imagined."

Rosa shook her head, glaring. "Not good enough for you and your friends?"

Holding the can securely, Rosa used the pointed edge of the knife to puncture the lid. Inch by inch she turned the can, cutting into the metal with each rotation until the lid came free. She bent it back slowly to avoid cutting herself, and snapped it off with a swift motion.

Mrs. Parker stared at her. "I've never seen anyone do that."

"I'm sure there's a lot you haven't seen." Rosa smirked, and raised the can to her lips, gulping the sweet liquid. She thrust her fingers into the juice and retrieved a slippery peach.

"Here." Rosa worked on a second can and handed it to Mrs. Parker, then laid the knife down. The fluid sloshed as the building shook; the metal blade rattled against the tile.

"Thank you." Hesitantly, Mrs. Parker picked a cherry out of the can, holding it between her thumb and forefinger. She took a bite, a look of disgust crossing her face. Rosa hunched over her meal and ate in silence.

"It's been so long since we've seen each other." Mrs. Parker cleared her throat. "How have you been? Since…"

Rosa looked up. She tucked a strand of hair behind her ear and stared at Mrs. Parker for a moment before she replied. "Since giant aliens invaded the world? I've been great."

"I wasn't referring to the aliens."

Rosa bit her lip and placed the fruit can on the floor. She reached into her pocket and removed a toy building block. Laying it in her palm, she ran her thumb over the chipped pink letter "D" painted into the carved wood.

"I've carried this with me, every day, for the past 267 days," Rosa said softly. "It was her favorite. 'D is for Dottie,' she'd say."

Mrs. Parker nodded, solemn.

Rosa leaned back against the shelves and hugged her arms across her chest as if to warm herself with a memory—Dottie, her only child, who'd shined with the life and light and love only a four-year-old could.

"She had my mother's eyes."

Mrs. Parker smiled. "She had your spirit."

Her daughter's zest, her light, was ended by a tumor that appeared as suddenly in her small body as the aliens did in the sky. Yet another predator, she thought. Satiated by pain. No purpose but destruction.

Mrs. Parker sniffled and played with the hem of her dress. "I'm sorry I didn't bring you back on after Dottie passed. You kept my house in order like no one else could." She paused, covering Rosa's hand with her own. "You were almost like family."

"That's rich." Rosa huffed. She snatched her hand back. "Let me guess. Being around *me* was too difficult *for you*."

"I didn't understand what you were going through," Mrs. Parker said. "The loss of your daughter was so tragic. But before... all this... I had never watched anyone die. I didn't know death."

"No one knows death until they've felt the absence it leaves behind." Rosa placed the wooden block back into her pocket. "It's like a hole in the sky."

Mrs. Parker reached up for a clean dish towel and dabbed at her nose. She continued, her breath catching. "It happened yesterday. He'd made up his mind to go outside. I begged him not to, but men like my husband are used to taking charge. Then, one of those... things... grabbed him. It tossed him away like he was nothing."

Rosa recalled the dead man lying on the stairs in the bloodied tux. *Mr. Parker.* She hadn't recognized his face. Death had robbed him of the confidence, the arrogance, she'd remembered him wearing so well.

"I understand, now, Rosa. And I'm sorry." Mrs. Parker grabbed Rosa's hand and squeezed hard. "All those hospital bills..."

Rosa sighed, a melancholy smile playing on her lips. "Maybe it was best Dottie left us when she did," she murmured. "Her light faded in its own time."

Like a sunset. Gradual and serene, sad and beautiful.

The ground shook hard. Mrs. Parker covered her head as linens bounced off the pantry shelves on top of the two women, covering them like a shroud.

A screech—metal on metal—pierced the silence.

Mrs. Parker gasped.

"Closer," Rosa said.

"What do we do?" Mrs. Parker whispered.

"We wait."

"For what? Those *things* to get us, too?" Mrs. Parker began to cry. "We can't stay in here forever."

"Forever is relative. Let's worry about now." Rosa leaned forward and embraced the older woman, one hand stroking her back to soothe her. Her sobs quieted.

Just like Dottie's had, at the end.

Rosa had clutched her daughter's hand as Dottie's small body wilted into the pristine white sheets of her hospital bed, and hummed a lullaby to calm the rapid, gasping breaths which ushered in their final moments together in a cold room far from home. A mother willing the hands of the ticking clock to slow, to stop, and to hasten—terrified of the inevitable but wishing it to come to end the pain. Rosa closed her eyes, pushing aside the memory and replaced it with a specter of happier times—Dottie's soft brown curls bouncing as she sang and played in her footed pajamas that last Christmas morning, her tiny hands building a tower with her precious blocks. Dottie beamed as the letters proclaimed her name.

Mrs. Parker straightened, her deep shuddering breath bringing Rosa from her thoughts. "I never thought I would die this way, hiding in some god-awful kitchen pantry."

"Eating canned fruit. With the help." Rosa chuckled. "Heck of a way to go."

"I always thought my death would be more... dignified." Mrs. Parker smoothed her gown. "I suppose at least I'm dressed for the occasion."

"Me too." Rosa tugged at her stained sweatpants. "See? No holes."

"You do know you're violating the club's dress code." She nudged Rosa. "Three strikes and you're out."

"But, Mrs. Parker, I didn't realize I was in."

"You are now. Please, call me Evelyn."

Brow furrowed, Rosa slowly nodded. "I'd be happy to. Evelyn." The name lay foreign on Rosa's tongue and, at the same time, comfortable.

"New Year's used to make me sad." Evelyn leaned her head back and smiled. "Every time the ball dropped, it was like a rock pushed itself through an hourglass. One year closer to old age. Seems silly now, sitting here as we are."

Evelyn closed her eyes and sighed.

In that moment, Rosa saw beyond the elder woman's glittering jewels. She noticed the fine lines cracking at the corners of Evelyn's mouth and eyes as if time had indeed caught up with her. She observed how the woman's shoulders, once perfectly postured, rounded as she sat slumped on the cold floor. Rosa envisioned an alternate reality in which Evelyn and William Parker glided across a glowing marble dance floor, their gazes fixed upon each other, hypnotized by the ghostly croon of a saxophone. She pictured an alternative life in which her own Christmas night had been spent gathering scattered toys under the glow of Christmas lights instead of grasping at memories in an empty room. And she thought about how shared sorrows connect us in ways shared joys never do.

She picked up the half-full cans of fruit cocktail from the floor, handing one to Evelyn as she raised the other in a toast.

"To the end."

Evelyn nodded. "To the end."

The metal cans connected with a soft *ting*. The women sipped the juice in silence.

"Promise me something," Evelyn said. "If these creatures should..."

BOOM.

The ceiling broke apart. Chunks of plaster rained down, the dust covering to their hair and eyes. The women clung to each other, a last hold on their humanity.

"They're here," Rosa whispered. She felt Evelyn's breath hot on her cheek, her body trembling.

"Do you think they'll—"

BOOM.

The tile cracked beneath them; fractures spread across the floor in a wave. Evelyn yelped. Rosa took a deep breath, desperate to calm the pounding in her chest.

BOOM.

Bright light leaked through a fissure in the wall, glinting off the knife on the floor. Rosa grabbed it, gripping the handle tightly. Her knuckles turned white as the blood drained from her face.

"This is it."

Evelyn reached out and grasped Rosa's taut fist. She spoke rapidly. "It needs to be on my terms. Not theirs."

Their eyes locked.

"Whether we succumb to the flames or leap into the abyss, the outcome will be the same." Evelyn squared her shoulders. "I need to die with dignity."

Rosa nodded, grim. She knew Evelyn was right.

"Will you do this for me?"

Rosa's breath caught like it did the moment after Dottie lay still. When time stopped, and the world was quiet. When the screams that threatened were quelled by the lingering peace of her daughter's final breath.

Soft wisps of silver hair entwined between Rosa's fingers as she placed her hand at the back of Evelyn's neck. Her pulse thumped against Rosa's wrist—steady, calm. Resolute. Rosa leaned in, feeling the woman's warm, even breathing, soft as a breeze.

"Thank you." Evelyn closed her eyes.

With a swift stroke, Rosa slit Evelyn Parker's throat.

Rosa kissed the woman's forehead and laid her down gently as blood and life drained from her body; death had taken her quickly. Peacefully.

BOOM.

Chunks of wood and splinters exploded as the pantry door blew open. The massive alien hovered, filling the doorway. Its claws clicked against the remaining tile. Rosa beheld her own face reflected endlessly in the multi-faceted surface of the creature's enormous eye. Green steam emanated from its gaping mouth. Its fangs glowed. Acrid breath enveloped her.

Rosa smiled at the creature.

She plunged the blade into her chest.

She felt the touch of a tiny hand.

A wooden block pressed into her palm.

And the light faded.

Fallen Hero

The man walked.

His scuffed work boots pushed pebbles with each step down the gravel path toward town. Ashen dust clung to his faded dungarees and the faint aroma of smoke lingered in the crisp fall air. Hands tucked in the pockets of his tattered black leather jacket, he strode beside the rusting tracks peeking through tufts of brittle overgrowth, the rails warmed but once per week with the slow rumbling of the CSX train as it passed through Mineville, brimming with coal. In the distance, endless rows of dilapidated houses settled beneath the shadow of shale mountains.

After twenty years away, the man returned to the only home he had ever known. Nothing changed here—*nothing ever changed here*. But, had he? His rounded and hunched shoulders betrayed his former stature; it was easier for him, *better for everyone*, to slink by in a world where he was no longer welcome than to rise to his true height, walk with purpose and show them that he was different now; he'd done his time, made peace with the past. The man welcomed the camouflage of age, his graying hair and beard painting him in a sad, non-threatening invisibility that he hoped would allow him to blend in with the landscape and help others forget.

His hazel eyes, magnified by the thick lenses of oversized and bent wire-framed glasses, fixated on the dust that swirled in eddies beneath his feet. He studied the impression his soles made in the terrain and the way the gravel reset itself as he marched forward, his presence as fleeting as his footsteps.

The boy emerged from the shadow of a burnt-out home in the distance. Its porch drooped in a macabre frown; the charred wood frame shedding history with each cinder that fell and drifted. Some relics aren't worth preserving, the man thought, wondering why the structure remained. *It's like propping up the dead among the dying.* The boy moved toward him with a bounce and a hop, a gait reserved for the very young. His cherry-red cheeks and curly, flaxen hair glowed in technicolor contrast to the decaying landscape beyond. Small fingers flipped at the lid of a tarnished, silver Zippo lighter. It clicked and snapped with each flick of the boy's thumb.

Click, click. Click, click.

Metal on metal.

"Hey, Mister!"

The man stopped.

"You got a lighter like this?"

The boy flipped the lighter open, producing a small blue flame, which he cupped to shield from the autumn breeze. The child's hands were rough and cracked, as if gloved in old-man skin.

Boys' hands should be plump and dimpled. Cradling fireflies, not fire.

The man shook his head. "No," he said, the train whistle in the distance drowning out his reply.

Sparks danced in the boy's eyes. "A lighter like this is dangerous, ain't it, Mister?"
A slow gap-toothed smile spread across his face as he thrust the lighter upward, just beneath the man's beard.

The man flinched.

"Shame, shame, I know your name!" the boy taunted.

"I think it's time for you to go," the man said, jaw tightening. "You don't want your mama worrying about you."

The boy licked his fingertips, extending them over the flame as if willing it to dance. He shook his head, mesmerized by the light in his hands. "Mama's not worried," the boy said, a reddish glow reflecting in his eyes. "She's sleeping. She's always sleeping."

The train whistle blared a warning. The man and boy looked up, their eyes locked as the ground rumbled, the vibration shaking the man to his core. The boy smiled and skipped toward the approaching train.

"Stop!" the man yelled, reaching for the boy, who leapt over the tracks just before the locomotive barreled through.

The man watched as a carousel of boxcars sped by, the clacking of the wheels a drumbeat against the whooshing and whistling that had devoured the silence. Amid the cacophony, the man lost sight of the boy; when the train passed, the boy was gone. The open lighter lay at the man's feet, its flame charring the dead leaves that blanketed the gravel road.

HEAD DOWN, THE MAN shrunk from the stares of the townsfolk shopping at the Five and Dime. He tucked his parcel under his arm—a carton of Marlboros, canned tuna, crackers, and three cans of wood varnish—and was met with the hard eyes of the shopkeeper. The meaning of his glare was clear: *Get Out of My Store.* This town's memory was as deep and unyielding as a barren mine. Perhaps it's better to be invisible to the world than to be remembered by it, he thought. The man pushed through the store's exit, the jangle of the bell a welcome respite from the cold silence inside.

Across the cobblestone road, three young firemen polished Mineville's newest engine, their arms coated in a sweaty sheen, their pride reflected in the gleaming red metal. The man smiled, wistful. His great grandfather founded Mineville Engine Company Number One in the late 1800s, in the days when horses pulled the rig. His grandfather, father, uncles, cousins, and brothers all heeded the call, just as he did in his eighteenth year. The brotherhood bound them with a force far stronger than blood—generations connected by the same yearning. *Seize power over fire.* But that bond was broken the day the man had left Mineville. Cousins and brothers drifted to unknown towns, faceless and nameless with the hope of starting anew. The uncles retired, retreating to their cottages on the outskirts of town, spending their final days rocking on creaky porches, swilling beer from sweating cans and talking about the old times. And his father—some say he died of a broken heart.

The man stepped off the curb, drawn to the fire station like a spark to kindling. He recalled the adrenaline rush that came with each call; the quick catch awakening his gut as he rushed to don his gear, his heart pounding like a caged eagle as he jumped on the rig. And the sweet euphoria of storming a burning building; he was a soaring bird whose talons reached through walls of flame, bold and unscathed. Beneath his wings the flames cowered, upon his back the helpless were whisked from harm. He breathed fire, taming chaos at will; a god whose actions determined who might live, and who might die.

Tires screeched as an oncoming sedan swerved around the man and slammed on its brakes. "Get out of here, before you get somebody else killed!" the driver yelled, wild-eyed and waving a fist through the open window. The firefighters paused from their work, shaking their heads and staring at the man, their lips pulled tight, eyes narrowed.

The man had dropped his parcel; the canned tuna rolled in the gutter. As he retrieved his package from the asphalt, he noticed the boy sitting on the hood of the fire engine, an oversized helmet falling over his eyes. The boy waved furiously, a red handkerchief balled up in his palm. "Hey, Mister," he yelled, releasing the fabric. Caught in a light breeze, it floated toward the pavement like an ember. "This belong to you?"

The man removed his glasses, his eyes following the cloth in its descent. As it touched the ground, the wailing of the fire signal mobilized the men. They pushed their buckets aside, the cleaning rags dropped and forgotten as they scrambled to gather their gear. The boy laughed as red lights flashed atop the firehouse and he clambered into the back of the truck; the firemen leapt into the cab and sped toward danger.

The wheels had rolled over the fallen handkerchief, leaving a filthy imprint in its center. The man crossed the empty street and crouched down to retrieve it. He spread the cloth over his thigh, dirtying his fingers as he ran them across the rough cotton.

THE MAN TRUDGED UP the rickety wooden staircase to the apartment above his great aunt's barn, a one-bedroom unit initially built as a boarding house for coal miners who drifted in and out of town. With few exceptions, those who were born in Mineville usually died there; newcomers were as transient as the seasons.

He had been homeless after twenty years in the state penitentiary. Great Aunt Martha was the only one who paid him any mind after he was released; she gave him a place to stay, though he doubted she'd visit. Like his life, the man's dwelling space was on loan. The furniture was mismatched and tired: a red velvet couch with cigarette burns and sagging cushions, a tan leather easy chair that began its life as ivory, a wobbly kitchen table. Wallpaper in the pattern of pink peonies curled down from the corners of the room. It wasn't much, but it was home, a comfortable solitary confinement after years of bunking with criminals.

When he unpacked his groceries, the man removed a crisp Marlboro from its carton. He reached in his pocket for the lighter that the boy left behind. It had belonged to the man, a gift from a long-forgotten fiancée. He hadn't seen it, or her, since the night of the Walnut Street Fire. That was his last night as a fireman, the last night of his life. The night he went to prison.

Where had the boy found it?

He ran his fingertips across the engraving. "J.D." His initials—the initials of the man he used to be. He flicked his thumb across the igniter, lighting a low blue flame. A plume of sweet smoke encircled his cigarette, and he took a long drag. He plopped down on the couch, sinking into the velvet. The lighter lay nestled in his rough palm, the luster of silver dulled by time.

Sighing, the man extinguished his cigarette in the ashtray, another loan from his great aunt. "Hero" was painted on the ceramic, along with a picture of a helmet and axe. That ashtray had survived through years of fire and ash, of guilty pleasures lit and snuffed out. The man recalled playing with that ashtray as a child, stacking burnt-out cigar and cigarette butts as he sat under his aunt's dining room table—the smell of stale nicotine absorbed into his skin. He leaned up against the legs of his father and his uncles that surrounded him like a fortress—*a prison cell*—entranced by their stories of rushing and rescue.

Heroes. All of them.

The man stood and stretched; there was important work to do. As part of his community service, he was tasked with refurbishing town relics damaged by a recent flood—starting with a collection of wooden plaques commemorating the history of the Mineville Fire Department. He lifted the first plaque from the pile on his kitchen table. "Fallen Heroes" was etched by hand at the top with his father's name, the name they shared, immortalized in the wood.

The plaque lay like a tombstone in the man's hands. With reverence, he laid it gently on the table. He reached for the can of varnish and dug his nails under the lid, pulling. The metal indented his fingertips, but the lid wouldn't give. He scratched his beard, intent on remembering where he left his screwdriver to jimmy it, when he heard a familiar sound.

Click, click. Click, click.

Metal on metal.

The man spun on his heels, knocking the sealed varnish can off the kitchen table.

"Hey, Mister!" The boy sat on the arm of the couch, his ruddy face rivaling the scarlet fabric. He held the lighter between his thumb and forefinger, opening and closing the lid of the Zippo in a maddening staccato.

"How did you get in here?" the man asked, his pale cheeks flushing. He looked toward the closed door, the deadbolt still secure.

The boy closed the lighter and tapped it against his forehead. "I've always been here." He grinned. "J.D."

The man shook his head, running fingers through his hair.

"I don't know why you're following me, but you need to stop." Fists clenched, the man stomped toward the door. He screamed as he touched the doorknob, his skin singed by a surge of heat. Pulling his hand away, he saw the knob glowing red. Blisters sprouted from his smarting palm.

The boy giggled as the man raced toward the kitchen sink and plunged his hand into a cool faucet stream. The man grunted with relief, and in pain.

"Get out of my house," he said through clenched teeth.

"Your house?" the boy said, materializing next to the man as he tended to his injury. "This is not your house. Nothing belongs to you any more, does it, J.D.? Except this." He ignited the lighter, dangling the flame in front of him.

"Scram." The man waved a shaking hand toward the door. "Get the hell out of here, kid."

"Kid? Why are you calling me Kid?" The boy closed the lighter and let out a belly laugh, clutching his stomach as it jiggled. "My name isn't Kid. It's Billy. Why are you making believe you don't know me?"

The man pushed past the boy, heading toward the wall phone. "I'll call the cops."

"9-1-1!" the boy said in a singsong. He skipped around the man.

The man reached for the phone, his uninjured hand resting on the receiver.

"That's who my mama said I should call if there's an emergency," the boy said. "9-1-1." He stopped moving and stood very still. His shoulders dropped, and he sighed. "And I did. I called them. But they were no help."

The boy clicked the igniter and ramped the lighter fluid to full strength. The man watched, wide-eyed, as the fire morphed from an innocent sliver of candlelight into to a brutal blowtorch. The boy dangled his pinky finger over the flame, then plunged it into the amber core.

The man retched at the acrid stench of burning flesh. He stepped backward, searching for the wall to steady him as the boy turned his head.

A crusted hole gaped open where the boy's left ear should have been. His neck was covered with festering blisters. Patches of flesh hung like cobwebs from his arms, revealing charred muscle beneath. He radiated heat.

"You burned my house," the boy said.

"*Your* house...?"

"I watched you do it. It was the middle of the night." The boy stared into the flame, yellow and red and blue dancing off his coal-black eyes. "I woke up. I had a nightmare. But Mommy made me go back to bed. I saw you outside the window in your fireman clothes. You had a red handkerchief in your pocket. You poured water on the bushes. And then you used this."

The boy thrust the lighter toward the man,

"No..." The man's voice was barely audible as he sank to the ground, burying his face in his forearms.

"I was really scared. I hid under my bed."

"Please don't do this," the man whispered. "I did my penance. I just want to be left alone."

"Mama told me firemen were heroes." A tear streamed down the boy's mottled cheek. "But not you. You're a bad man."

The boy's face scrunched up in a twisted grimace. "I miss my Mama," he said. His lower lip quivered, and he squeezed the lighter, as if willing the tears away.

"I miss my Mama!"

The boy flung the fireball toward the can of varnish that lay on the floor. It blossomed in a plume of blue heat. Tufts of wallpaper ignited and rained down upon the mismatched furniture. Fire licked at the couch. It pushed across the table in a wave, consuming the plaques. The man's name—*his father's name*—melted away as the wood crinkled into a charred mass.

Fallen heroes.

The man gasped through the billowing smoke that obscured the boy's face. As the heat entombed him, he recalled the heavy, endless weeks before the Walnut Street Fire, how he trudged through each day as if dragging a charged line uphill. There were only so many games of Spades a man could play down at the firehouse, so many jokes he could tell, before losing his mind. The summer heat had fueled his hunger for fire; the caged bird raged, yearning for purpose. And that night, as the man walked, he saw an opportunity.

What he hadn't seen was the little boy who pressed his face against the window on the third floor to watch the fireman *watering the bushes* with a large red can outside the house. The little boy who stood before him, twenty years later, avenging a mother who would always sleep—staring down the nightmare that robbed him of his rest. This brave boy who breathed fire through a gap-toothed smile.

"Please. Forgive me." The man lay on the floor, his body spasming with each cough. Black smoke curled around him like a shroud. "Billy." He reached toward the boy, straining against the effort of breathing.

"No."

"I'm so sorry."

The man gasped his last. The fire he had so craved over the years turned on him, devouring him not in a blaze of glory but of retribution, his death a release for a young boy who had been long trapped, invisible to the world.

Nothing changed here—*nothing ever changed here*—but, perhaps, it had.

The boy walked. He smiled as he pushed onward, through the flame.

The Last of the Kalachi
A Story of Exodus

The NOGD DARTED INTO the night. Ears flapping and tail wagging, it blazed forward like a comet in a blur of yellow fur.

Racing past a menagerie of creatures and cargo, the Nogd whizzed through a door that sprung open when the hovercraft transporting it abruptly stopped. It ignored the whistles and shouts of the four Kalachi crew members imploring its return. It rebuffed promises of treats and toys, blissfully ignorant of the enemy territory beneath its footfalls. It thought not of curfews, or boundaries, or the Cretean sentries in the surrounding watchtowers.

The Nogd yearned for freedom.

MARI jogged across the empty plains on the fringes of Kalach, her holstered laser-pistol thumping against her thigh. Like a drumbeat, it reminded her to be vigilant. Though silence skulked around her, enemy Cretes could ambush at any moment, and the longer the hovercrafts in her caravan remained exposed, the greater the likelihood of their capture. She tried to quash the ache she felt for the city she was leaving behind, her home for twenty life-years. It was all she knew and now, its lights shone dull behind her, distant as the shadow of a dream.

She squinted through the haze—searching. Seeking movement. She stopped to catch her breath, heart thudding in her parched throat. If Mari didn't locate that missing Nogd soon, it would be left to die alone in the barren city outskirts.

Twin moons poked through the sky, tiny beacons in a murky and uncertain future. It had been almost one life-year since the Cretes had discovered Kalach. Their vast ships floated through Kalach's night-clouds in a shimmering affirmation that the Kalachi were not alone on their small planet. Or in the grander universe beyond.

In the Kalachi spirit of *kukoma*—kindness without question—they had offered the Cretes a peaceful refuge. The visitors claimed they'd been driven from their home planet by a great pestilence. Yet, like a dormant disease awakened, the Cretean occupation crept through the city with a gradual poison. Dark tendrils of betrayal wrapped around the soul of Kalach, the embrace of these strangers devolved to a crushing grip intended to pulverize its people until nothing remained but an empty husk—without a hint of why.

Mari tried to forget the women slashed by Cretean laser-blades as they waited in the market for slim rations that seldom came. She squeezed her eyes to blot the image of families obliterated beneath the walls of their homes as the bombs fell. She shook her head to rid visions of the hands of those fallen—young and old reaching from the rubble for help that never arrived.
But the stench of bodies left to rot in the streets still haunted her. And the blank stares of small children, orphaned and hungry, wandering the city until they simply disappeared.

Sadness and guilt entangled in an intricate, leaden knot within Mari's mind, twisting away any relief she might have felt from being among the Kalachi chosen. The caravan would build a new life on the dark side of the planet, far from the city. Far from the Cretean vise. With cloaking mechanisms activated, the caravan's five Advance Reconnaissance Crafts, or ARCs, crept through the darkness in a clandestine exodus to ensure the preservation of their race. Though the Elders deemed Mari worthy to live, she couldn't shake the sheen of death plastered upon their flight. Leaving Kalach marked the certainty of its demise.

And it was impossible for Mari to forget the boy who'd begged them to take him, too. He appeared, pale as a phantom, when the caravan was secured. Rags covered his body; he shivered in the cool night. Bruises reflected the indigo hues of his eyes, dark and deep—unnatural for one so young. He couldn't have been more than five or six life-years, but centuries of Kalachi culture and love resided in his gaze. "Please," he'd said. But Mari had turned away. Her eyes weighed heavy, burdened by the strain of brewing tears and a grim vision of the boy's future. She could not respond with anything but silence, her tongue unable to shape even an empty apology.

It wasn't for Mari or her crew to choose the Kalachi whose lives would take root in their new home. But they were tasked to ensure those lives chosen had the chance to be lived.

She needed to find the Nogd.

RHEE grasped tight to her laser gun. The cool metal grounded her in the moment, in the mission. Her life spun in three orbits—the time before the invasion, the time after, and the time now. She'd never sought to be a soldier; hell, none of them had. Kalach had barely maintained any semblance of a police force. But they were chosen and trained, a ragtag army born of people who neither knew hate nor war until the Cretes delivered it, wrapped in a package of deception.

The Elders had seen something in each one of them—Rhee and Mari, their partner co-pilots Tomak and Emon. They'd taken a solemn oath to carry Kalach forward and left the city as unwitting warriors, pioneers paired two by two, their genetics matched to ensure viable offspring.

Rhee felt a twinge of envy as she glanced at Tomak, Mari's designated partner. Sweat glistened over his tattooed skin as he worked to repair the cloaking device of ARC-4. He was an excellent mechanic and a gentleman, always offering to help Mari and Rhee carry heavier equipment or holding the door of the ARCs, allowing them entry first. He 'yes ma'am-ed' and 'no-ma'am-ed' in a gentle school-boyish way, despite his rough looks. Rhee could tell he'd be considerate to her friend, that he'd make a good father to the children they'd sworn to conceive.

Rhee, however, would not be as fortunate. Her partner Emon was a weaselly man; she wondered if he'd bribed his way onto the ARCs. He wasn't much of a co-pilot, a sharp critical tongue his only asset. But agreeing to the genetic pairing was the only way to secure passage from the city, and they were a match.

Rhee scowled at the barbarism of it all. But she knew she'd never survive if she remained in the city. Emon was a necessary burden if she wanted to live. As a Pilot, it was her obligation to transport the chosen ones to safety. As a woman, her role was even more critical: to ensure the Kalachi would persist, if—no, *when*—the city fell.

"Why does that girl care so much about some dumb, scruffy beast?" Emon swaggered toward Rhee, blaster slung over his shoulder. Rhee shuddered under his ogling stare.

There's only one beast in this caravan, she thought.

"That 'girl' is one of the best pilots we have. And the 'scruffy beast' will be among the last of its kind." Rhee said. "We were *chosen* for this mission—you and I, as much as that Nogd."

"How I ended up on ARC-4's pet patrol is beyond me," Emon scoffed. "At the very least, they could have assigned me to ARC-5. The transportation of cultural relics is much better suited to a man of my stature."

Ignoring him, Rhee glanced toward the two parked crafts, the cloaking mechanism of ARC-4 still pixelating in and out of sight. The journey of the Kalachi people on ARCs 1, 2, and 3 hadn't stalled with ARC-4's cloaking failure; Rhee was grateful that Mari and Tomak stopped ARC-5 to help them. She glanced over the plains. Mari's light pink hair shimmered in the distance.

"We should leave that Nogd to its fate," Emon said.

Rhee's eyes burned red. Though she was smaller than Emon, she rushed at him, gritting her teeth inches from his face. He took a step back, paling. "Look around," Rhee said, the tremble in her voice giving life to her anger. "We left the city to its fate, and all its people. We're not leaving here without the Nogd. Or without Mari."

Emon huffed, his expression cracking before it settled into his characteristic resting sneer.

"There, there, now, dearest." Emon stroked Rhee's cheek; she yanked her face away from him, glaring. "I'll make sure the idiotic brute gets that cloak up and running ASAP. After all, someone needs to be in charge—especially with one of our Pilots off chasing some mongrel through the brush."

He turned on his heel. Rhee squeezed her blaster hard. Its ridges dug into her fingertips and as much as she wanted to shoot him, she knew she wouldn't. Couldn't. She turned away to hide the violet teardrop rambling down her cheek. Anger was such a futile emotion.

Futile, yet unequivocally real.

EMON stalked toward Tomak. His feet moved toward the bigger man, though his eyes fixed on the skyscrapers in the distance. How defiant those structures stood, despite the endless bombings that crippled them. It was the city he loved; yet its façade nauseated him, like a crisp apelfruit rotted from the inside.

The city was dying at the fault of its Elders.

Pathetic, they were. Their infinite wisdom hardly served them when people started disappearing not long after the Cretes landed. First, it was the street urchins and the beggars, then the peddlers. As benevolent as they were—or, claimed to be—the Elders only took notice when the city began losing its more prominent citizens. Clergy and professors, artists and musicians.

People of importance. People like Emon.

By then, it was too late.

It wasn't enough for the Cretes to slice the heart from Kalach. Instead, they crushed it in their palms—their ensuing onslaught so severe the streets rained slick with its blood. Emon had huddled in a filthy safe house, night after night, as the echo of ion cannons jolted him from a restless slumber. He'd prayed that the centigods would spare him from capture, or at the very least, that they'd offer a swift death.

Until the bombing ceased and the Cretes presented an offer of truce, thought to be a ruse with an undefined endgame. Yet, it was the signal he'd been waiting for, a call to the chosen for salvation.

Emon had surrendered his collection of rare art and first edition Kalachi texts for a co-pilot's seat in the exodus from the city. It was an expensive proposition, timeless Kalachi treasures bartered for his life. Well worth the price of his ticket to the new civilization, though their intended destination was hardly civilized. Even the ARC hovercrafts were crude. Once the vehicle of Kalachi plains hunters, the crafts still bore the lingering odor of slaughtered carcasses that previously hung in the cargo holds.

Funny, how the essence of prey lingered; mocking their hunters, who were now the hunted.

Every moment their caravan spent grounded presented an opportunity for the Cretes to find them. Without an operational cloaking device, the caravan's journey would end in the worst possible way.

The idiocy of his crewmates astounded Emon. They were almost as bad as the Elders.

Almost.

Panting, **MARI** scanned the landscape, devoid of cover, save for a few crumbling bushes that rose from the ground like specters. She wished her memories were strong enough to bend reality; that with hope, all would be restored, just like in the ancient tales her grandmother had once told.

But her family was gone, the ancient tales frivolous, grasses scorched by Cretean ships. Knowledge of a world bigger than themselves had once filled the Kalachi people with awe and hope. Now, only the smell of burnt foliage endured.

She willed herself forward, longing for the Kalach of her childhood, the shining marble streets upon which she'd run, chasing her schoolmates to the city's highest points. They'd watched the azure grasses of the great plains shimmer in the distance, unable to find the line where the land ended and the sky began. But now those streets were rubble, and the plains, nothing but a wasteland.

A dormant enemy watchtower rose in the distance; moonlight glinted off its glass. Mari prayed that its Cretean inhabitants slept soundly—lulled by the promise of truce, as much as the inhabitants of her city had.

And then she saw it, the sole life form nestled into the burned-out field. The Nogd curled up, as if in slumber, its fur shimmering gold amid the surrounding chaff.

Mari broke into a full sprint, her steps crackling through the brush.

TOMAK yanked the wrench. Sweat streamed from his temples; he grunted, turning the bolt that linked the ARC's control panel to the cloaking device's converter until the connection was airtight.

Fried connection sent this mission into a tizzy, he thought. Not gonna happen again.

"Almost finished?" Emon scowled, scrunching his pinched features. He shone a light into the control box.

"Little more," Tomak said. "We need to be tootin' sure this cloak ain't gonna give us more trouble. 'Specially when we pass those Cretean battalions." Straightening, he wiped his brow.

Emon nodded and tapped a transmitter strapped to his belt. "The other ARCs are halfway to the Turen Wood." He sneered. "Civilization, born in the wildlands."

"It's the only safe place," Tomak said. He lowered his voice and glanced around, in case someone—*something*—was listening. "They say when the Cretes tried to burn those woods, those woods breathed fire back at 'em."

"Too bad we couldn't weaponize that power." Emon sighed. "But that would never have been tenable under our *benevolent* leaders. Our Elders would've taught the Cretes how to use it against us. *Knowledge is a dish best shared.*"

"Complaining ain't gonna get us nowhere," Tomak said. "Gettin' this cloak up and running, now that'll get us where we need to be."

"What I wouldn't give to be relaxing in my hoverchair, smoking a willowpipe and listening to the city chamber orchestra's performance outside my penthouse window." A scowl pinched Emon's face. "Instead of here, sweating in this wasteland. How I look forward to the dirt pile, the grime that awaits us in the Turen Wood."

Tomak grunted, shooting a glare at the little man. He's got small hands, Tomak thought. Beady eyes. Emon was useless as a mechanic, probably a pain in the ass co-pilot, too. Must've aced his virility test, Tomak mused.

Tomak thought of the children selected for ARC-1. Two by two, males and females, aged one life-year through young adulthood. *Those kids must be scared, their mamas and papas left behind in the city. But then, most of 'em probably don't have mamas and papas anymore.*

Emon shuffled his feet. Tomak saw him glance at Rhee, staring a moment too long as she stood watch, laser-pistol in hand. She was young. Athletic. Attractive, with long violet hair flowing down her back.

"The city looks peaceful," Emon said. "Quiet. Perhaps the truce is legitimate and these precautions unnecessary."

"What good does a truce do the Cretes?" Tomak tapped the wrench into his palm. "They had the upper hand."

"The incompetence of the Elders may have failed us yet again." Emon said.

"When someone's pummelin' you in a bar brawl and they just... stop... bet your life they're bidin' time for bigger men with bigger swords to come cut you in half." Tomak shook his head and frowned. "Elders were right to send us out now."

"Civilized Kalachi do not engage in... bar brawls." Emon tsked. "We should be on our way."

"And leave Mari? That ain't gonna happen, man."

Emon glanced toward the craft, his gaze narrowing as it fixed on the cockpit. "I say we fire up the engines now," he said.

"We ain't leavin' no one behind." Tomak felt his hands curl into fists.

Tomak looked over the plains for Mari. Though it was awkward to consider what was to come once they reached the new world, Tomak had resigned himself to his duty. His heart would always stay with the wife he'd hidden in the city catacombs, the woman whose body he'd cradled until her skin grew cold.

Tomak rubbed a deep scar that extended across his forearm; it burned with the sorrow and regret that simmered within him. He knew he was luckier than most. Though he'd been unable to stop the onslaught that ripped away the love and the life he'd intended, Tomak had been given another chance.

A swath of pink cut through the night. Mari's hair swayed as she hurried in the distance.

She was awfully nice, if not a little careless, for chasing down that runaway pup.

Pretty too, Tomak thought.

MARI hastened, her leg muscles burning. Crushing the deadened earth with each step, she felt alive. The faster she ran, the louder her heartbeat, the more confident she became that she'd save that Nogd. The Cretes couldn't take everything. She wouldn't let them. And they'd go on. The Kalach Mari knew and loved would carry on.

In the city, most Kalachi never would have noticed one stray Nogd roving the streets. Nogds were as plentiful as people. Neither caged nor tethered, they simply roamed, wandering in and out of homes, enjoying the care given by the Kalachi people. That was the Kalachi way. *Kindness without question.*

It was why Mari needed to save that Nogd. In the caravan, one being carried the burden of thousands. To save one was to save all. But she ached for those who remained behind. How much longer until the Creteans swallowed them whole, until the city's lights were snuffed out, one by one?

What an empty end we face when no one remains to tell our tales.

She shook away the thought, focused on the Nogd lying in the brush ahead. What was life without a Nogd nuzzling under your hand to be petted or snuggling up beside you on chilly nights?

The capacity for joy—it bridged the divide between surviving and living. She couldn't—wouldn't—imagine a world where Nogds didn't exist.

The Nogd's head rose through the brush. Mari was close enough to see its nose wriggling. It burrowed deeper into the withered grass.

The watchtower's searchlight clicked on. Mari dove beneath a crumbling bush; she laid her hand on the holster of her pistol.

The light rolled over them, and Mari held her breath. She held still.

She prayed the Nogd smelled her fear and froze in its place, too. Willed the Cretean sensors to interpret them as field debris, not intruders.

The light passed.

She exhaled.

"It's okay," Mari whispered. "I'm coming."

Mari crawled on her belly toward the Nogd, the hardened grass digging into her hands, scraping against her cheek. She stayed as low as she could, lifting her eyes to follow the path of the searchlight that stretched into the fields to pluck them out and punish them for their trespass.

Reaching over the coarse ground, Mari's hand met soft fur. The Nogd whimpered, as did the two newborn pups snuggled at her belly.

"That's why you're here," Mari whispered.

Mari pushed herself up and ran her hand down the Nogd's smooth back. Fine hairs stuck to Mari's palm as the Nogd licked her arm with its long, spotted tongue. The pups wriggled into their mother.

Another whimper.

"Good girl. We'll keep them safe."

Mari picked up the small bundles and tucked them into her jacket, zipping them, snug. She stood tentatively, surveying the night.

Still dark, the watchtower remained quiet. Motionless.

The mother Nogd leaned into Mari's leg as they began their trek back to the caravan. Her boots crunched through the brush; ARC-4 and ARC-5 hovered within Mari's sightline.

And then she heard it. The hum of drones suspended behind them. Mari pivoted; laser-pistol drawn.

TOMAK had just run the last test of ARC-4's cloaking device when he saw the light trolling across the Cretean plain. He held his breath, hoping it was far enough away for the vehicles to remain hidden in darkness.

"See that light?" Emon asked, scurrying next to Tomak. "It was a bad idea for your girl to run off after that worthless beast."

Tomak set his jaw. "*You* breakin' the cloaking gear on this hover was a bad idea."

"I did not break the cloaking gear," Emon said, straightening.

"Co-pilot who can't handle a cloak ain't worth his flight suit." Tomak leaned in, a growl in his voice. "And Mari ain't no one's girl. Best you learned some respect."

"Quiet!" Rhee crept toward them. Emon's ears flushed. Tomak couldn't imagine a more unlikely pairing. She holstered her weapon, retrieving night vision binoculars.

"Whaddya see?" Tomak asked.

"Mari's reached the Nogd," Rhee said. She smiled. "They're okay. On their way back."

Emon scowled. "Took her long enough. We should get the ARCs fired up now."

"Wait." Rhee adjusted the dial and leaned in toward the open field. She dropped her smile.

MARI obliterated a drone with a single shot. Shrapnel erupted from the fireball, the blast an endless sound wave that crashed over the night. The tower burst with a light that raced over the landscape like a barreltrain. The Nogd howled at her side and they sprinted, desperate to stay out of the beam.

Another drone chased behind them, shadowed by a swarming horde.

"Halt, trespassers!" a tinny voice warned.

The Nogd pushed against her as they ran, its warm body urging her forward, away from the ensuing drones. The nearby ground exploded in a cloud of dirt and rock, and the dry grass ignited. Flames spread around them. Mari raised her laser-pistol over her shoulder and fired.

Missed.

Another blast. Another miss.

Her third shot hit the drone's vocal box; warbling in slow-motion as it fell into the fire.

Mari cradled the pups close. Rhee raced toward Mari and her charges, blasting the drones that followed. She drew their fire as Mari and the Nogd advanced, Mari shooting furiously and blindly over her shoulder through the smoke. Laser shots whizzed past her from the direction of ARC-5; Tomak's gamma gun cut holes through the enemy wall.

Their efforts were barely enough to contain the pack of attacking robots.

"Emon!" Through the din, Mari heard Tomak's plea. "Help us!"

Close within Mari's sightline ahead, the image of ARC-4 flickered in and out of night. If they could lose these droids and the cloaking device was operational, they might have a chance.

Emon sprinted from behind the pixelating craft, his blaster raised over his head. Mari watched Emon turn toward the open field; saw the terror freeze on his features as the robotic wave crashed toward him—Mari and Rhee both riding its crest. He dropped his weapon and sprinted toward the cockpit door. The engine hummed to life, and the craft vanished.

With an invisible whoosh, ARC-4—and Emon—took off.

"You bastard!" Rhee's voice shrieked, a whistle through a whirlwind.

The drones surged toward her, swallowing Rhee in a surge of metal.

"No!" Mari screamed.

Rhee's body jerked with each close-range blast that ripped through her; her wasted, limp form sliding to the ground like refuse.

Mari choked back a bile-laden sob, smoke burning her eyes and coating her throat as she ran. She forced herself forward—if Mari stopped running, she would die.

The Kalachi couldn't lose them both.

The Nogd turned back, then; her howl a mournful song. Running toward Rhee, she dove to the ground as she reached the body.

With her nose, the Nogd nudged at the fallen pilot. Blasts exploded above them.

Mari reached Tomak at ARC-5 and together they downed the mechanical assassins. Drones dropped like fallen stars. Yet, with each one destroyed, another arrived to replace it. Until the drones stopped firing.

For a moment, the machines hovered, an army of miniature Cretean crafts surveying them with red cybertronic eyes. A heartbeat later, they turned, racing through the flaming plains toward the city.

The night was silent again. The Nogd padded over to them.

"They stopped." Mari's breaths heaved. "Why?

Tomak shook his head and glanced toward the city. Mari followed his gaze. The mass of drones pushed toward Kalach.

"They got somethin' bigger planned, alright," he said.

Mari laid her palm on the Nogd's head and rubbed behind her ear. The Nogd stretched her head up under Mari's hand; Mari drowned her fingers into soft fur, staunching the tears that threatened. Rhee's fallen form rested small and still, like a stone in the field. Someone so brave deserved so much more.

The Nogd emitted a low whine and leaned its weight against Mari's thigh. It offered its warmth as respite.

That's what Nogds do. They heal our souls.

Mari turned toward Tomak, her eyes meeting his melancholy gaze.

"Can we—" Mari started, glancing toward Rhee's body. Kalachi death rites had all but been abandoned since the invasion.

"We should go," Tomak said, resting his hand on Mari's shoulder. "She would have wanted us to carry on."

Mari's breath caught as she said a silent goodbye to her friend—her courage, her sacrifice, her drive to save the mission, to save the Nogd, even as it cost Rhee her life. Mari also thought of that boy she'd rejected in the city, knowing that she'd see his eyes every time she looked up at the twin moons through the foliage in their new home.

No one could save them all.

Quietly, they slipped into the cockpit of ARC-5. Tomak held the door as Mari slid into the pilot's seat, followed by the Nogd. Staring ahead, Mari gripped the controls. A chill sidled over her skin. The Nogd rested its flank against her.

"To those we've left behind," Mari whispered.

Mari and Tomak glanced toward the city as a heavy green mist rose through its spires, choking Kalach in a toxic cloud. One by one, the lights of their civilization extinguished, the final breaths of their people exhausted. Mari said a silent prayer for all the Kalachi who closed their eyes that night, wrapped snug in the false hope of a promised truce. Perhaps it was better they didn't know. At least they'd sleep easier at the end. Yet, their absence would carve an enduring chasm as deep as the craters on the dark side of the planet.

Whimpering, the two small pups wriggled themselves from Mari's jacket.

Tomak's eyes widened.

She offered him a weak smile, grateful for small miracles.

"New life," Mari said.

Tomak rested his hand on her arm. Mari's skin tingled beneath his warmth.

"New life."

Mari pushed the throttle forward, and ARC-5 raced onward, invisible, through the night.

A Longing for the Old Days

Esther had married her high school sweetheart.

For most of the fifty years she and Marvin spent together, they'd looked ahead to what came next: their wedding day, the house with a white picket fence, the birth of their children. But when the children grew, she and Marvin were left to stare at each other on their matching recliners and Esther longed for the old days. Marvin didn't say much, but when he did, he talked about what was, rather than what would be.

The new drive-in theatre in town was just what they needed to bring them back, perhaps even bring them forward, together. It was almost romantic.

Almost.

Cane draped over her arm, Esther shuffled from the concession stand. Liver-spotted hands held the tray of treats that Marvin liked most—lightly salted popcorn, candy-coated chocolates, and the gooey caramels that always stuck to his dentures. Esther hated that Marvin needed to remove his teeth to eat them. The last time they visited the drive-in, his dentures slipped to the driver's seat floor and wedged beneath the gas pedal. Marvin hadn't noticed until he started driving. Broken teeth scattered about like Chicklets falling from an open box. It was a wonder they got home that night.

Small steps, Esther thought, as she weaved through the minivans and sedans parked on the open lot, avoiding the darting children and adults distracted by their cell phones. She never understood the allure, why grown adults needed to escape their lives by staring into a device they kept glued to their hands. Living inside a screen was unnatural.

But she supposed she was just old. And it was easier to mutter "back in my day" than it was to recognize that the world had changed. Or to change with it.

Esther's knee began quivering. It wouldn't be long until it would give out on her again. Only a few feet away from their Grand Marquis, she needed to stop. Rest that leg. Knee surgery was inevitable, but she'd tried to put it off as long as possible. Who would take care of Marvin if she were laid up for weeks?

She heard him snoring before she saw him through the window, his head tilted back, mouth gaping open. He always sounded like a buzz saw when he was asleep, yet he denied ever making a sound in his slumber.

As children giggled and pointed at the tired old man in his car, a strange sensation overtook Esther. Her body chilled, gooseflesh rose on her skin, and it felt as if every pore on her body opened to suck in the night air. Her feet lost contact with the ground, and she floated, feather-light. The tray slipped from her fingers and crashed to the grass. The light on the movie screen flickered, as if charged by an electric current.

Darkness overtook her; swallowing the drive-in and everything in it.

She emitted a slight gasp, reached shaking fingers to her chest. She felt no pain, but her heart thrummed like a bass drum. It reminded her of high school Marching Band, of cheering Marvin on as he scored the winning touchdown of the championship game.

Her best self, in her best days.

In the distance, a pinprick of white light shone through the dark. Brilliant spires flashed from its core like starfire. It grew—*breathed*—as illumination poured through. The pinprick became a circle that stretched in a whirlpool of radiance, until the movie screen glowed. Esther reached for the light; it stretched toward her, entwining a smoke-like ribbon through her fingers, around her hand, her arm, her waist. She drifted through darkness toward that rectangular beacon—it called to her, it calmed her. She closed her eyes, surrendering to the sensation of butterfly wings fluttering in her gut, balmy breezes blowing through her mind.

Esther landed softly. Silken sand oozed between her bare toes.

"Where am I?" Esther whispered.

She opened her eyes, wide, surrounded by lush palm trees and mountainscapes, a pink sand beach, and the clearest turquoise water she'd ever seen. As birds cawed in the distance, she glanced down at her own body, clad in a bikini. Her stomach and legs were smooth, her body lithe. The spots had dissolved from her hands. She felt no pain in her knee or joints. She touched the red curls that fell from her shoulders, twisting her fingers through locks she hadn't felt in decades.

When am I? she wondered.

Through the rolling waves, Esther heard a clicking, like keys from an old-fashioned typewriter. She glanced up to the azure sky, where the words "The Choice" was typed into a cloud, and in smaller print, "Starring Esther Morris."

This can't be.

"Turn around, Esther," a deep voice boomed.

Hugging her arms to her chest, she obeyed. The islandscape gave way to a vast field, dotted with miniature cars and people, small as toys. She squinted to make out the words over a tiny building. "Concessions," it read.

"I'm... I'm on the screen?" she asked.

"For the moment," the voice said. "Stay, and you become writer, director, and star of your perfect, eternal story."

"I have a choice?"

"Always," the voice said.

"And if I return?"

"Simple as re-setting the reel. You keep the life you have. We simply find another story."

She thought of Marvin, alone in the car. Of a life well-lived. Of their years remaining.

"Take me back!"

"Very well." Sand splayed over Esther's eyelids. She closed them tight. When she opened them, she was back in the darkened field, holding a tray of candy and popcorn.

Esther glanced through the shadows toward the Grand Marquis. It was empty.

The screen lit up again, to the cheers of patrons around her and the blares of car horns.

Esther gasped.

"You left me," she murmured.

She looked up to the face of seventeen-year-old Marvin on-screen, securing his football helmet under the glare of stadium lights.

An Uprising of Stones

The Old Stonecutter lived in the center of Village Placid with his young Apprentice, in the cottage his ancestors built in the time before time was recorded. Callused hands had carved stone blocks with care, scoring shapes with hammers and chisels blessed by the ancients, a prayer whispered with each beauteous piece curated. Stone by stone, the forebears had laid the foundation of the Village and the community born within its walls.

In the daytime, the stones shimmered with the sun's fire; at night, they breathed frost in the moon's icy glow. The rocks forming the cornerstone of all Village Placid were not comprised of ordinary mineral or sediment, but an amalgam of magic originating deep in a cave in the forest glen. The stones permitted only the most righteous of heart to mine from their quarry; the most capable hands to build from their bounty.

The rewards for such reverence were immeasurable.

To smell the sweet smolder from hearths burning in Village Placid was to imbibe strength from the stones' power; tendrils of smoke tasted with each breath tickled the mind and swaddled the heart such that memories persevered, and hearts pumped strong long past the natural progression of old age. Water from the well, built of the stones, nourished the soul; nary a dark glance or ill word was ever exchanged among neighbors. And when the wrinkles of time finally weighed a villager's lids heavy with eternal sleep, the community offered the body to the cave from which the stones were procured. They placed a glowing pebble in the palm of the dying, to light a path to the ever-after. To fuse the spirit with the salts that powered the earth.

Indeed, the inhabitants of Village Placid led a quiet, yet privileged, life. By day, yellow yisminbuds and pink lylack flowers dotted the lush green land under cloudless teal skies and at night, the humming of stone lulled the villagers to sleep. Fortressed by mighty Evergreens in the deep woods, they lived free from the dalliances of interlopers.

Until the day the Old Stonecutter's young Apprentice grew restless of his work and followed the call of a curious blue bird twittering in the trees. Defying the Village's established boundaries, he chased its melody through the forest, reaching a parched and foreign valley littered with the detritus of withered trees and decomposing brush. It was a world neither the boy, nor any villager, had ever encountered. A pall of gray sucked all color from the land, and an army of Centaurs circled, ravenous for their next pillage.

A THUNDEROUS ROAR SHOOK the grounds of Village Placid. Villagers burst from their homes, eyes widening at the treetops swaying in the distance, as if a puppeteer from the heavens pulled strings to make nature dance at its whim. Dust swirled as the beasts appeared through a sepia haze.

Cradling a half-carved commitment stone he'd been craft-ing for a betrothment, the Old Stonecutter emerged from his dwelling and stepped forward to address the intruders. The largest of the creatures held the Apprentice, bound and gagged, over his shoulder like a bag of sand.

"Release the boy," the Old Stonecutter said. The villagers whispered amongst themselves. A baby wailed; its mother hushed its cries with panicked urgency.

The creature—a Centaur—cackled. He squeezed the Appren-tice so tightly the boy yelped. "On whose authority?"

Taking another step forward, the Old Stonecutter squared his shoulders. The stone he still held in his hands, the stone walls of all the buildings in the Village, emitted a deep indigo mist, as if releasing their breath. "On the authority of this village."

"A village that exists unauthorized by the Grand Tyrant, di-vine ruler of all lands of Timeron." The Centaur sneered and spat; the emerald grass turned black and shriveled in its wake. He glanced at the walls of the Stonecutter's cottage and the homes that surrounded it, at the massive well that occupied the village center and the intricacies of the carved statues of sun, moon, and stars that adorned the space. He spotted stone benches, pottery, and children's toys, carved through the ages by Stonecutter hands. The buildings and objects grumbled under the creature's gaze, mist dissipating into a shining sil-ver sheen, like armor. "And your sorcery, equally forbidden. Though you look more like a common forest rat than a man of any power."

The troops laughed at the Old Stonecutter; his wild white hair, his dust-addled clothing.

"I am but a simple artisan with a deep reverence for nature's gifts," the Old Stonecutter said. "My Apprentice has done you no harm. Release him and return to the land from whence you came."

The Centaur scowled and threw the boy into the crowd. Village women scurried to tend to his wounds. "He is of no use. However, you—and your people—owe a great debt to the Grand Tyrant."

Murmurs slid through the crowd, a ribbon of confusion.

"We owe no such debt."

"The Tyrant permits you to live, for a price." The Centaur motioned toward his troops and the line of creatures pushed forward, flanking him. "Take the tools and all the trimmings. Anything you can carry."

As the army trotted toward the villagers' homes, the Centaur snatched the half-carved stone from the Old Stonecutter's hand. The rock sparked and sizzled in the creature's palm. Screaming, the Centaur flung the stone to the ground. It glowed as it bounced, landing cool and smooth at the Old Stonecutter's feet.

"Such power! Our supreme leader will take great interest in this place and its offerings."

❖

TEARS BRIMMED IN THE bruised and swollen eyes of the young Apprentice as he worked beside the Old Stonecutter in the cave, a Centaur standing sentinel behind them. The stone sighed as the old man and the boy struck it with reluctant precision, their chisels apologetic to the task.

"This is my fault," the Apprentice said, his voice a hushed whisper. "If only I'd stayed focused. Ignored the call of that strange bird…"

"Not every birdsong is pure," the Old Stonecutter said, resting his roughened hand on the boy's shoulder. "Our life's vocation weighs heavy. With time, you will learn."

The boy choked back a sob. "See how the stone weeps with each strike of our hammers?"

"The stone mourns with us."

The Centaur cracked a whip. "Work faster. The Tyrant bears no sympathy for the lazy."

❖

A graveyard of Evergreens lay still on the outskirts of the Village. Under the Centaurs' glares, young men and women stacked stones in the clearing, building the foundation for the Grand Tyrant's new castle. Sweat intermingled with silent tears as they toiled, placing each slick block atop the other. The Old Stonecutter and his Apprentice emerged from the cave with armfuls of newly curated stone. With another whipcrack, the two joined the others in packing and filling, laying gravel and mortar between each layer to solidify the structure.

As the moon rose that night, the laborers had squared off the foundation. The thick shells of castle walls, double the height of men, rose steady. The Centaurs pushed the workers to the Village center where they rested beside the Elderly and the Young who'd sat shackled and beaten, collateral to ensure the castle was constructed to the Centaurs' liking—and to the Grand Tyrant's demands.

❖

THE OLD STONECUTTER STARTLED awake, a flash of pain blinding him. He cried out and grasped his bleeding cheek, the lash of the Centaur's whip smarting with ear-ringing agony.

"What is the meaning of this?" the Centaur shouted.

The Stonecutter struggled to his feet; his Apprentice clung tightly to his arm.

"It's nothing but… sand…" the Apprentice said, gaping.

As his world returned to focus, the Stonecutter glanced over at the castle's foundation, reduced to dust. Speckles of glitter shined through the rubble, as if taunting the Centaur guards who circled the site, their thick brows furrowed in knots.

The Old Stonecutter smiled. "Let the rebellion commence," he whispered.

"Charlatan!" The commanding Centaur gripped the Old Stonecutter's frail shoulder and shook him. "You bear responsibility for this vandalism. In the name of the Grand Tyrant, you are to be punished." The Centaur grinned maniacally, his sharp incisors protruding from his jaw. "Death, by public stoning."

"Leave him!" the Apprentice said, stepping between his guardian and the oppressor. But the beast shoved the boy aside; the Apprentice fell to his knees.

The Centaur turned to the villagers, who trembled with the raging boom of the creature's voice. "Let this be an example to you all. Your village, your lives, are and always will be the property of the Grand Tyrant." With a dusty hoof, he kicked the Apprentice, hard, in the gut, and grabbed him by the hair. "You will cast the first stone."

"No." Despite his struggle to breathe, the boy glared at the Centaur, defiant. "I refuse."

"You WILL cast the stone of MY choosing," the Centaur roared.

"Dear boy, you must," the Old Stonecutter implored as troops dragged him toward the well and shoved him against it. "For the sake of Village Placid and all who dwell here."

The Centaur pushed the Apprentice face-first into the earth. Shimmering gravel embedded in the boy's cheek, his skin stained with luminescence. As he pushed himself from the ground, the beast retrieved an irregularly shaped, spiky stone from the dirt. It was unlike all other stones in the land—dark as the blackest night, heavy as death. The Centaur kicked the boy again. Writhing, the Apprentice rolled onto his back, his eyes imploring the skies above. The Centaur cackled and tossed the stone toward the boy's chest. Instinctively, the boy raised his hands to catch it; he cried out in both fury and pain as the rock cut into his palms.

As the boy struggled, a small girl with blond ringlet curls and wide blue eyes tottered toward the Old Stonecutter. Gasps, followed by murmurs of assent, rolled over the crowd. The Centaur and his minions stopped, staring at her, as if mesmerized. With a delicate hand, the child placed a tiny, perfectly round and smooth shimmering gold pebble in the Stonecutter's palm.

"To light your path to the ever-after," she whispered. "A gift from the ancestors."

The Old Stonecutter closed his hand around the pebble and nodded as the girl disappeared into the crowd like a shadow under a cloud, as if she'd never existed. The Centaur blinked hard and shook his head, attention returning to the Apprentice on the ground. He hulked over the boy, who struggled to his feet, grasping the stone so tightly his flesh bled.

"I've failed you once again," the Apprentice said to the Stonecutter, his features twisted and twitching with regret. With shame. Sadness.

The Old Stonecutter smiled at the boy. "Aim here," he said. "Right here." He rested roughened ancient fingertips upon his chest, tapping on the tender spot where his heart resided.

"Do it!" the Centaur screamed. "Or the children of this village will suffer the same fate!"

"I'm sorry!" The boy's voice cracked with a sob as he fired the dark stone at the Old Stonecutter—the man who'd raised him, the mentor who'd taught him to revere the stone and respect its sovereign power. The Old Stonecutter closed his eyes as the projectile rammed into his chest, propelling his body deep into the well.

The villagers gasped. There was a great splash, and then, silence.

The Centaur chortled as he kicked the Apprentice back to the site of the Tyrant's castle. "Return to your tasks immediately. You will not rest until what was lost is rebuilt and your efforts triple, elsewise others will join your beloved old sorcerer in death."

With quick and steady hands, the villagers resumed building the Tyrant's castle. But each stone that was laid cracked and crumbled to dust. The faster the villagers attempted to build, the more rapid the dissolution of stone. The Centaurs bucked and yelled; the foundation devolved to a luminous powder that swirled around them. It formed a blinding cyclone; the voices of village ancestors whispering in the wind as their spectral hands constructed iridescent spires of a sandcastle high into the sky.

A red glow radiated from the cave; every stone in the village smoldered. Water boiled inside the well and a fine mist ascended from within, raising the soul of the Old Stonecutter. He floated toward the Centaurs, the round pebble in his palm bursting into a flaming boulder. He hurled it into the hovering sandcastle, and it exploded. Grains of earth rained down; they soothed the villagers with tranquility and scorched the intruders with a million pinpricks of fire. Screeching with both agony and rage, the Centaurs galloped off, smoke trailing them in chains of torment.

The Old Stonecutter floated toward the boy. For a fleeting moment, the old man's body adopted its corporeal form and the Apprentice embraced him.

"The uprising of stone," the boy whispered.

"And of spirit," the Old Stonecutter replied. "I am one with the salt of the earth. It is your time, now."

The boy nodded, resolute, acutely aware of his station—no longer Apprentice but now, The Stonecutter, charged with preserving the village's treasure.

White Noise

THEY HAVE SILENCED THE wizard who dwells across the hall. The cadence of his spells—ancient words booming with the power to awaken fire from a dragon carcass—have swathed my nights in a mantle of stars, reminding me of who I was.

What I was.

Before they brought me *here*. They call this house a halfway point toward healing; yet I feel nothing but pain.

A hushed vortex whirls across the threadbare carpet outside our chambers, gulping the wizard's nightly incantations deep within its belly. The doors—*one two three four*—tremble in the dull hum that spreads like steam from a cauldron.

White noise, they call it.

For peace and quiet.

Lights extinguish after midnight; hands of the clock marking witching hour, frozen, until dawn. Magic snuffed under a muted spell of rules; all powders and potions forbidden.

For our betterment. For our rehabilitation.

My body quakes in the endless, droning silence. The sepia-laden darkness crushes my chest, forcing my body into the punishing coils of a decrepit mattress.

In this room, there is nothing.

As they've intended.

I crave the forbidden nectar that once filled my spirit. How it lightened my steps to dance across rainbows and tingled my fingertips to pull tulips from stone. My world was violet and fuchsia, my skies teeming with light. I miss the faeries, whose fluttering wings tickled my shoulders as we played; the unicorn whose horn shimmered as it chewed morsels of the leprechaun's gold. I miss lying among the clouds, floating sweetly free over a universe that embraced me as a limitless child. A magic child, seeking nothing but the potions and powders that sustained my reality.

Rested bodies yield quiet minds, our Keeper says.

I close my eyes, and I fall.

❖

SUNRISE THRUSTS ASIDE THE curtains of night, and my eyes flutter open. I lay twisted on this small cot, the battle of my night-mares evidenced by the cotton nightdress strangling my torso, the scratchy gray blanket crumpled, defeated. Righting myself, I stretch and tiptoe across the cold, dusty floor. I palm the metal knob; hinges creak in protest when I open the door.

The wizard appears outside his chamber, as if summoned by my motion.

I freeze.

Ruddy skin has replaced his long, white beard; his hair, close-cut and bristling on a scalp once covered by a glimmering black cap. He wears khaki pants, a white shirt, and brown shoes—*peasant's clothing*—hardly the attire befitting a wizard of his stature.

"Good morning, Joy," he says. "Sleep well, I hope?"

"Your face...?"

"Oh, this." He touches his cheek. "It's amazing what a shave and a haircut will do. I feel like a new man."

"And your robes?" I swallow back the shock that seizes my throat.

He chuckles. Despite the incongruity of his appearance, the timbre of his laughter remains enchanting.

"Can't stay in pajamas forever." He pulls a bronze medallion from his pocket. "Besides, it's about time I let this little nugget work its magic."

I stare at the trinket. It is somehow familiar, though I cannot recall where I've seen it before. Its glow rains over his fingers, engulfing his arm in light. Mesmerizing.

"Token to a new life," he says.

I cross my arms, feel my hair swish across my back as I shake my head. He stares, green eyes widening, as if attempting to extract my thoughts.

"Ever consider cutting your hair?" He reaches toward me and stops as I take a step backward. "Change is good. You would look cute with a pixie cut."

The pixie! I had almost forgotten the tiny girl, ensconced behind the door brandished with a "2." I motion toward her chamber.

"Have they forgiven her transgressions?" I ask, lowering my voice to a whisper. It has been days—weeks, perhaps—since I've last seen her. They had scolded her for absconding with delicacies from the dining hall, remanding her to her room.

"Poor kid just wanted a midnight snack. But you know the rules." He hunches over and squinches his face, wagging his finger. "Residents are not permitted unsanctioned food or drink."

"She hasn't caused additional mischief? You know how pixies are."

"Pixies... no." I see a storm brewing in the wizard's eyes and wonder at his converging brows. "Are you feeling alright this morning, Joy?"

"A rested body yields a rested mind," I say. "And the goblin in the corner chamber? Is he well?" The white noise had consumed his snoring, too, and I wonder if he is still alive.

"Old William? He might be offended by that term."

"But... that is what he is." I reach for the wizard's hand and squeeze, searching for the sparkle in his eyes. "Don't you see? This place... it's draining our magic. I cannot hear your voice at night. That white noise—"

"—saves us from ourselves. It's why we are here."

No, no, no.

"I never chose this!" My head tingles, as if trapped in an ogre's grasp. "I was hexed!"

"Dear Joy," the wizard says. "There is no such thing."

❖

THE KEEPER OF THE House smiles as she hands me a glass and places two shiny pebbles in my palm. "Take these, dear. To calm your nerves."

"No."

"Non-conforming behavior extends your stay." She gestures toward the pixie cowering in the corner. "And hers."

Ice crystals fall from the pixie's violet eyes. Her shoulders slump as the shimmer of her aura dulls; a gray cloud eclipsing her lavender soul.

I cannot let her light fade.

Steeling myself, I shuffle toward the filtered water dispenser.

Even the water is distilled.

Like sound.

Like magic.

The Keeper watches me place the pebbles in my mouth. Cool liquid carries their acid through my body. The wizard grins beside her, flipping his coin—*up, down, up, down.*

I feel a tug at my nightdress. Old William grasps the fabric with his gnarled goblin hand, his eyes wild with terror.

What have they done to us?

Thirteen Steps

Forty-five paces from our walkway to the Rations Dispensary. Twenty-three from there to Mrs. Smith's; eighteen more to the Martinez family; ten to old Mr. Hubbard. Thirteen steps from Mr. Hubbard's stoop to our garage door.

To the safety of home.

Twice each month, my heart cinches as I watch you walk into that sepia cloud connecting earth and sky, into that haze of toxins consuming oxygen and life. I squint through thick layers of plastic taped to the windows and follow the orange-clad form that is you. I pray I've zipped your anti-contamination suit tight enough, that I've sealed taut every potential crevice to secure you inside.

I curse the unfairness of it all. Fifteen-year-old girls should be gossiping with friends, sending Snapchats and experimenting with makeup. Not risking their lives to deliver a pittance of government-ordered food rations to a neighborhood starving for survival. But no fathers remain to brave this radioactive world to deliver us sustenance; the government couriers long since relieved from their duties. Only the very old and young and the enduring frail *(like me)* huddle inside duct-taped homes hoping for some miracle of nature—a typhoon or tornado or hurricane—to spawn and blow the toxins away.

We all await your delivery to help us live another day.

"Mommy, help me fix Dolly's dress?" Your little sister Grace tugs at my shirt, but my gaze remains magnetized to your form, tottering like an astronaut over Earth.

Breathe in and out, baby. In and out.

"Not now, sweetheart." I nudge her away. "When Sissy comes home, okay?"

In my peripheral vision, I watch Gracie shrug and retreat to a corner, baby-fat knees dimpling as she sits cross-legged, consumed in her make-believe musings of women who dress to go *out*—who yearn for glamor and adventure and dreams that no longer exist. I wonder if she remembers anything of the days before. If she remembers her father's smile; the way the corners of his eyes would crinkle when he laughed or the feel of his strong hands lifting her high above his head on sunny days at the beach.

I cannot think of him; nor of sun or sky, or the sweet and pure sea-kissed air we drank with innocent abandon.

When food delivery was nothing more complicated than a pepperoni pizza arriving in an hour or less, or it was free.

Not a husband's life sacrifice. Or a teenager's death-defying walk through the neighborhood.

"Mommy, Dolly's dress keeps falling."

"Shh, Gracie. A few more minutes."

You slide a box through the delivery slot built into Mr. Hubbard's door.

Thirteen steps.

One.

Breathe.

Two.

Breathe.

Three.

You pause. Wobble. Fall to one knee.

Breathe.

"Mommy?"

"Not now, Gracie!"

Your sister thrusts a half-naked Barbie into my sightline. A glittery button hangs from a square of duct tape at its neck; the waist wrapped in a jaggedly cut, bright orange swath.

I push the doll away, unable to...

breathe.

The Angel's Death Knell

Twilight crept over a weary sky, beckoning the night to awaken. Death had gone missing in the graveyard, and Charmeine was tasked with finding him.

She tapped long, alabaster fingers atop the cold granite crypt, thinking. Paschar was last seen kicking tumbleweed through the field of crumbling, nameless headstones, dragging his scythe, leaving singed grass behind him. But why would he be here? He was the only Death Angel in his ranks with an aversion to cemeteries (*rotting wastelands*, he called them, *recycling centers for bones*). And why now?

Charmeine scanned the landscape, awash with overgrowth and marble and wilting roses. Decaying leaves blanketed the monuments of those who had moved beyond—many of whom had taken their last steps, their first steps, guided by Paschar's loving hand.

Under Paschar's watch, no one ever languished in wait for death. He stood waiting to catch the final, icy breath of his charges, to infuse them with warmth from the moment of their transition.

His cloak was a hearth, his scent like June rain, his blue eyes a beacon. A good concierge, Paschar accommodated all their final whims—daffodils sprouting in the snow, butterflies fluttering with a goodbye kiss, blustery windstorms to announce the start of a journey onward.

A scrawny rat scurried across Charmeine's feet. She recoiled. *Wasteland indeed.* How she wished Paschar would materialize! As a Death Angel, he was everywhere and nowhere, proximal and distant—like a lone snowflake pushing through a blizzard. Which is what made his absence so palpable.

Merciful Death, he would never forsake the souls assigned to his care. Of that, Charmeine was certain.

She paced, her mauve satin cape fluttering in the autumn breeze, brittle fallen leaves crackling around her. Owls hooted in the distance in unison with a howling coyote, its mournful cry heralding the rising moon and, Charmeine thought, perhaps something more.

She floated across the decaying terrain toward the creatures' siren and found the missing angel slumped against a mausoleum wall, ivy falling over him like a shroud. A spider scurried across his shoulder, stumbling over the folds of his royal blue cloak. Elbows resting upon his knees, he peeled the bark from twigs and snapped them in succession, tossing the jagged wood to the side. His scythe lay discarded, like the toy of a fickle child.

"Paschar." *Peel. Snap. Toss.* "Why are you here?"

Paschar pulled his cloak around him tight, settling deeper into his cocoon. He closed his eyes, ignoring both Charmeine's question and the luminosity she cast over the shadows.

She inhaled deeply, repeating her query.

Silence.

Charmeine regarded the scythe laying in the dust. "What's this?" she asked, extending her hand toward Death's unwanted tool. The blade glimmered under her gaze, as if awakening, and the scythe floated toward her. She tapped Paschar's shoulder with the pointed end; his body jerked as a blue arc flashed between Death and his abandoned weapon.

The angel lifted his head. Paschar's gaze attempted defiance, almost shielding his evident sadness.

Charmeine crouched down, her cloak blanketing the crunchy grass as she allowed the scythe to fall on her lap. "Paschar," she whispered, her voice velvet. "What's happened to you?"

Paschar winced, his expression waffling between a smile and a frown. "Don't you find it amusing," he said, chuckling softly. "An Angel of Mercy delivering a death knell to an Angel of Death?"

"The Master is worried about you, Paschar. I'm worried. This," she waved her hand in disdain, "is not *you*. You don't belong here."

"I am an Angel of Death. Perhaps this is where I should be." Paschar sighed, his shoulders dropping. Charmeine noticed hints of gray faulting his chestnut hair, tiny lines etching the corners of his eyes. The Angel of Death had aged.

"The journey's changed, Charmeine." He retrieved another twig from the ground, bending it until it snapped. "Death has changed. Perhaps I have, too."

Paschar tossed the broken pieces. "I walked away—I came here—after my last charge forced me to use *that*." He gestured toward the sickle resting across Charmeine's lap. "I hadn't touched it since my fledgling days."

"Oh, Paschar…"

"His soul was cold, Charmeine. Colder than hell. I offered him mercy and warmth; he countered with chaos and pain."

She reached out to him. "This is not your fault. Some souls struggle to separate the wheat from the chaff at the end, you know that from your training."

"In his eyes, I was simply a thief, robbing him of the life he knew. And he attacked me for it." Paschar wrung his hands together, his brow crinkling. "I took this job to bring peace and comfort to those embarking on the most amazing journey of their existence. But, I can't do that without their trust. I'm not sure I belong here anymore."

Charmeine sighed and laid her hand upon Paschar's shoulder. "You are an old soul, my friend. You're white-glove service. Handwritten love letters. Lemonade on the front porch. Dressing for church on Sundays. An emissary to simpler times."

"Better times."

Charmeine shook her head. "Different times. But it is your obligation to carry the charges assigned to you into the afterlife, as wild and manic as they might be. You cannot choose them." She took his hand. "Just as I have no choice over the fallen angels assigned to my watch."

Paschar nodded, his jaw tightening.

Charmeine moved the scythe from her lap and leaned in, breathing the sweet summer storm that was Paschar. She brushed her lips across his forehead.

"On behalf of the Maker," she murmured, "I relieve you of your duty." She retrieved the scythe, tracing a circle in the air above Paschar's head. The tip of the blade sliced a hole in the night and a halo rose through, crowning Paschar in celestial light.

Paschar smiled. He faded in a beam of bursting radiance that bathed the cemetery in the warmth of a summer sunrise.

"Go in peace," Charmeine whispered.

A Menu of Moments

AGNES HUGHES HAD NEVER considered herself old. Not when the first brushstrokes of age painted gray-white streaks into her tresses. Not when her knuckles knobbed like tree roots or crows' feet etched time into her thinning skin.

But on this, her one-hundredth birthday, Agnes felt tired. Elderly.

She perched at the edge of her facility-issued twin-sized bed, waiting for Nurse Mary to retrieve her for the party. Health aides had curled Agnes's hair and attired her in the pink dress reserved for Sunday Mass and holidays. Her Luckenbooth brooch, an engagement gift from her late husband Charles, adorned her frock, clipped below the collar.

Near to her heart.

Agnes sighed. "I wish you could be here today, Charlie."

"But I am." A deep, gravelly whisper emanated from the silence. "I've always been."

Agnes stiffened, tapping her hearing aid as she turned her head and fluorescent light coalesced beside her; her beloved materializing, translucent, from its core. She recognized the squared stubbornness of his chin, the broad shoulders of his youth, the strong posture that defined his life. The undying brilliance of his smile.

"Am I dreaming?" she said.

"No."

"Am I dead?"

Her husband chuckled.

"Not in the way you're imagining."

Agnes reached out, stopping just before she touched him, as if Charles were an open flame. "I've missed you so much," she said. "The years have been long without you."

"I never left your side." He took her hand, kissing it. "Never will."

"But how... Why are you—?"

"It's time for decisions, my love." A flat glowing rectangle appeared on Charles's lap; he lifted it and handed it to Agnes, who took it with trembling hands. A buzzing sensation, like a low-voltage charge, warmed her palms; a screen appeared on the object's surface with a drop-down menu: *Emotions. Core Moments. Everyday Life.*

"An iPad?"

"God has a talented IT staff."

Charles gazed at Agnes, his eyes aglow. "Today is your last day. Your first day. You choose the soundtrack. How it begins..."

"...how it ends."

"Your life does flash before your eyes when you take that next step," Charles said. "But *you* select what you wish to see."

He gestured toward the tablet. Agnes leaned into his light as she scanned the main menu, her choices quick and easy.

Joy. Breathless wonder. Laughter through tears.

A first kiss. A pin, a promise. White wedding roses. Babies' first cries.

Breakfast in bed. Playing Scrabble. Walking the dog. Autumn sunsets.

Extraordinary, ordinary, beautiful days with Charles.

Agnes closed her eyes, the tablet heavy.

"But my party. Everyone's coming."

Charles's lips brushed her forehead, tingling. "See you when I see you."

❖

AGNES SLUMPED AT THE edge of the bed, chin to her chest, palms empty and open on her lap. She never heard Nurse Mary knock as she entered the room—instead, a whisper, soft, like an angel's call.

"Agnes, are you ready?"

Fluorescent lights flickered.

The clock stopped.

Sun set, and Agnes took Charles's hand.

229

How I'd Wished

I STAND IN A virtual room that is blank-page white. Walls, floor, and ceiling a canvas awaiting my whims. Paintings, palaces, arias, accolades. New chapters in a life unwritten.

How I'd wished.

I stand, pencil-straight, in the center of the room; the tight embrace of a carbon-colored bodysuit stilling the tremors that threaten to surge from within me. The mask I've designed rests feather-light in my palms. I await the moment it becomes part of me—when it transforms me—delivering the technicolor dreams I've carried since childhood.

Orchestral swells reverberate through the walls; elation sings in full vibrato. I'm a voyeur to the soundtrack of yearnings well-fulfilled. I swallow my breath to quell the urge to hum along in joyful allegiance to this club, where its chosen members barter with the founders for the chance to roll dice laden with hope. Plucked for entry into an exclusive organization where we are promised the constructs of our greatest imaginings; dues are not limited by monetary capability but are paid with something much simpler: intellectual capital, emotional intelligence. And a binding agreement to don a mask of our own creation.

❖

THE BLANK FACE GLEAMS in my hands. *What will it take from me? What will it give?* I'd painted the mask in shining crimson, adorned it with shimmer for beauty and power and vivacity—privileges stripped from my rights by birth. Could I blame my mother for her station in society? For her inability—her lack of ambition—to break caste? She'd accepted a mundane world of dismal tasks; taken pride and pleasure in thankless servitude. Considered it noble duty to collect refuse and clean toilets of those better than herself for nothing more than a pittance. *Take pride in your work, Alexandra.* Grateful, she was, when offered scraps from the feast; she'd fluttered like a bird tossed days-old bread.

Throughout my childhood, others had poked at my secondhand clothing; they flashed shiny sushi-filled lunchboxes while I ate peanut butter crackers from a crumpled plastic bag. And though I'd complained, Mother never saw our sad existence as anything but wonderful, attempting to quash my protests with warm embraces and soothe my embarrassment with time-worn clichés: *You are enough, Alexandra. We are enough.*

Foolish prattling of a woman content to bathe in raindrops when there were oceans to explore.

Within these walls, I stand united with my brethren—each of us yearning for something grander. My mind-numbing office job, hourly pay, punching an unforgiving timeclock—

All are shackles I'm desperate to shed.

I'd sell my soul to whatever devil offered the key to freedom.

Natural intelligence, artificial intelligence, man, or machine—does it matter who or what I've bargained with, when the trade is quid pro quo?

❖

THE MASK ALIGHTS WITH life.

It is time.

I raise it toward my face, staring into the hollows of its potential. My head recoils from its heat, like summer haze over scorched pavement; but even so, my hands continue to push the mask up, up, up until it connects with my skin, branding me and melting into every pore. It is I and I am it and I shudder as a great knot unravels inside me.

"Connection established." A voice, calm as an unrippled pond, speaks within my mind—not my subconscious inner monologue but something else. "Welcome to the Human Emotion and Intelligence Capital Club—an exclusive membership extended to those who desire *more*. We sense greatness in you, Alexandra Covette. Thank you for accepting our invitation, cryptic as it was. Our existence is founded upon discretion."

One click on a random social media post; from dusk until dawn traversing a litany of personality questions to help me unlock my potential. Leading me here.

My cheeks stiffen inside the mask. "It's an honor," I mumble, despite my intent to project.

"Silence, please, as we remand your data as remuneration."

The tingling initiates in the bone between my eyes; a buzzing bounces through my forehead to the top of my skull like an entrapped fly. A stock market tickertape marches across the tops of the walls, presumably assessing my net worth.

My value to the machine.

"Avarice: 57%. Anger: 20%. Determination: 18%. Empathy: 5%," the voice says. "Subject data within two standard deviations of humanity's norm. Enjoy your membership."

"That's all the information you want?"

"The algorithm adapts through progressive learning on the human species."

Numbers dissolve. The room's starkness is smothering.

The voice is silent.

"Hello?"

White walls pixelate and swirl around me, blizzard-like. I spin into the cyclone and fall into my own bed in my dingy apartment.

My rage bubbles—this is not the life I've paid for!

Yet, in a blink, the space expands. Chipped paint seals and smooths, crown molding bursts from all corners. French doors open to a garden of roses; their sweetness intoxicates with my every breath. Creaking mattress springs beneath me melt into a plush pillowtop covered in satin and gilded mosquito netting drifts from the ceiling like a cloud. A princess bed in a room worthy of royalty.

Worthy of my grandest imagining.

I rise up in paradise and notice a maid scrubbing my marble tile floor.

I have a servant!

I cackle with joy—my energy like lightning. "Work faster! Or I will dock your pay." My voice booms with the thunder of power. I barely recognize it.

But, it is *my* time, now.

The servant startles, knocking over the pail and spilling sludge as thick as blood across the floor. She looks up, observing me. Fat tears drip into the mess from her tired eyes.

My mother's eyes.

There is no judgment, only pain in that stare.

Empathy: Five percent.

What have I become?

My screams shatter this AI-generated illusion. Walls crumble. Windows crack. Regret sings in full vibrato.

I tremble in stark emptiness.

How I wish...

I claw at my mask, imploring the database that owns my soul.

My mother was right—we are enough. Humanity is enough.

But for me, it's too late.

JOEY

Mommy says I live in a magic room.

All it takes is a tap of my finger, and poof! Whatever I'm thinking about becomes real. If I want to build a raceway for my toy cars, TAP! It's there. Stretch the lanes out to make it a great big highway? Easy peasy.

Mommy says it's like dreaming, but better.

And boy, do I dream. About cars, mostly. Race cars and sports cars, sedans, even minivans! I have diecast cars, plastic cars, Matchbox cars, and model cars on shelves that almost touch the ceiling. I thought it'd be cool to build a car elevator to reach the ones at the tippy top. So, I closed my eyes and touched the wall and, ta-da, there it was.

My room is cool like that.

Mommy says my mind is special; that I'm a special little boy. But she hasn't been here in a while. She doesn't answer when I call for her.

I sure hope Mommy didn't go on a business trip like Daddy. I'm still waiting for him to come back so we can play with the yellow Lamborghini I keep on my dresser. It's his favorite.

I miss Mommy.

I'm too big to be scared, but I can't help it.

✦

Marjorie Williams couldn't stop staring at Dr. Kepler's ears. His image glitched in the videoconferencing system they were using to discuss a clause in her mother's will—Kepler to elaborate on the technical aspects; her attorney, Allen Gleason, to ensure the details were legally sound. Those ears morphed from normal, to potato-like, to balls of fuzz resembling the earmuffs her daughter, Daisy, wore in winter. Balancing the five-year-old on her lap, Marjorie attempted to focus on the scientific mumbo-jargon the neuroscientist spewed from halfway around the world.

"Mama, when is this gonna be over?" Daisy asked.

Marjorie plopped the girl on the worn living room rug, unchanged since her own childhood, when this house was once her home. It still had that same desperate, neglected feeling as it did the day she'd left—like a withering vine clutching to brick.

"Soon, baby."

"Can I go play with Joey?"

Marjorie's breath caught with a jolt.

"That little boy in Grandma's special portal." Daisy prattled on. "He said next time we'd play with his truck, and…"

"Absolutely not." Marjorie pulled her lips into a thin line, attempting to staunch her rising furor. A year prior, her mother had guilted Marjorie into 'meeting her only grandchild,' and against her better judgment, she'd allowed Daisy one visit—*one!*—with the understanding they'd only spend time together in the real world.

Mother's definition of "real" vastly differed from Marjorie's.

"Play with your tablet while Mama does her conference call."

Dr. Kepler smiled, the convoluted video flickering across his mouth. Teeth, no teeth, pixelating lips. Technology at its finest.

"Your mother's contract with INC Technologies has been extended multiple times. We continued the experiment at her request, in exchange for data on your brother's vitals." Kepler paused. "The subject has resided in VirtuSpace longer than any other human."

Marjorie glowered; her mother would come back from the dead to haunt anyone who referred to her brother as a *subject*.

Gleason cleared his throat and leaned toward the camera. "Marjorie, as executor of your mother's estate, you have legal authority over her dependents and assets. Definitions established in the contract with INC Technologies classify your brother—known as Experiment 0978—as an asset. You have full power to determine his future."

The future. The past. The present. What did it matter to a being who was considered nothing more than a number; whose existence straddled the boundaries of reality? Was he a person? Did his soul still live somewhere in that virtual cocoon, or was it an illusion augmented by the artificial intelligence pumping life into his mind? It built while it extracted—breathing adaptable code in, exhaling data out.

Marjorie had spent most of her childhood grieving the brother she'd lost; her teen years pining for the father who'd abandoned them and the mother so obsessed with the "experiment" that she'd seemingly forgotten Marjorie's existence in the living, tangible world. She'd learned to navigate those pain chasms in her life, some days tiptoeing around them, other days leaping across. Yet, now the familiar floorboards of her childhood home creaked beneath her, and she was left to play God.

Against her own free will.

VROOM! VROOM! MY MCLAREN F1 diecast is the coolest. The motor sounds like a lion roaring all around my room. I think I'll make a race. McLaren F1 against all the Formula Ones in my closet. Boy, will that be a fun matchup! Gotta get to work if I want the track to be ready for them to go, go go!

I hope that little girl will come back and play with me. Her name is Daisy, like the flower. She liked my monster truck and Mommy promised to take us to the VirtuPark so we could ride in it.

Mommy hasn't taken me to the VirtuPark in a long time.

Another little girl used to play with me, too, but Mommy said she moved away. Her avatar had blond hair just like Daisy. She liked my McLaren F1 the best.

Maybe Mommy went to pick up Daddy from his business trip. I would like that very much.

❖

"Mama, video's done!" Daisy climbed onto Marjorie and waved into the laptop's camera, making funny faces.

"Hello, Daisy," Dr. Kepler said. "You look just like your uncle when I first met him."

"Dr. Kepler..." Marjorie warned.

Daisy raised her eyebrows. "I don't have any uncle, Mister." She wriggled in her mother's lap. "Who are these people, Mama?"

"It's grown-up stuff, Daisy." Marjorie tapped at the tablet again. "Go, play some games."

Daisy shrugged. Tablet in hand, she scampered across the room and plopped cross-legged against a worn denim couch.

"Parenthood is the world's most challenging job. Which is why I decided to get a PhD in Artificial Intelligence and oversee hybrids instead. So much easier." Kepler laughed at his own joke.

Marjorie shook her head. Gleason raised his eyebrows.

"I've reviewed the terms of the current contract," Gleason said. "My client wishes to better understand the implications of her decision on the..."

Kepler spoke over him. "The impact on the *subject* is quite simple. Should you decide to extend the experiment—as your mother had—nothing changes. Joseph's mind will continue residing within his room, and the algorithm will support his need for mental stimulation. You will have unlimited access to the portal, which will remain open in perpetuity—or until the software is no longer supported. Of course, there is the matter of relocating his body should you choose to sell your mother's house."

Marjorie nodded. Selling Mother's house was a top priority—it was nothing more than a casket of empty memories.

"Now, of course, there is the issue of companionship." Kepler retrieved a handkerchief and blew his nose loudly, without muting himself. "Your mother spent 90% of her waking hours in the portal with your brother from the time we connected him to the network after his accident..."

Shuddering, Marjorie closed her eyes to blot that image she'd obscured for so long. Her eight-year-old brother broken on the pavement. Blood—*so much blood*. The Soapbox Racer he and Dad built together flattened under the wheel of a sedan. Her mother shrieking in her bathrobe, barefoot, on the street. That breathless, *this-isn't-real* heat—searing, crushing like a vise.

"... would be fascinating to see the impact of solitude on his cerebral growth. He's aged one and a half mental years since initiation, but that was with intense nurturing." Kepler wiped his nose again, an oddly wistful grin emerging beneath his handkerchief. "Would but the daisy wilt with adequate water, but without sunlight?"

Gleason smirked. "Rather poetic for a man of science."

Marjorie observed Daisy, intent on the tablet, and wondered what it would be like if her daughter were trapped in some contraption—playing alone without anyone to talk to, save for someone checking in once a day, once every other day, no better than the world's most irresponsible pet sitter.

"What happens if I choose to terminate the contract?"

❖

Daisy's here!

I see her hair first—it's fuzzy and yellow, just like mine! Then her eyes and her nose and the rest of her—poof!

Magic in my magic room.

"Daisy!" I wave the cars I'm holding like airplanes. Airplanes are like flying cars—cars can do anything.

"Hi, Joey!" she says. "I can't believe I'm here!"

I'm so excited!

"Have you seen my Mommy?"

Daisy shakes her head.

I feel sad, but then I'm not. My friend is here now.

"I can't go to the VirtuPark without Mommy, so we can't ride on my truck."

"That's okay," she says. "There's so much to play with!"

I hug Daisy and make her sparkle. Her giggles are glittery.

"Let me show you one of my favorites," I say. "The McLaren F1. This car broke a world record. Over 240 miles per hour!"

Daisy claps her hands. "This is gonna be fun!"

❖

"ENDING THE EXPERIMENT IS nothing more than flipping a switch," Kepler said. "Like turning off a light and walking out of the room."

"But you're talking about a person's..." Marjorie clamped teeth into her tongue, silencing the word that wanted to follow.

Life.

All these years, she'd struggled to reconcile what, exactly, Joey had become. It was easier to consider him dead—and by some medical standards, he was.

It was easier to forget the times they had played together in this house, running down the halls shooting laser tag or preparing pillows for an epic fight. Four a.m. Christmas mornings, Mom and Dad chuckling at wrapping paper that flew like confetti as they tore through their gifts. Hours spent helping Joey build his model cars; organize his collection of diecasts, or stage drag races. Kneeling on the cold garage floor watching Dad assemble that Soapbox Racer.

It was easier to lock each loss inside so she wouldn't *feel* it. Now, her mother's heavy urn resting inside a brown paper bag was a tangible reminder of the death—the many deaths—Marjorie had carried for years.

"Marjorie, the law does not recognize Joey as a person, but rather as a hybrid entity powered by artificial intelligence and sustained by medical equipment," Gleason reminded. "As your attorney, it is my responsibility to help you remain objective."

Marjorie forced a weak smile. "Thank you, Mr. Gleason." She glanced up at the video square occupied by Dr. Kepler. Sometime during the discussion, he had changed his background from a model of the human cell to a complex circuitry board. *Fitting*.

"Dr. Kepler, what happens if that switch is flipped?"

"Well, I'm not entirely sure," Kepler said. "Certainly, the physical body ceases to function without the ventilator. But your brother's presence in VirtuSpace—and the time that will remain for him—is largely dependent on the extent to which the AI algorithm has taken over his mind."

"You mean, the less of *him* that's in there, the longer he might stay in the portal, even after—"

"—that's exactly what I'm saying."

"77% AI, 23% Joseph," Gleason added, "based on the latest data."

The three sat on the conference call in contemplative silence, until Daisy's outburst startled them all.

"VROOOOM! VROOM!" Daisy squealed before collapsing in a fit of laughter.

"Daisy!" Marjorie jumped from the chair, grabbing the tablet. On screen, Daisy's avatar knelt on the floor of an all-too-familiar bedroom with Joey—*oh, God, Joey!*—surrounded by a parking lot's worth of toy cars. Cold panic enveloped Marjorie; it was dangerous, so dangerous, so terrifying to see the likeness of her daughter *in there*.

"Turn it off!" Marjorie screamed, stabbing at the Power button until the screen went dark.

❖

Daisy? Daisy? Where did you go?

I'm not scared.

I'm too big to be scared.

❖

The door to Joey's room creaked with age as Marjorie and Daisy entered. The conference call ended; Marjorie had made her decision—e-documents signed and filed.

One task remained.

It was time to say goodbye, to pay respects to the brother she had buried in her mind so many years before.

The space was a memory plucked from a distant dream. A time capsule. Posters of race cars adorned the walls, yellowing like old newsprint, edges curled and crumbling. Dusty artifacts stood on display—the toy Lamborghini Dad gave Joey for his fifth birthday, his prized McLaren F1 diecast.

"I was here, Mama. But it was brighter." Daisy wrinkled her nose. "And cleaner."

Marjorie draped her arm over her daughter's shoulders as she led her over to the twin-sized bed. The thin, gaunt body of a middle-aged man lay beneath a child's race car sheets; graying chin stubble indicating his need for a shave. A series of round electrodes protruded from his bald scalp, beeps and blips signifying the AI feed. Whooshing white noise from the ventilator permeated the room. Various tubes snaked from under the sheets—a catheter, a feeding tube—Marjorie couldn't imagine what else. Joey's nurse had left when Marjorie arrived, leaving her brother alone.

He'd served thirty years in this prison cell for nothing more than being a victim—for being loved so much by a mother who couldn't let him go.

Marjorie squeezed Daisy's shoulder. Blinking back tears, she wondered if she would have made the same decision for Daisy, had they encountered such tragedy. Her mother had sacrificed everything—her marriage, her daughter, a life in the living world—for the opportunity to keep Joey close, eternally a child. Yet, this body—this man—who should have been buried years before lay in his childhood bed, his mind a machine trapped in an infinite loop, the memory of his mother's avatar his only companion, a virtual room his only home.

"Would but the daisy wilt with adequate water, but without sunlight?" Marjorie whispered.

Daisy glanced up, her eyes wide and moist. "Mama?"

"Daisy, this is your Uncle Joey. He was my best friend in the world when we were little."

"Is he gonna die?"

"Everyone dies in their due time." Marjorie closed her eyes and breathed deep in the stagnant air. She pressed a large red button next to Joey's bed. "Initiate code Charlie Alpha Roger 0978."

"Confirm," a tinny voice replied.

"Confirmed."

The room silenced. Marjorie hugged Daisy as the ventilator's whooshing dissipated and the absence of beeps and blips marked the official dissolution of her mother's contract with INC Technology, and the final moments of Joey's existence in the real world.

❖

I THINK I'LL MAKE a race. This time, Lamborghini takes the lead. I'm sure Daddy won't mind. Mommy should be coming back soon. Maybe Daddy, too.

Wonder why my head feels tingly, like pins and needles.

But I'm not scared.

I'm too big to be—

Seeing Utopia

QUEEN ACLARA HAD LOST track of how many days she'd languished in the dungeon. She knew the number of stones on the walls and ceiling of her cell. She'd counted the number of iron bars behind which she wasted away, even took comfort in tallying the links of the chains that bound her. But the days eluded her. They'd relented to one endless night of suffering, punctuated only by the howls of anguish echoed in the halls of the castle above and the Sorcerer King's demonic laughter.

She couldn't remember the last time her voice had succumbed to her own screaming as she tried to quash the sounds of the pain she had blindly welcomed into her kingdom. Her cries reminded her she was still alive, still human; but in the silence when she lay with cold stone pressed against her cheek, she wondered if Death had crept into her cell to take her next.

Just as Death had taken her kingdom when she'd pledged herself to Elwin of Erylo. His whispered promises had fallen sweet, like rose petals, and she promised her life and love and the kingdom of Videre to his care. But the skies changed the moment they'd said their vows, yielding to a darkness that consumed the stars. Aclara hadn't realized she kissed death until their lips parted and she tasted blood. Thunder boomed, knocking her to the ground as he peeled back his mask, revealing a demon camouflaged under the guise of a nobleman with a smile as bright as the River Moon rising over azure waters.

No, Aclara had not seen through evil's clever disguise. Wedding bells blunted the death knell that resounded across the kingdom, over the people and land she loved.

And he took everything.

Aclara pulled her legs to her chest to quiet the pangs that churned her gut, the need for water and food overpowered only by a yearning for her people's freedom. In the darkness, she felt something brush against her leg and pulled her body in tighter, knowing the rats shared her hunger.

She thought she heard a voice. Faint. *'Hello?'*

Aclara teetered on a shaky precipice, hovering between life and death. *Perhaps I am dreaming? Hallucinating?* A man materialized beside her, morphed from the shadows, flesh and blood with large, soft hands. He released her chains and lifted her from the floor, cradling her like a child. She tried to speak but could only choke out a raspy cough.

The man's image flickered as he carried her up the steps leading her from hell. His form dissolved in the shadows. Aclara lay, limp, in his invisible embrace, as if she were floating back up to the living.

He pushed open the door, and Aclara gulped in the night air. It tasted of fire and ash, smelling not of the yensi flower whose vines climbed over the castle walls, but of smoldering wood and pulverized stone.

She squinted in the twilight and held tight to the man's vest as a crowd cheered around her. Her invisible savior held tight to her waist as he lowered her to the ground, her bare toes nestling into ash. She opened her eyes to the cacophony, but saw no one, save for the Sorcerer King, whose head was perched on a stake, his green eyes as wide and menacing in death as they were in life.

The man who'd saved her flickered back into view; his face round, adorned by a graying beard. He had kind brown eyes. With a flick of his hand, he produced a ladle of water and as Aclara drank, he introduced himself as Mollo, Wizard of the Hamlet Andle.

Cheers again erupted in the empty courtyard. Aclara was confused.

A hundred patches of dust shimmered around her. The golden boots of as many peasant soldiers materialized, followed by their sweaty, exhausted bodies. They knelt before her.

Aclara smiled weakly. The Sorcerer King's pride blinded him; he never would have suspected an army of commoners to rise against him.

She gestured toward the severed head glaring at them from the stake. Mollo followed Aclara's eyes.

"We must burn it," he said. "Spread the ashes deep in the sea so this evil never returns."

Aclara nodded. Mollo murmured an incantation unintelligible to the Queen and raised his hands. Blue flame engulfed the head in a demonic halo. Amid the conflagration, the Sorcerer King's eyes glowed emerald green. Aclara stared deep, silently willing those eyes to close one final time.

She let go of Mollo's grasp and walked forward, her steps tentative as a baby dragon in the snow.

"Your Grace?"

But Aclara didn't hear Mollo above the fear that reduced his voice to a whisper. She didn't see anything but those eyes that hovered in the inferno, pulling her closer. Aclara reached toward the radiance emanating from those eyes, her fingertips smarting as her hand approached the flame.

And with a burst of light, the skull of the Sorcerer King imploded, leaving a swirling plume of black ash that moved above them as if it were breathing. Sucked inward by a violent centripetal force, the remains of the Sorcerer King contracted into a tight bullet that fired directly into Aclara's wide-open gaze.

GERARD tapped the tip of his cane against the Queen's chamber. The cane was crafted from the wood of the Degal tree, bent and knobby yet sturdy as steel—just like Gerard himself. His joints ached from the strain of a century's use, but as Royal Valet, he was committed to the needs of the rulers he served. Never was a request made nor a challenge presented that Gerard did not oblige—even for the Sorcerer King, who saw service and servitude as being one in the same. Gerard remained true to task even as the King spat on him, cursed and kicked him. His body and spirit ached; each movement a reminder of his years. But Gerard was a survivor, and would carry on.

It had been a fortnight since the Sorcerer King's fall, yet the kingdom still felt his presence in the mantle of despair that lay upon it. Scouts described villages quiet as the grave, as if entire communities held their collective breath against evil that lingered in the air. Commoners holed up in damaged homes, peering through windows as broken as their souls. Nobles kept their bridges drawn;

wizards and witches stayed close to their oracles, waiting for a signal of changing winds. And at night, the cries of hungry children harmonized with the distant howls of wolves.

The Queen had not left her chamber.

Gerard tapped louder. Beyond the thick oak, he heard shuffling and finally, a click, as the door cracked open.

"Gerard?" Aclara stretched her arm through the opening, grasping until her hand touched Gerard's shoulder.

"Dear child." He slid his arm through hers, leading her back into her quarters. She stared ahead, eyes glowing opaque white, as Gerard brought her to a settee near the window. He frowned as they walked past the royal family's coat of arms—a purple dragon shimmering atop a river of gold—and rich tapestries depicting the verdant orchards of the South, knowing that Aclara would only see them again in her dreams. And the Queen's own paintings: sunrise and sunset over the Sea of Delas, rainstorms and rainbows, and faces—the faces of the people, the youthful, the aged, the elated and downtrodden. The kingdom she beheld in a way no other ever had.

"Have you rested?" Gerard squeezed her hand. Her slumped shoulders, slow breaths, and pallor saddened him. Though she was his Queen, Gerard regarded Aclara as he would a niece, perhaps even a daughter. He silently cursed the fates.

"How can I rest?" She lowered her head, red curls a veil. "My kingdom bleeds and I've no way to stop it."

"Indeed, the pain persists." He frowned. "But your kingdom is free."

"Freedom does not heal the wounds that brutality leaves." Aclara rubbed her wrist, the fresh purple bruise a reminder of her captivity. "I can't see the way back, Gerard. Nor the way forward."

"Your love for your people will be your beacon." Gerard leaned on his cane, kneeling beside her.

"The Sorcerer King took more than just my sight." She shook her head. "What is a leader without a vision? One cannot build a castle with a single stone. Or fill an ocean with just one raindrop."

Gerard patted the Queen's hand. He'd lived long enough to know that when hope was needed, hope would arise. "You need not carry this burden alone. Sometimes we see more clearly through the eyes of others."

MYTH hummed as she sat at her work table in a cottage deep in the Dorwol Woods. She'd first heard the tune upon the kingdom's liberation, when the twitter birds proclaimed the good news, and it stayed with her. Waving her wand in harmony with the song, the silken threads hovering above her danced under her spell, weaving themselves into a shining cape. She was surrounded by multi-colored tapestries, bejeweled cloaks, and hats of various fabrics and sizes. Rows of shelves spanned floor to ceiling, holding dozens of identically-styled shimmering gold boots that intermittently blinked in and out of sight.

"Can you believe it? The Queen herself, calling upon the likes of us. Papa would be so proud."

Myth's twin sister Janin materialized on the empty bench across from her through dust motes that coalesced, as if magnetized. Though they had shared the womb, Myth and Janin could not be more different. Janin was svelte, with a shock of midnight blue hair cropped close to her scalp, the color matching the steel in her eyes. Myth was plump. Bright yellow, green, and orange hues danced within her amber eyes; her pink hair, soft as a fairy's wing, grazed the floor.

Ankles crossed, Janin rested her feet on the table. She wore the same golden boots that lined the shelves.

Myth pursed her lips and sighed. "How many times did Papa tell you to keep your boots off the table?" *A witch's table is a sacred space.*

She brought her wand down. The unfinished cape fell across Janin's legs, but she didn't budge.

"Father was a better wizard than he was a soldier," Janin said. "But, without his sacrifice, we'd still be under the rule of King Crazy."

Myth frowned. She didn't like to think about how her Papa died, how there was nothing left of him to bury. Instead, she preferred to remember how he lived. "When I was a little girl, Papa told me stories of the Great Oracles. He said they'd predicted I was destined for great things."

Janin snorted. "He only said that so you'd stop feeling sorry for yourself every time I beat you in Cauldronball."

"I never felt sorry for myself." Myth shook her head. "Besides, you didn't *always* win."

"Believe what you'd like." Janin slid her feet off the table and stood, stretching. "The Queen's entreaty is logical. Of course, she would consult us." She gestured toward the footwear on the shelves. "The army never would have infiltrated the castle without the Cloaking Boots I designed."

Myth cleared her throat. "You mean, the boots *we* designed. You and me." Her voice came out in a squeak. When Myth wasn't standing in her sister's shadow, Janin often seemed to find a way to make a shadow find her. And Myth much preferred the light.

"I should have been there," Janin said. She had ambitions to lead the charge against the Sorcerer King, but Papa had forbidden it, casting a sleep spell over his daughter until the siege was complete. As Janin awoke and the fog lifted, Myth saw in her sister's face a pain that seemed sharper than a thousand thorns. Though they never spoke of it, Myth wasn't certain if Janin had been more upset about her father's death, or that someone beside herself had sealed the King's fate.

Myth lifted the unfinished cloak from the table and raised it, fabric spinning, threads weaving at her whim. "It's up to us to create a new fashion for the Queen, to lead us back to brighter days." Myth threw a splash of pink on the garment; it sparkled in the dim light. "Dear sister, our design will color the destiny of all of Videre!"

Janin sat on the bench, her features pinched with thought. She thrummed her fingers on the table. "It should be sturdy. Tailored for the Queen's long-term aspirations."

"Something beautiful." Myth sighed. The gold and pink hues of the fabric hovered above them like sunrise. "Something whimsical."

"Practical," Janin said. "Probing. Sleek, yet authoritative. An accessory of wisdom and strength. To bolster the crown."

"Stylish, yet inconspicuous." Myth ran her fingers through her hair and smiled. "An accessory of beauty and grace. A complement to the crown."

The two witches sat upright. The spinning cloak floated across the room toward an empty shelf, slinking away from the tension brewing beneath it.

"True vision entails seeing the world for what it is." Janin folded her hands and leaned in toward her sister. "Our design will help the Queen find truth."

Myth shook her head. "To rebuild the kingdom, the Queen needs to see its rebirth. Its possibilities."

Janin pushed herself back from the table, scowling. "Possibility is what plunged our Queen, and our kingdom, into despair. It is time to look deep into the heart of the darkness, to prevent it from ever rising again."

Myth stood, glaring up at her sister who stood a head taller than she. Myth levitated until they were eye to eye. "Only light can cut through the darkness."

Janin folded her arms across her chest. Myth mimicked her sister's body language; together they were a mirror image of stubbornness.

"And I'm sure that if Elwin of Erylo had only felt the light of Aclara's love, they would have lived happily ever after." Janin smirked. "You are soft, dear sister. And your magic suffers for it."

Myth felt her ruddy cheeks flare. "And you are as cold and unyielding as a... as a..."

"Good luck with your design," Janin said. Her form flickered, then dissipated, leaving Myth alone.

Myth floated down and settled back in to the bench. The unfinished cloak glided toward her, wrapping her in a hug.

QUEEN ACLARA listened to the murmuring crowd that had gathered in the courtyard. She wiped sweat from her brow as the heat of the summer sun beat down. With the King gone, daylight had finally ventured out like a child emerging from her hiding place. Aclara's time in the dungeon had given her an appreciation for the warmth she had long taken for granted.

"How many are there, Gerard?"

"Maybe two hundred, your Grace. Mostly peasants. Some nobles, few wizards." He squeezed her hand. "It's a start."

"And the two witches? Have they arrived?"

"They have. Each with her own design. Apparently, there were creative differences."

"Sisters." Aclara smiled. "It's to be expected."

"And their quarrel is to our advantage." Gerard laughed. "Sometimes a friendly competition is all you need to bring a kingdom back together."

MYTH raised her hand to her eyes as she looked skyward. Purple and gold banners—the Queen's colors—rustled in the breeze. She felt a nagging tickle in her stomach as the Queen's valet led her and Janin, whom she hadn't seen in weeks, to a large platform. Myth grasped tight to the pink satin sack that held her design; Janin carried one similar in dark blue.

Myth's hated the way they'd left things and was anxious to see Janin's creation. But based on Janin's stony expression, rigid as a castle gargoyle, she suspected that her sister didn't share the same feeling of goodwill.

The crowd quieted as Queen Aclara stepped forward to address them. It was her first public appearance since her captivity, and the first time Myth had ever seen her in person. Though slight in stature, her movements betrayed a heaviness that only tragedy, and uncertainty, bring. Nonetheless, Myth thought that Aclara was the most beautiful woman she'd ever seen.

"My loyal subjects," the Queen boomed, her voice belying her mousy exterior, "today we celebrate our lives and our freedom."

Aclara's subjects cheered tentatively, as if they feared excessive joy would conjure the evil that had enslaved them all.

The Queen continued. "Standing before you are two witches whose vision, expertise in the art of magical design, and unparalleled bravery helped to break the chains that bound us under the Sorcerer King's reign."

Myth smiled. She had never considered herself brave. Father was brave. Janin was brave. But she? Optimistic, perhaps. But not brave. She glanced again at her sister, who nodded, solemnly.

"The evil that impaired me under the guise of love is irreparable, my blindness his final act intended to break our kingdom." The Queen paused and drew in a deep breath. "But we will not be broken."

Myth stood close enough to see that Aclara's jaw quivered. Before the Sorcerer King had seduced her, the Queen had been an artist, a poet, and the type of ruler who governed like a master chess player. Myth blinked back hot tears as she realized all that the King had taken, the shell left behind, and how difficult it must have been for her to stand before them today.

"I will never regain my sight. But today, Myth and Janin will share the magic of their vision. And the one I deem most worthy will stand by my side as Royal Seer of the Kingdom of Videre."

Myth's eyes widened. She watched Janin shift her weight, a twitch in her cheek the only hint of her sister's surprise.

JANIN scowled, standing on the hillside outside the castle walls. The crowd had followed through the gates to witness the first challenge, and though she was secretly pleased with her odds at becoming the Royal Seer, she felt like a pawn. Aside from a proper match of Cauldronball, Janin didn't much like games. These festivities were far better suited for her sister, who enjoyed this type of pomp and circumstance. Janin just wanted to get on with things.

Gerard hobbled forward, supported by a cane bearing the pewter head of a dragon on its handle. His back was crooked and arched; time etched into his skin with wrinkles as deep as the bark of the Dorwol tree. "Your first task will demonstrate your vision of the life force."

Gerard nodded toward Janin. "Fidelis the dragon, Queen Aclara's lifelong companion."

Guess I'm leading this jester-fest, she thought.

The purple dragon snored beneath a willow bush. He wasn't much bigger than the shrubbery. Faint puffs of smoke wafted from his nostrils. His scales were molting, his snout graying, and a large black bruise the size of a watermelon blemished his neck.

"People of Videre," Janin said, raising her voice loud as a trumpeter's call, "behold the Shade of Perlustrate." She retrieved a sleek black satin beret, placed it on her head, and pulled down a dark shade, like a knight's mask save for its translucence. "True vision entails seeing beyond the surface. We need to delve into the depths of our humanity to unmask our shortcomings. Eradicate our weaknesses."

The shade flashed and midnight blue granules beaded on the mask. They detached, darting in the air above the crowd as if in pursuit of an invisible foe. They flew toward the dragon's chest and disappeared, burrowing into his skin. He emitted a low groan, breath unsteady, as he exhaled.

Brows furrowed, Janin squinted through the shade and observed a green aura around the dragon, rising like a poison mist. As she probed deeper, she felt the weakening pulse of his turquoise veins, she watched the blood trickling through them like a stream about to run dry. A parasite the size of a tortoise, with legs spindly like a spider's, squeezed his heart. She lowered her chin and removed the apparatus, her hairline moist with sweat.

"Good Witch, what did you see?" Queen Aclara brought her hands together, as if in prayer.

Janin glanced at the waiting crowd, and at her sister whose gaze was fixed on Fidelis. She shook her head.

"I'm sorry, your Grace. His heart will not beat for much longer."

The crowd mumbled disapproval. This was not the vision they sought, nor the news they had hoped for. The Queen turned away.

Gerard motioned toward Myth, who had been trying to capture Janin's attention since their arrival at the castle. Though Janin had not welcomed her sister's emotional distractions, she didn't want Myth to paint herself the fool. With a sharp nod, Janin attempted to warn Myth to control her exuberance.

Janin held her breath as Myth stepped forward. "My fellow citizens," she said, her voice quavering.

"Louder!" someone shouted.

Myth cleared her throat and raised her chin. "I am honored to present to you The Spectacles of Hope."

She wiggled her chubby fingers over the bag's opening. Rose-colored glasses, adorned with rubies and quartz stones, floated from the sack and hovered above Myth's head.

"True vision lies in seeing the potential around us. Viewing the world for what it can be."

The jewels glowed, a prism of color exploding from their core. The glasses floated down, feather soft, until they rested on Myth's smiling face. The gemstones glowed, bringing out the color in Myth's cheeks. She moved closer to the dragon, regarding it with wide eyes. Myth frowned, wringing her hands.

"I'm afraid my sister is correct," she said. "Your Grace, this dragon is gravely ill."

She approached the Queen, laying a hand on her shoulder.

"But I do see a happy creature, spending his last days with joy," Myth said. "It may be past, it may be future, it may be a dream, but Fidelis sees himself in a meadow of adaflowers surrounded by children who tickle his belly." She gestured toward the dragon and smiled. "Did you know that dragons can giggle?"

The Queen grasped Myth's hand.

"You have given this dragon a very happy life," Myth said.

"Thank you," the Queen whispered.

Janin scowled. From anyone other than her sister, Janin would have thought the vision contrived, a testament to that which the Queen and her people wanted to hear. But Myth was different.

MYTH strode toward the crumbling village of Yobho for their next task: to convey their vision of the kingdom. The shuffling of the crowd's feet behind her nearly drowned out her own breaths.

Closest to the castle, Yobho had suffered the worst of the Sorcerer King's siege. Myth prayed to the deities that her magic was strong enough to cut through the gray cloud that still hovered over this hamlet.

Myth brought the glasses to her face. The world glowed around her, her body draped in a pink halo. Like a specter, she moved from the crowd and looked outward. The gray swath dissipated, revealing above a cloudless, cerulean sky. Rubble wriggled from the ground, filling the cracks of damaged buildings until the walls were smooth, transfigured from stone to marble, a kaleidoscope-burst of color painting each in a shimmering mosaic. Vines rose and flourished in the village center, bearing fruit three times the normal size. Children splashed in the clean water flowing from a fountain of unblemished porcelain.

And in the forest beyond, dead evergreens righted themselves. A flock of singing twitter birds swooped by in symmetry. Well-groomed coyotes sat watching, swaying in the delight of their song.

Myth turned toward the crowd, breathless.

"Ours is a kingdom of infinite beauty," she said. "Magician, noble, and commoner eat the fruit from the same lush vine. Dragon and dog sleep side by side and bird and coyote are friends. With unity and love, we can be whole again."

Gerard pushed through the crowd with Janin by his side. Myth struggled to read her sister's countenance. The rigidness of Janin's jaw, the thin line of her mouth, her perfect posture—all classic Janin. But there was a heaviness in her eyes that rivaled all the stones in the castle walls.

Once again, Janin pulled down her visor. The granules formed and flew into the village and the forest beyond.

"Buildings on the verge of collapse. A patch of dirt in the village square, overgrown with weeds of poison. Starving animals, starving birds seeking sustenance. All potential predators. Dangers everywhere."

Janin removed her visor and rested it on her hip. "Your Grace, it will take an army—carpenters, masons, botanists, experts in animal husbandry, and a visible police presence to rebuild." She looked toward Myth. "This village needs more than love."

Myth hung her head. Once again, Janin cast a shadow. Her sister clearly didn't understand.

QUEEN ACLARA took both Myth and Janin by the hand. Though she had never seen either with her own eyes, she painted each in her mind, just as she had captured her people in the care of her brushstrokes in a time that seemed so long ago.

In her imaginings, Myth was the girl with a perpetual smile, the best friend who ran beside you, never overpowering even as your own gait slowed. She transformed dandelions to roses, tree bark to chocolate, always laughing. Warmth emanated from her like the summer sun on the beaches of Matee. And Janin, she was sharp. Smart. She ran ahead, not to win, but to push the rocks aside and warn you of errant roots rising from the forest floor. From her, Aclara felt the cool, swirling breeze that signaled the start of winter. She was the rise of the moon, the setting of the sun, steadfast as the ancient Dorwal trees.

Janin's vision validated Aclara's suspicions about Fidelis; she knew the dragon was dying, but Myth's assurances offered her comfort. Royal scouts affirmed the persistent dangers wrought by the damage to the villages that Janin identified; and Myth's vision provided perspective on how she, as ruler, could inspire the kingdom to flourish once again.

Perhaps Gerard was right, she thought. We do see things more clearly through the eyes of others. But Aclara needed them to pass one final test—the one she had failed.

Aclara addressed the crowd. "People of Videre, this final challenge is perhaps the most important. For it is one thing to envisage life, and another to have the vision to rebuild a kingdom. But without the ability to see the true character of those around us, lives and kingdoms can be lost."

JANIN hadn't expected the Queen to admit her failings in public; the tittering crowd and Myth's wide-eyed stare validated that others shared the same view. So much easier to confess one's sins in darkness, Janin thought, like in ancient times. The Queen trembled as she adjusted the crown that seemed too large for someone of her stature. Janin wondered which burden was heavier for Aclara to bear—the guilt of her prior mistakes, or the fear of making new ones?

"Dear Myth," the Queen called. "What is your vision as you behold your sister?"

Janin opened her mouth and just as quickly closed it, setting her jaw tight. She swallowed hard to quell the flutter rising from her stomach, and wished she had the good sense to wear her Cloaking Boots. A clean disappearance would have been more valuable than all the gold in Videre. Janin's steps were always sure; she never stumbled down any path she chose to travel. She never doubted the veracity of the looking glass. But the mirror had never talked back until today.

Myth approached, grinning. The gemstones on her glasses shimmered, reflecting the changing color of Myth's eyes. A kaleidoscope of color burst from her spectacles, bathing Janin in a rosy haze. Myth was like sunrise over a snow-covered field. Janin felt warm gooseflesh creep over her skin in a sense of calm she had never experienced before.

"I see a woman with strength I could only dream of," Myth said. "Bearing the intelligence of a kingdom within an erudite mind.

A truth teller, brave enough to voice her opinion, even when her viewpoint is not favored."

Myth removed her glasses, but her glow lingered. "In my vision, the newest member of the Queen's royal counsel stands here before you."

Janin's lower lip quivered, and possibly for the first time ever, she didn't resist it. Without invitation, she donned her visor and peered back at Myth. The granules rose and darted over her sister, surrounding her in a cyclone. The black spheres burst into diamonds as the centrifuge spun around her.

"I see a woman with warmth I could only dream of." Janin's voice cracked. "Bearing the kindness of a kingdom within a selfless heart. An artist who sees beauty all around her, whom the oracles have marked for greatness."

Janin removed her visor and cupped her sister's hands within her own.

"I am honored to stand before the Royal Seer."

ACLARA was swept away by the crowd's cheers, unbridled as the crashing tide. The magic kindled by these two witches would light the torch that would lead Videre through these long, final hours of night to a dawn painted with gold. And though Aclara would never see the sun rising with her own eyes, she would feel it warm on her skin. She would taste the sweetness of morning, thick like the juice of the mayca fruit. Videre would be rebuilt. It would flourish. Its people would persevere.

"Faith and fact, potential and practicality—the cornerstone upon which our kingdom will be rebuilt. Myth and Janin, together your vision will help us see our utopia."

Aclara repositioned her crown. For the first time since she suffered the Sorcerer King's kiss, it rested lightly upon her. She held her head high.

A Time for Understanding

I lay your bulky, yellow head on my lap, your labored breaths hot against my nightdress. Your massive Labrador paws thrash against an unrelenting hardwood floor, as if you're trying to run to a place without pain. I press my cheek into your soft fur; it cushions the fear that strikes with each violent spasm that threatens to take you from me. I pull you close, wrapping myself around you until the yelps subside to whimpers. Your body shudders. You exhale, deep and deliberate, pushing out the hurt. Your body calms. It is quiet.

I lean back against the cold wall, the chill a respite from the icy-hot adrenaline that pulled me from my dreams to your side. I pet you with long, careful strokes. Your muscles twitch beneath my fingers. A plume of your fur, like dust, hovers above my touch.

As the moon through the bay window bathes us in a ghostly light, I watch you breathe.

I will myself to linger in this moment, to relish the warmth of you.

I run my fingers over your ears and down your neck. I kiss your nose. Still wet.

You offer a single tail thump in thanks.

We huddle together until dawn. I'm grateful for another sunrise.

I can't lose you. I won't lose you. You're everything to me.

❖

WE LEAVE FOR TOWN early. It's a snowy Saturday morning and the village bustles with shoppers; their mittened hands grasp plastic bags bulging with toys and sweaters and trinkets from the Five and Dime. A couple argues as they struggle to tie a freshly cut balsam fir to the top of a red Volkswagen Beetle. A weary mother balances a crying toddler with a grocery bag as a young child skips around her, catching snowflakes on his tongue. You stop to say hello and wag as he gives you a friendly pet. The mother yanks him away, and he cries, his cheeks red with cold and tears.

It's funny how people choose to carry their burdens. Some wear them boldly, like a red knitted scarf on an overcoat. Others bundle them deep within their layers, keeping them close to the heart as they go about their everyday lives. You and I, we blend into the wintry landscape—young woman, old dog, out for a stroll in the snow.

"Almost there, Cody." I graze the top of your head with my fingertips as we tread gingerly across the salted sidewalk. We skirt the ice patches and slush missed in careless tosses of crystal rock. I sense your insecurity with each step. I slow my pace, our gaits parallel.

Marco's Marvelous Pets is on the first floor of a two-story brick building that has stood on the corner of Main and Fifth for over a hundred years. Though time has dulled the structure to the color of cardboard, the window display glows with life. Across the generations, passersby have been drawn to the den of misfit puppies romping in the storefront; litters born to strays on the street, small miracles the world never intended. Children press their palms and foreheads against the glass, hoping for a closer look.

When I was really little and *seen but not heard*, Mother would let us stop for a minute to watch the puppies play while we ran errands. Mother called it the Canine Circus. One by one we'd name the pups—Acrobat and Lion and Clown. She never smiled much, but I remember the way her eyes shone in the reflection of the glass, like some kind of magic trying to break through her frown. Each time, I begged her for a puppy and each time she said no, the moment lost as she tugged me away from the window.

But on my twelfth birthday, my dad brought me to Marco's to choose my puppy. Instead, you chose me.

Barreling out of the kennel, you tripped as you galloped, knocking past Dad and sliding into a display of rawhides. You were as gangly and awkward as I was. My braces and bad perm were a perfect match for your oversized paws and lolling tongue. You wiggled out from under the mountain of bones and leapt to greet me. Bouncing off my kneecaps, you knocked me to the floor and buried me in barrage of puppy kisses.

From that moment on, I was your person.

We huddle under the awning to shield ourselves from the snow. I stomp ice cakes from my boots. You wiggle and shimmy to free yourself from the frigid wetness, too weak for a glorious full shake. I brush the snow from your back and open the icy glass door. The metal of the handle tingles my skin, sending a slight shock through my bare hands. Together, we enter the shop, and its warmth embraces us.

Francis Marco IV is the current proprietor. Shriveled and gaunt, with a complexion like paste, he may be the oldest man I have ever seen. A cloud of cottony hair encircles his scalp, and a faded gray sweater hangs from his diminutive frame as if it were intended for a more robust man. Deep wrinkles form rivulets down his cheeks and around his eyes. He looks at us through thick, horn-rimmed glasses; his deep-set blue eyes belie his age. Marco shuffles loafered feet across the worn floor, a weathered wooden cane supporting his weight in one hand; a bag of Puppy Chow in the other.

Your nose twitches and you sneeze. The smell of must, wet dog, and slush clings to the wood-paneled walls. I adjust my eyes; flickering fluorescent bulbs buzz overhead. The store is crowded with pet supplies, but absent customers.

Stacks of silver dishes, walls of rawhides, a fortress of sheepskin beds pile almost to the ceiling. Despite the retail disarray, I've always been able to find just the item I'm looking for, as if it's risen through the mess just for me. There's always been something special about the things that Marco sells. With a box of his dog biscuits, even the unruliest dog behaves. Marco's chew toys make a dog forget the temptations of wayward shoes and children's homework. And one drop of Marco's Special Salve heals even the ugliest of ear infections.

The magic pill we're looking for must be hiding somewhere on these cluttered shelves.

Eyes focused intently on Marco, you attempt to sit, as if on command. Painstakingly, you lower your hind quarters to the ground.

You wince as your tail approaches the floor. "Good boy," I say, scratching the soft fur behind your ears.

"Nice old dog you have there," Marco says.

You bark once, as if in agreement.

Marco chuckles, his throaty laugh almost too strong for someone of his stature. "Age hasn't robbed him of his personality." He leans in, peering from you, back to me, as if examining us. "Been a long time since I've seen you."

I pause, caught under an embarrassed spotlight. I've been purchasing Cody's food and toys online for years. It *has* been a long time since I've been to Marco's.

"We haven't been out much, other than to go to the vet." I frown. "We've been to every one in the county. But no one has been able to help."

Marco's eyes take in your expanded girth, the hot spot growing from your right paw, your hind legs trembling with the pressure of sitting. You return his gaze, tilting your head slightly. Something about Marco amuses you.

"What makes you think we'll have anything helpful here?"

"Well, I just thought... you always seem to have just what Cody needs, whenever he needs it."

"Oh?" His eyes widen.

"Maybe a special kind of treatment? Something... holistic... that the vets wouldn't consider?"

Marco chuckles. He rests his skeletal, liver spotted hand on your head. You turn to lick it as he whispers to you, "How silly. She thinks I'm some sort of old shaman for dogs."

"I didn't mean it that way." I kick at the floor with the toe of my wet boot.

Why should I think this small-town pet shop owner could provide an answer that so many doctors couldn't? Desperation is the enemy of logic, and although I learned at an early age that doctors were far from godlike, I just needed someone to help me. Even if it was an old man in a musty old shop.

"I'm sorry. It was a stupid question."

He places the Puppy Chow on the scratched Formica counter. The bag crackles as it settles in place. The puppies tussling in the shop window halt their willy-nilly ear-biting play, whimpering at the sound of the bag.

Marco slides his glasses up to the bridge of his nose. His eyes narrow; scrutinizing us. He turns a heavy gaze toward you and back to me, where it rests uncomfortably. "I have what you need," Marco says. "If you're willing to trust me."

Trust—that fog-laden bridge between promise and truth, navigated by the very young or the very foolish. I learned to avoid that path long ago. It's like being handed a bouquet of roses and having them wilt in my palms; the last viable bloom reserved for a coffin at a gravesite. Or believing mother's words that she'd always be there, never realizing "there" was on the dirty tile of a bathroom floor, her fingers wrapped around an empty bottle of booze. The surest way to align promise with truth was to bypass bridges, finding my own way with you by my side.

It's impossible to trust anyone.

Your nose twitches as you sniff the air in the direction of the puppy food.

Anyone, except for you.

❖

MY FATHER'S DECLINE BEGAN just before he brought me to you. Not that I recognized it at the time; I was too wrapped up in my own pre-teen priorities. It wasn't until much later, looking back on those photographs of your puppy days, that I saw what wasn't evident to a child's eyes. Dad's tanned skin, bronzed from years of working in construction, had faded to an ashen pallor. His bright eyes had lost their spark, sunken in behind cheekbones that had become too prominent.

I remember now how his hands shook during those fleeting and frustrating days when we were housetraining you, and the way his pajamas hung from his frame as he tended to your nighttime whimpers. I can still see the tiny bruises on his ankles left by your needle-teeth as you explored the world by mouthing it—I'd always thought it odd how the marks your nibbling left on me were short lived, and with Dad, how they seemed more permanent. But nothing was permanent for him, and at the same time, everything was. I suppose it's like that when people reach the end.

Around the time you had grown into your oversized paws, Dad stopped laughing. The sound of him changed. *He's got a cold,* Mother told me. *Chronic bronchitis. It'll go away.* His weight loss was explained as *a much-needed diet to lose that belly of his.* The days and nights he spent on the couch, my mother attributed to a bad economy. *No one builds houses in a recession.* He spent hours in silence, just staring, the TV remote in hand. Tissues piled up and spilled from the tray table to the floor; meals were left untouched and cold.

Mother told me to leave my father alone, to keep "that dog" away from him. She took up residence in the kitchen, chain-smoking until her voice adopted the raspy timbre of a woman twice her age, gin and tonic on the rocks her constant companion.

My dad was dying, and I didn't know.

Maybe I didn't want to know. Maybe I wasn't ready.

At the very end, when machines pushed the air into my father's chest, I spent my days doing homework in the cold antiseptic loneliness of a hospital room. Nurses came to check in, but they said little to me about my dad. They would help with the occasional math problem or pat my head and offer me some Jell-O. As if that would make me feel any better about the alarms that rang off from the machines almost hourly, or the stale, urine-tinged air that made me sneeze.

You were the only thing that made me feel better. Rolling together in the cool grass as we picked you up from the neighbor's house, your muddy paws on my shoulders were as strong as any hug. I didn't even flinch when the neighbor yelled at me and demanded my chore money because you'd dug through her gardenias. She called you a naughty puppy, but I knew better. Flowers could be replanted, but you, you were a good puppy.

I wished I had been able to bring you with me on those long days I spent at my Dad's side. Your nose, working hard to find him hiding deep in his work boots or tucked away under the knitted afghan on the couch, told me how much you missed him.

I pictured you on my lap, nudging my hand to be petted as I sat for all those hours on that lumpy pleather hospital chair. The nurses would have brought you cookies—the good stuff—with some extra for me. Dad would have been happy to have you there, even though those machines kept him from saying anything at all.

I thought about that a lot, and one day, I suggested to Mother that we sneak you in to see him. *My backpack's big enough*, I said, stowing you inside. You whimpered and scratched at the canvas until I unzipped the bag just enough for you to poke your head out and lick my cheek.

Mother just shook her head at me. She did that often, especially when I asked her if my Dad was going to get any better. And when he'd come home. When life would go back to normal.

She refused to tell me anything. She answered every question with *He'll be fine. Trust me.*

Mother sent me home from the hospital early one cloudy Saturday afternoon. You and I had run around the yard most of the day, playing soccer, until the rains came, and we huddled together on the couch. We watched movies and ate popcorn. Doing nothing special was what made it special. It felt good to snuggle with you, lay my cheek against your head, feel the familiar for just a little while.

Dad died that night, just about the time I was brushing my teeth. I was thinking about how good I would look when my braces finally came off as my dad fought against his final breath, alone. Mother called me from the local pub to tell me the news.

I never said goodbye.

❖

Marco removes his glasses. Reaching over the counter-top, he places a hand on my arm. A feather pokes out from the fabric of my down jacket, grazing his skin.

"I'd like to help you, Allison. But I need you to do something first."

I nod, feeling my brows furrow.

"I'd like you to take a good look at your dog."

You yawn and slide to the floor with a thud, laying your nose between your front paws. You fight the gravity and fatigue that weigh upon your eyelids. With a soft snore, you surrender to your nap.

"I'm looking at him," I say. I wonder what point Marco is trying to make. "He's tired. He's an old dog." I feign a smile. "Just like you said."

"What is he telling you?"

"Telling me? I'm not sure I understand." Awkwardly, I wriggle away from the old man's touch. Gooseflesh fights the layers of my winter clothing, leaving my skin cold. "How can he tell me anything? He's a dog. Last time I checked, they don't talk."

"He'll tell you what he needs, if you are open to it." Marco leans on his cane. He purses his lips and stares at me—through me—as if he's trying to read my thoughts.

I hold my breath to fight the sigh—or is it a laugh?—that threatens to push through and wonder if Marco is just a lonely old man desperate for company. Or maybe he's senile. It's the only explanation for why he continues to speak nonsensically instead of doing something to help you, as he said he could. My gaze rests on the merchandise surrounding us. I need Marco to stop talking and hand me that wondrous potion, that rare salve or special bandage that we came here for.

I glance at you. Our time together is finite. I feel its tug with each passing minute.

Marco shifts his weight and appears to sink further into his sweater. "What you need, what he needs, is right here, just as it's always been," he says. "If you're not afraid to find it."

He fixes his gaze upon you; you raise your head, open your eyes, and blink. Twice.

"Why would I be afraid to help my dog?" I'm tiring of Marco's word games. And there's something about his countenance that burrows into me like a determined tick. Old people seem to think that wisdom is built by the number of footprints they leave on the earth. But the truth is, it's the weight of the imprints that matters most. And how well they withstand the tide. Francis Marco IV doesn't understand me at all.

"Fear distorts our judgment, my dear. It is the thief of faith."

You lay quietly at my feet. Fully awake, your knowing eyes shift from me, to this frail man who speaks in riddles, and back to me again.

"I've been all over creation trying to find something that will help cure Cody." The walls of useless pet goods are suddenly stifling. "What he needs has nothing to do with fear. Or faith."

"The time for cure has passed. He needs something more." Marco picks up the Puppy Chow and resumes his scuffing walk, turning his back to us. The patter of dry food pelts off the metal trough. The sound of the puppies' crunching fills the silence.

Heat spreads across my cheeks. Marco's speculative nonsense is wasting valuable moments that could be spent seeking a solution. I grab your leash with both hands, tight, to stop them from shaking. This man is no better than the veterinarian who handed me a pamphlet with that ridiculous poem about rainbows. Or that neighbor who told me, as I cried at my Dad's casket, he was in a better place now. Unfulfilled promises of help, empty words, they leave me with nothing but hopelessness. Tears threaten as I tug on your leash, imploring you to rise on tired legs.

"I'm sorry we came here. Let's go, Cody."

Marco peers over his shoulder and smiles. "Please don't leave. I've been expecting you for a while, now, Allison."

I lean down and wrap my arms around your middle, desperate to pull you up and get out of this place. You won't budge. *I may have to carry you*, I think.

Breathless with the fruitless effort of moving you, I stand. You look up at me apologetically. I cross my arms and glare at Marco. "Why would you expect me, when I haven't been here in years?"

Marco turns away, ignoring my question. He dangles a smooth hand into the puppy den. A fluffy brown dog toddles toward him, sniffs Marco's flesh and opens her tiny mouth wide. She nibbles

Marco's index finger like it's rawhide. You bark and thump your tail, your curiosity piqued by this small creature as much as mine is by the man who feeds her.

The puppy enjoys a final taste and, abandoning Marco's hand, wiggles her way back in through the pack, nose first, to her dinner. Marco retrieves his cane and limps toward the front door.

"They always come back, when it's time," he murmurs. His reflection in the glass glows an icy fluorescence as Marco turns the lock and flips the sign to *Closed*.

"What are you doing?" I ask, my voice quavering.

Slow-motion panic percolates within me; legs poised to run, feet rooted to the fading tile. Then adrenaline overwhelms like a winter squall. I lift you as high as I can off the floor. Feet scrambling, you writhe for freedom. I fall back, cushioning your body as we crash to the ground, trapped with this strange old man.

Marco leans in. The glasses that rest halfway down the bridge of his nose magnify his eyes; his pupils an eclipse that demands my gaze.

"Helping Cody. Helping you." His voice is a whisper. "Your father came here because he knew you'd need someone very special to love after he was gone." He bends slowly toward the floor, aged knees creaking with effort. His outstretched palm strokes your head. Your ears flutter, as if lifted by a breeze.

"Cody was his final gift to you."

"We've always been together," I whisper. "I can't lose him, too."

You stretch your neck and close your eyes as Marco's hand runs over your fur, his caress so light it seems as if he's not touching you at all. And I recall the days, months, and years after my Dad died, when you lay, warm next to me, as I sobbed into my pillow. The sunsets we watched together on the front stoop, my arm draped around you, as summer faded with the turning of leaves. How you wagged and wiggled, greeting me as I returned from school to an empty house. How your head tilted with interest, as I read you my salutatory address before graduation, knowing you'd listen when Mother would not. The way you held your head out the window, as if defying the wind, as you sat in the front seat of my car when I first got my license. Waiting for your treat outside the bank as I cashed my first paycheck. Munching on cardboard boxes as I moved us into our apartment.

Sadness and fear converge and morph to tears that threaten to fall from a precipice I've hidden behind years of resolve. After my Dad died, there was no knight to rescue me from the tower of bad dreams; no healer to kiss away the pain of skinned knees or broken hearts. I grew up lonely as an orphan. You were my family, my friend. My only joy.

"Your father's love for you flows through Cody." Marco inches upright, two hands grasping the curve of his cane to support the weight of his timeworn body. "It's everything you know. It's part of who you are. But it is time for understanding, now." He taps the cane on the floor for emphasis. "It is time to listen to Cody."

"But that's impossible." This is a place I am not ready to visit, an indulgence I'm unwilling to grant to this stranger who knows too much.

This stranger who has shown more interest in us than any other human has, in a very long time.

Marco removes his glasses. He stares at me with wide eyes. "We cannot see love with our eyes, Allison. But does that mean it does not exist? That it is impossible?"

I shake my head, my throat dry.

You emit a whining, yearning bark and swat a beefy paw at me, batting it against my leg. An invitation. The eagerness of puppy-hood glimmers behind your old-dog eyes.

"I'll be waiting." Marco looks at you, laying loyal at my side. "Whenever you're ready to listen."

Marco turns and shuffles toward the back of the store. Together, we watch him stroll down an aisle that seems to lengthen with each labored step, his form shrinking until he vanishes into the stacks of pet supplies.

"Come on, old friend," I say. You push forward off your hind legs. Your limbs quiver and bow, failing as gravity grasps with a cruel hand. I bend next to you; I feel your hot breath on my cheek and smell the acrid scent of illness rising from within you. You pant rhythmically; your soft brown eyes imploring my assistance in an embarrassed silence.

"It's ok, buddy." I crouch down and wrap my arms around your middle. Gently, I pull you upright. Your front legs flail beneath you as you scramble to regain your footing. "I have you. I won't let you fall." Your tail twitches in thanks.

We haven't much time. Words alone will not heal you. Whether it's medicine or magic or some impossible miracle cure, I need to keep searching for an answer not to be found in a small-town pet shop. Time was a steep price for this fool's errand.

I tug your leash in the direction of the exit. "Come on, Cody. We've got to keep trying." You stop, four paws planted to the linoleum. Your legs are rigid, feet dug in firmly. Your tail extends in perfect parallel to the floor. Like a chiseled marble statue, you stand immobile, unmalleable, and defiant.

"Come on, boy." I pull again, more emphatically. You whine and sniff the air in the direction of Marco's departure. I squat down and lay my head on yours. "We're going to find someone who can help you." Your ears pull pack and your nose twitches.

I stand. You sit.

Woof.

You bark with a resolve I haven't heard in a long time, with the same determination you showed on a day long ago, when you'd found a burrow of baby bunnies in our yard. You stood over them, rooted and protecting them, taking kicks from Mother's landscaper as he tried to push you away. *He's trying to tell us something!* I'd shouted.

Those bunnies lived because I listened to you. And because you didn't give up on them.

Woof.

Are you trying to tell me something now?

I shake my head. That old man's gotten to me. If I'm not careful, I'll start speaking in riddles, too.

"I must be losing my mind. Time to go."

Woof.

Desperation *is* the enemy of logic, but this shop, this old man—they've been anything but logical. And despite the exasperating poetic conversations and odd platitudes harnessing us since we entered the store, I know we're just about out of options.

We've come this far. Might as well see it through—whatever *it* is.

"Okay, Cody," I say, once again helping you to stand. "Let's go find Mr. Marco. You lead the way."

As we work our way down the aisle in the direction of Marco, a stray red rubber ball falls from a crowded shelf, bounces, and rolls to a stop in front of us—as if the store is beckoning you to play. You push at it with your nose.

"Want this?" I ask.

You lick your chops in affirmation—*in anticipation?* I shake my head and retrieve the toy. We continue toward a narrow hallway at the back of the shop. Worn brown paneling buckles toward us; the walls push further inward with each step we take. My shoulder scrapes the warping wood as we reach a door at the end.

You stand stoic, watching me. "Ready?" I ask you. But for what, I'm not sure.

I crouch down until we are at eye level. I extend a hand to you, open-palmed. You take hesitant steps forward, just as you did the day we brought you home and you first walked into our kitchen, overwhelmed by the cacophony of foreign smells and sights. You lick my wrist, the warm flesh of your pink tongue easing the drumbeat of my pulse.

Woof. Your tail wags side to side, increasing its rhythmic tempo.

The door creaks open, releasing a burst of frigid air from within. I'm met with a chill I've never felt before as Marco waves us inside a small, windowless room the size of a storage closet. Except for two metal folding chairs, the room is empty. A lone lightbulb hangs from the ceiling, its pull-string sways gently above us. Marco shuffles toward me and places a metal dog whistle in my hand. *Another of Marco's marvelous pet supplies.* My palm tingles; it's as cold as ice.

"Please, sit." He gestures toward a chair. As I wonder what we're doing in this odd little room, and why I decided to stay, I obey.

He takes your leash and pets your head. Together you take a few steps toward the wall opposite me; your tail is raised, your gait peppier than I've seen in years. He settles you into a *down* position. Your descent is slow but easy. Paws forward, head erect, you stare at me, eyes wide. As you pant, you look like you're smiling.

Marco shuffles toward the empty seat. He leans on his cane for support as he lowers himself.

"When you are ready, blow into the whistle."

I nod at the old man and cough to stifle the laugh that bubbles in my throat. Perhaps it's the solemnity with which Marco handed me the dog whistle, or simply the tickle of nerves in my belly, desperate for release. Either way, I feel a full-on belly laugh threatening—an urge as strong and inappropriate as a scream on a cross-country flight.

That is, until I look at you.

You lay your head down on your paws, nose twitching, tail thumping. Waiting, like you used to wait next to your supper dish, back in the days when dinner was more than just a necessity for you, it was an event.

I take a deep breath as I raise the whistle to my lips. I blow out, hard. A tinny screeching pierces my eardrums. I grab for my ears and drop the whistle. It clatters to the floor and transforms from silver to a brilliant white; bright light bursts from within it. The room dissolves around us—walls, ceiling, and floor morphing until they're indistinguishable. I squeeze my eyes against the light as I fall. An icy tingling enshrouds me; it hurts as it soothes.

Voices vibrate above, below, and around me. I crack open my eyelids and hold my hands up, seeing only a faint outline of myself, like a child's chalk drawing before it is brushed away by time. I am suspended in space, in non-space. I feel your presence. I sense Marco is near.

And then I see you. You're like a hearth ember floating through the mist, feather-light, *down, down, down.* We hover side by side and land together in a cloud that's as soft as your angel fur.

"Allison? Allison?"

A voice. *Cody?*

Your words burst in a staccato outpouring of discovery. Your speech sets fire to logic.

"Allison! Why are you lying down?" You nudge me with your nose, slipping your head beneath my arm. "Time to get up! It's time to play!" Your voice is gravelly, like that of an old man—poignantly misaligned with the vibrant, wiggling dog nuzzling into me.

I pause, not quite knowing how to engage in an impossible conversation. With my dog.

You tug my sleeve so hard I almost fall over. I can't remember the last time I've seen you this animated. Your nose is cold; it tickles my skin. "Okay, Cody. I'd love to play."

It really *is* him. The puppy of my youth.

"Allison? Do you have that ball?"

It *was* an invitation.

"I do."

"Yippie!" You leap straight up, pitching forward into a somersault. "Lemme have it. Lemme have it!"

I reach out and catch you; you're light as air in my arms. I stroke your head; your tail beats against my thighs. Your panting intensifies. "Take it easy, Cody. That was quite a flip." I feel your chest tense as you breathe in. "How are you feeling?"

You pause. All your life, you've been asked what you need. Dinner? A walk? But never how you feel.

"Allison, I feel... funny. But not ha-ha funny like when you laugh. I like it when you laugh, Allison."

Sometimes it's the wonder of the little things we do, the things we don't notice ourselves, that makes all the difference. Like the way my father fluffed out the morning paper while he had his coffee, insisting that the window stay open just a crack, so he could *feel* the new day. Or the way he'd chuckle as he read me the Sunday Funny Pages.

For all these years, you've watched my every move, heard every sound, perhaps memorized every gesture. Just as I did with my Dad.

"Allison, when can we play? I want to play. It's all white in here—like snow! Let's run!"

You wriggle in my arms and stop, wincing. I feel your low whine quaver against me.

I stroke your back to calm you. "Remember our first winter? We had so much fun."

"You called me your little snow dog."

I smile. "Remember I brought you a top hat, a scarf, and even a carrot for a nose?"

"I ate the carrot. It was crunchy."

"That was a long time ago, Cody."

You pause, contemplating. "Why don't I run in the snow anymore, Allison?" You look up at me with sad eyes. "I don't really run at all, do I?"

"It's been hard for you, my friend." I recall your tentative, hobbling steps; your nighttime restlessness. "It hurts my heart to see you in pain."

"You hurt, Allison? Maybe you should ask Mr. Marco for a Band-Aid. I promise not to pull it off you."

I stroke your ears and roll the tips between my fingers like I used to when you were a puppy. It was our special signal of quiet time. And now, my time to listen.

"There's a lot we need to talk about, Cody."

"It's about your shoe, isn't it? I'm sorry. I know it was your favorite. But you weren't home, and it smelled like you. Chewing it made me feel much better."

I exhale slowly to ease the flow of words I'd rather not speak. "Cody, we're here now. Wherever here is. And I've seen you do things I'd never have thought possible." I lower my head and look away from you, into the void. "It's like somehow you've become young again."

"Young, Allison? But I'm an old dog now." You giggle. A dog's giggle. "You're silly, Allison. How can an old dog be young?"

"I don't really know." Silence. You lean into me. Your warmth exudes home.

Marco appears beside me, materializing through the light. His voice is a whisper, a cool, circling breeze.

"Cody, how would you like to go to a place where the sun will always shine upon you? Where you can run and frolic across endless fields, and never tire." He strokes your head. "I can bring you to this place."

I bite my lip and turn away, closing my eyes to squeeze away the tears before you see them fall. You deserve this life—the effortless existence I always hoped my father had found.

"Allison! That sound like fun! Like old times. Let's go, let's go, let's go!"

I remember the sound of your nails tap-tap-tapping on the hardwood of my dining room, how you held your blue leash between your teeth, letting it hang down as you waited for me to grasp the end. The whole-body wiggle of joy I never thought I'd see again.

"Cody." I sigh. "I can't come with you."

Your tail droops. You whimper. I'm reminded of that first night when my home became yours, the sad cries subsiding only when I invited you to snuggle in the warmth of my bed. Until that day, I never knew puppies cried.

"Cody?"

"Allison, I don't want to go without you. Mr. Marco can keep his sunshine and his fields."

I shake my head and try to resist the knot twisting in my throat. The ice engulfing us does little to dull the pain. I'm watching. I'm listening. And you've been holding on, so hard, for me. As I know my father tried to, for as long as he could.

How difficult must it have been for my dad to lift a hammer and drive each nail into your doghouse? The weight of a paintbrush like an anvil with his every brushstroke, knowing that this would be his final creation? Yet each day, we worked together until the evening sky turned pink and the cicadas serenaded us; a small, active puppy curled up at our feet to snooze in the grass. Dad and I speculated on the many adventures you and I would have together. Halloweens spent in matching human and canine superhero costumes. The excitement of Christmas morning—you, tearing through a pile of presents seeking a bone wrapped up just for you, complete with a bow. Future memories my father designed but would never build. The foundation of my life lived without him.

I look to Marco. We lock eyes. In this moment, I see. I hear. I understand. The past, present, and future converge in Marco's gaze, and I realize that we're standing at the foot of a bridge to a place I stopped believing in a long time ago. I grasp the peace that has eluded me for years; it's woven like silk through my fingers as I reach out and run my hands through your fur.

And I hear my words echo before they leave my mouth.

"Cody. My dad will be there, waiting for you."

Your ears perk up, your head tilts slightly to the right with interest. *My Dad*. One of your favorite phrases. And after all these years, his imprint remains strong. He's still one of the people you cherish the most.

"Do you remember when you were a puppy, my Dad used to nap with you, outside in the sun?" I recall the image of you—wiggling as you dropped a ball at my father's feet, nuzzling his hand, determined to play. But my dad's hand lay limp and useless beside him. He had only the strength to brush his fingertips down your side.

"How far is this place? I'm tired, Allison. What if I fall down?"

"I will never let you fall."

I lean down and lay my head atop yours, wrapping my arms around you. I inhale the sweetness of you—fresh snow and summertime and falling leaves and newly-cut grass—and allow the tears to wash over the precipice of my grief and into your soft fur.

"Cody, it's okay for you to go." I breathe in, deep staccato. For your heart to flourish, I know that mine must break. "Run free, my friend. Goodbye."

Goodbye. A word that stops time. I wasn't ready then. I'm not ready now. I clutch you tighter, willing the light to linger as I absorb the last vestiges of your warmth. You turn, nose pressed to my eyelids, sniffing out my sadness. A final kiss.

❖

I'm sprawled on the floor of the dimly lit storage room. Ice crystals cling to my drenched hair and clothing. My face has lost all feeling.

You are gone.

Marco shuffles over and takes your leash from his back pocket.

"Time is finite." Marco's whisper is soft as cashmere. "But for just a moment, I can offer you a glimpse.

"A glimpse?" I sit up, holding my head.

Marco touches my wrist, bringing my hands down to my lap. He places your worn Nylon collar in my hands and retrieves the dog whistle from his pocket. He blows into it gently, silently, producing a small cloud. In the mist, I behold an emerald field, an azure cloudless sky and you, Cody—strong in the innocent determination of your puppyhood. You bound effortlessly, intently, despite oversized paws that threaten to trip you in a roly-poly bliss. You run free, determined to catch the rubber ball that sails like a red comet through the pristine sky.

The red rubber ball tossed effortlessly by my father.

❖

I TRUDGE TOWARD THE exit of Marco's Marvelous Pets. Wiping my cheeks with the back of my hand, I wonder what the world will look like when I walk through those doors. If time will stop, if the clocks will keep ticking. If everything will be different. Or if it will all be the same, and it's just me who will be different. Will others know what I've seen? What I've done? Will they even care?

"Wait, please," Marco says, shuffling toward the puppy den. He lifts a fluffy brown dog and offers me the squirming bundle. "This puppy needs a home."

He places her into my arms. Small paws bat at my long, loose hair as she wriggles in my embrace.

I observe her wide eyes staring at me, the way her brows lift in the wonder of a new human. I snuggle her close.

She will never be you, Cody.

But she needs a home. And I need a friend.

"How much does she cost?"

"What is the price of faith?" Marco smiles and turns from me, moving once again toward the back of the store.

"Faith," I say. The puppy yaps in reply. "It's got a nice ring to it."

Acknowledgements

Many say that writing is a solitary journey, but for me, it's like running a marathon where every participant is rooting for you as much as you are for them. To finish the race. To win, in whatever form winning takes. It's having people pick you up when you stumble, tell you when your shoe is untied, hand you a towel when sweat's dripping in your eyes, and make you take a water break before you pass out.

I've been blessed to have so many amazing people who have been part of this life-altering race with me. Family, friends, teachers, co-workers, neighbors, fellow suburban moms... In the eight years since I've been writing regularly, support has come from both expected and unexpected places.

This is now the second collection of short stories I've sent out into the world. (As if I wasn't a glutton for punishment enough the first time...) I learned a lot from my experience with *Core Truths*—some things went well, some not so well—either way, I decided to do it again. There are a few more collections in the works, too, because I'm a little nutty like that. But since I was a little girl, I'd always dreamed of "writing a book." Never did I think the book(s) would be comprised of microfiction, flash fiction, and short stories, but here we are.

I'd like to thank my husband, **DAN FOX** (note: acknowledgement in big, bold, flashing letters... :)) for celebrating the wins with me and being the voice of reason on days the writing hasn't gone so well. As I've said a million times, I always know I'm on to something good when I'm reading Dan one of my stories, and he turns away from his fantasy sports stats to really listen to my words. To my boys, Ryan and Aidan, for serving as my inspiration every day and showing me the meaning of unconditional love. To my family, especially Debbie and John Fox, Frank and Grace Billings, and Olivia Verdon, for their endless encouragement. (Special thanks to my father-in-law, John Fox, for reading *Core Truths* cover-to-cover and asking me some great, engaging questions. Can't wait to keep the conversation going with this collection!).

Thank you to my two amazing writing "tribes." To LF and WAB, I am grateful every day for your encouragement and support—for pushing me to become better. I might have quit doing this a long time ago if it wasn't for all of you.

Thank you to Lydia Collins and Nora Wilson Fry, my accountability partners and to Talia Camozzi and Paulene Turner for generously volunteering as alpha readers for this collection. To MM Schreier and Myna Chang for your amazing beta reading for so many of the stories in this book, thank you. To the WAB Bus Stop Café brunch crew, Charlie Rogers and Stephanie Lennon and everyone else who's joined in the NYC fun (from near and far and through extreme heat and cold!), I'm so glad for our meetups and your friendship. Extra special unending thanks to Andrea Goyan for being an amazing critique partner and friend—I don't know where I'd be without you, in writing and in life!

I dedicated this book to my parents and godparents whose guidance, love, and support brought me to and through the passageways leading me to where I am today. I love you, I miss you, and I appreciate you more than you'll ever know.

Finally, I'd like to extend massive thanks to you, the reader, for traversing these *Passageways* with me.

Publication History

Her Memory Uncloaked, in *Uncharted Magazine*

In the Image of Evie, in *New Myths*

On the Canvas of Dreams, in *Bright Flash Literary Review*

Unfinished Business, in *Second Chance Lit*

Here, There, Everywhere, in *All Worlds Wayfarer*

The Victory Garden, in *72 Hours of Insanity*

Self-Actualization, in *Theme of Absence*

False Hope, in *Theme of Absence*

Aunt Tessa's Special Blanket, in *Bards and Sages Quarterly*

And the Light Faded, in *Alien Days Anthology*

Fallen Hero, in *Halloween Party 2019*

A Longing for the Old Days, in *Sledgehammer Lit*

The Angel's Death Knell, in *Metastellar*

Seeing Utopia, in *Luna Station Quarterly*

PASSAGEWAYS

A Time for Understanding, in *Metaphorosis*

297

About the Author

Lisa Fox is a pharmaceutical market researcher by day and fiction writer by night. She enjoys crafting short stories across genres, but most of her work can best be described as literary speculative fiction. For Lisa, there's no greater thrill than creating something out of nothing, in transforming life's 'what ifs' to prose that flashes a mirror on the human condition. As a writer, nothing makes her happier than having readers say that her work made them feel something or look at the world in a different way.

Lisa won the 2018 NYC Midnight Short Screenplay competition and, over the past several years, has had work nominated for a Pushcart Prize and Best Small Fictions. Her first collection of short stories, *Core Truths*, was published by Crystal Skipper Press in April 2023.

A resident of northern New Jersey in the USA, Lisa navigates the everyday chaos of suburban life with her husband, two teenage sons, and a quirky but lovable double-doodle dog.

You can reach Lisa in a variety of ways:

Website: lisafoxiswriting.com

Twitter: @iamlisafox10800

Facebook: lisafoxiswriting

Instagram: lisafoxiswriting

Email: lisafoxiswriting@gmail.com